Illegal Activities

A mafia romance

Holly Guy

Amazon

Contents

Title Page
Content Warning:
Chapter One   1
Chapter Two   4
Chapter Three   12
Chapter Four   20
Chapter Five   27
Chapter Six   31
Chapter Seven.   37
Chapter Eight   41
Chapter Nine   53
Chapter Ten   60
Chapter Eleven   65
Chapter Twelve   75
Chapter Thirteen   82
Chapter Fourteen   96
Chapter Fifteen   106
Chapter Sixteen   111
Chapter Seventeen   117
Chapter Eighteen   124

Chapter Nineteen	129
Chapter Twenty	133
Chapter Twenty-One	140
Chapter Twenty-Two	146
Chapter Twenty-three	149
Chapter Twenty-four	156
Chapter Twenty-five	167
Chapter Twenty-six	170
Chapter Twenty-seven	176
Chapter Twenty-eight	186
Chapter Twenty-nine	192
Chapter Thirty	196
Chapter Thirty-One	204
Chapter Thirty-two	217
Chapter Thirty-three	227
Chapter thirty-four	233
Chapter thirty-five	238
Thirty-Six	246
Books By This Author	259

Content Warning:

Hello, Reader.

If you've read my other books, you'll be aware that some of my books include a little more spice. These sexual scenes may be vanilla, but other scenes not so much.

In 'Illegal activities', there is also talk of abuse, violence, and other topics some may find troubling.

Please read with caution.

Are you still here? Wicked!

Now for the good stuff...

Chapter One

MAYA'S POV:

Everything hurts. My legs ache, my heart throbs and my lungs shriek for me to pause, to take a deep breath and restore my oxygen levels. But I can't. I'm too far gone now.

Startled, I skid to a halt. I freeze and strain to listen out for any movements around me. The howling wind sweeps away any noises. It even hides my desperate sobs. The mud beneath my bare feet slithers between my toes and makes me feel sick. The stench is much worse; like decaying shit and dirt all washed up into a disgusting sludge. I force down the bile and tear my gaze back towards my home. *No.* Alessio's house.
My prison.

The cold, wet night drenches my thin jumper and flimsy leggings. I shiver and hug myself protectively. With one final glance at the beautiful castle, I continue my escape. I stumble forward towards the tree line. Huge oak trees strain against the assault of the wind. The thick tree trunks
offer me no way past them onto the main road. Like soldiers guarding me from the outside world. More like forcing me to remain inside this hell hole.

Desperately, I peer up at the mighty tree. The rain picks up its attack on my shivering body. It's freezing and I can barely feel my fingers as I reach up for the first branch. Thankfully, it doesn't snap as I haul my weight up. It takes a lot of effort, but I finally make it to branch one. My body heaves as I struggle to regulate my breathing. I have already run a mile and a half as fast as I could, weighted down by the harassing rainwater. I've barely eaten, and sleep has been unkind to me for the past couple of days. I mean: *how can you get a wink of sleep when the man lying next to you is planning to kill you?*

And yet I'm forcing my exhausted body into flight mode. Contrary to popular opinion, the adrenaline doesn't remove pain. If anything, it increases it. I feel sick and dizzy. The tension is a constricting snake, quickly wrapping itself around my neck. It squeezes more, *more*. A choked sob spills from my lips. Everything within me wants to fall off the tree and sulk back into Alessio's arms. But I can't. I *won't*. I was made to survive, not to make easy prey.

I force another limb onto the branch above me and struggle to heave myself onto it. I'm much higher now. A huge gust of wind threatens to knock me off. My numb fingers grip tighter into the small grooves in the tree trunk. Shakily, I stretch my foot onto another branch. I place all my weight on it. Then, it snaps.

Suddenly, I'm falling out of the tree. As I tumble through the leaves, it scratches and cuts at my skin. Shrieks of pain leave my lips as I finally hit the ground. The agony is exquisite. Mud splatters up my cheeks and I can even taste the awful sludge in my teeth. My body snaps in two as I cry out. Thankfully, the wind muffles the moans.

In the distance, I hear a siren. Like the devil himself roaring out for Persephone, the sound is gut wrenching. It blares and red, flashing lights quickly follow. Red like the blood dripping down me. This is all I need to break into action. I force my numb limbs upwards and towards the long-tarmacked road. My road to freedom.

I sprint towards it and tear out of the treeline. My muddy feet stumble onto tarmac and I sigh a breath of relief. Finally, I'm free! Finally, I can breathe again.

Searching for which way to go, I tear my gaze left, and then right. I didn't have time to plan my escape out in detail; it could have been a costly mistake. Then again, I've always been an impulsive woman. Plans and restrictions do not work well with my mindset. One-foot stumbles in front of the other as I finally decide to jog down the hill and see where it takes me.

However, in the darkness of the night, a shadowy figure emerges. Crossed arms, my husband stands there with his overbearing, powerful presence. I can feel the rage from here. My entire body shakes with anticipation of my pending punishment. Menacingly, he takes a step forward.

"Hello, *Juliet*." He smirks.

I gulp and throw myself backwards. Fear is an understatement. The Devil has returned to take his wife back to hell.

Who am I kidding? I can never escape the mafia. It's not an occupation, it's a lifestyle. My dear Alessio would never change. *Could* never change. He is too far gone. The jagged rabbit hole has swallowed his black heart up.

And me?

Once a prisoner, always a prisoner.

Chapter Two

THREE MONTHS AGO:

MAYA'S POV:

Tap.
Tap.
Tap.

My scarlet heels scratch the dance floor as I stumble towards the small bar. Like a small carving knife sinking into a lump of clay, my heels carve patterns into the cheap floorboards. In this club, it stinks of warm humanity oozing out of every sweaty pitted man and woman, shamelessly grinding on one another. I bite my lower lip to prevent the scowl. My eyebrows betray me. The thick slugs on my forehead jump towards each other.

As I push my way to the front of the queue, I stick my elbows out, jabbing anybody in my way. A drunk teenager offers me a dirty look but it's nothing an innocent smile can't fix. With one bat of my eyelashes, he simply stops his protests. *Pathetic*, I think bitterly before shoving another elbow into his side.

"Another one!" I bark my order at the bartender. Loose curls tumble into his eyes and cling to his sweaty forehead. His face flushes red. I peer down at his smart looking suit. There are far too many layers on his pudgy body for this club. Half of the people here are naked. *And even we are too hot.*

"Another one? Already?" His eyes widen in despair as he casts his gaze over the dozen other people in the queue calling to get his attention. As usual, only one bar staff worked the Saturday night shift. It is why I chose this club. They barely have time to pour drinks let alone scour the place for thieves. The bartender begins to protest but I get their first.

"I asked for another one."

A patronising smile stains my lips when I look down at his name badge.

"Please, *Carl*." I add, batting my lashes. His mouth opens and closes like a fish out of water, but the rest of his body quickly moves to make me my usual double vodka cranberry. No ice and half a stir. The bar staff know exactly how I like it. Anything else, and It will go over their heads. Nervously, he slides me the drink. I offer him a half nod to say my thanks. He gulps before pressing at some buttons on the till.

"That will be five pounds forty." He pulls the card machine towards himself to type in the number before pushing it out towards me. I scrunch my face up at the card machine. My head nods to the man next to me,
"He'll get it."

The stranger's jaw drops slightly as he looks between me and the bartender. I tilt my head to the side, challenging him to say no. A smile kisses my lips; the siren within me hisses to escape. To start a fight, to give me a reason to let out my pent-up rage. A short pause drifts between us; like the silence before a battle.

Then, the man gulps before scrambling to pull out his debit card. I pat him on the chest patronisingly.

"Good lad."

Drink in hand, I return to the dancefloor, searching for my next victim. Drunken bodies stumble into one another. I dodge them effortlessly, sipping at my drink, as I slip further into the crowd. Red stains tint the top of the glass and I have no doubt my lipstick is smudged around face. Perhaps I resemble a wild beast who has just finished one meal and is now stalking the next. My lips curl at this idea.

Like a moth hypnotised by a flame, the music takes control of me. The alcohol slowly seeps through me, warming my insides and removing my inhibitions. I lift my glass to the air and sway my hips back and forth. A lazy smile licks my lips as the music consumes every inch of my being: the flashing lights, the alcohol, the deep vibrating rhythm. Every component pulls me into my fantasy of being a free woman. Saturday nights are for freedom! *Kind of.* But just because I am working, it doesn't mean I can't have a little bit of fun. My Father doesn't know this, of course. It's my little secret.

A pair of calloused hands slither around my waist. They are cold and make me shiver. Steadily, I take a deep breath to control the panting monster inside of me. I long to break his arms for assuming that he can touch me. Like twigs, I'd snap each one backwards into a pattern of my choosing. Perhaps I'd create a penis. Symbolism. I'd cup his hand into the head of the penis, and then break his shoulders to round out the balls. Yes, that's what I'd do. That will teach him some respect.

The smell of whisky and rich cigars storms my nose. Disgusted, I look down at the stranger's hairy arms and go to pry the invaders off. But then my plan is quickly frozen in place. On his wrist, a customised Rolex. Without hesitation, I finish the rest of my drink before letting the plastic cup fall to the ground. With one small kick, it hurdles across the dancefloor out of my way. Then I twist on my heels to greet my new, hairy guest.

"Hello, handsome." A lazy grin licks my lips. I run a hand through my curly, raven hair to make myself look a little more presentable.

His drunk, oceanic eyes transfix themselves on my body. Heavy wrinkles stain his skin like a rash, and his eyebrows look like they have never seen a pair of tweezers. Worst of all, his thin lips have dry skin peeling from them like the stringy bit of an orange hanging off. I resist the urge to gag in his face.

Mischievously, his hands drop down and they squeeze my bum. They roam over my body and for a moment, I'm too stunned to act. He takes my silence as an invitation to continue, and smiles. A golden tooth jumps out at me. *Boy, is he ugly! But rich too.* Tonight, I can make an exception to my rule of 'no flirting with ugly people'.

Pleased with my find, I scan him to locate different points of where I can steal from. He is a little too well-off and put together to be coming to this club in the small town, two miles away from Venice. But how can I turn down such a tempting offer? His pocket bulges with a full wallet and his wrist shimmers under the club lights, further revealing diamonds etched into the clock face. My heart skips a beat.

"What is your name?" The man brings his face closer to mine. His Russian accent is thick. I wince as his bad breath harasses my senses. *Ever heard of a mint, asshole?* Quickly, I gather my bitter thoughts. He is too good of a find to let my attitude prevent the job being completed.

"Zara." I lie with a winning smile. His eyebrows pull together and for a second, I think he's going to challenge my lie. But then his grip tightens around my hips, and he returns the smile. Longingly, he stares down at me.

"How much do you charge for a night, Zara?" The man slurs as he talks. My jaw drops.

"Excuse me?"

"For the night? Or I can just pay for a couple hours."

"No! Not happening." I spit, backing away from him.

Mortified, I stare down at my little black dress. Okay, *fine*, it *is* quite short, and the bust *is* very low. And maybe there are *some* decorative holes dancing up the side. But that doesn't make me a whore!

A drunken woman stumbles into me. *The perfect opportunity.* I purposely fall into the man's chest acting like the lady fell into me harder than she actually did. Without him even knowing, I slip my hand into his pocket and retrieve his wallet. He is too distracted glaring at the lady behind me to notice anything, so I slip the watch off too. Quickly, I regain my balance and send him an award-winning smile.

"I should go find my friends. I'll see you later."

It's a quick exit. He lungs to grab me and hold me close but I'm much faster and can weave in and out of the crowd like a dog in an agility course. I have had much practice with these escape routes. Even if I closed my eyes, I could still find my way out of the club before he did.

I take the back exit, slipping past security and drunk teenagers throwing up in the toilets next door. My smile grows as I stare down at my find. Two thousand pounds and a brand-new Rolex watch. *Just another successful day in the office.* Father is going to be very impressed!

I resist the urge to jump for joy as I stuff them down my bra. Kicking my heels off, I shove them under one arm and begin my long walk home. I live five miles from here. My personal nightly mission is to get home before the sun rises. Tonight, my body aches from dancing for six hours straight. Tomorrow, I will have to do it all over again. I can grant myself an early night with this huge find.

Stones scratch at the bottom of my feet but I ignore their tickling touch. The salty sea fills my nose, and the sound of crashing waves calms my achy body. I sigh. Above me, the crows call out to one another. They fly in a triangle formation, all heading north. I home in on one bird at the back. It struggles to keep up. It flaps its wings as fast as it can, but it is no use, she's miles behind the others. I mean: *It* is miles behind the others. My jaw hardens and I avert my eyes.

Suddenly, the quiet street roars to life. A black BMW shrieks to a halt as it pulls up beside me. My head snaps right and then left, searching for an escape route. Two massive men slip out of the car door. Within seconds, I am sprinting away from them. But they give chase.

My ankles threaten to buckle from the lack of support and my lungs heave. I am not used to running. Dancing is my cardio. *And theft.*

"Fuck!" The word leaves my lips as another car blocks off my path. I look left and I start towards the alley way. But it's too late. An enormous force slams into my side, sending me to the ground. The rough tarmac kisses my skin, leaving nasty gashes. I kick my legs around violently and land a couple solid hits to the man suddenly on top of me. I am quickly outnumbered as the other two men catch up. They drag me off the floor as if I'm weightless.

"Let go of me, Assholes!" I scream, "Help! Help!"

One of the burly men aims a punch at me but I'm more agile. I throw my body forward, shocking the men on either arm. They stumble into each other. Furious, I spin around to continue the fight. I am too slow to outrun them and maybe even too weak to win the fight... *But I will give them their fucking money's worth.*

"Come on then." I spit, raising my small fists. Each of the meat heads look at me with a twisted grin. It's like looking at triplets. Big, broad, and brooding. *Bastards*. The one of the left lurches for me. I force a foot into his stomach before throwing my elbow back into the face of another one. Their grunts echo through the night, and for a moment I feel alive.

My fist connects with the last man's cheek. His head snaps right and blood pools from his lips. I aim again. And again. Each time, landing a successful punch. A wave of pride storms through me.

"Come on then tough guys, I know karate!" I shriek, trying to intimidate them. A lump throbs in the back of my throat. Something deep inside of me screams that these men are not your average rapists or murderers. Hell, they are three times the size of a normal man! Usually, your average assholes would give up at the first sign of a successful fight.

The words of my Father swamp my mind. *Fight dirty, and you will live.* Pulling strength from him, I thrust a foot into the groin area of the unlucky bastard in front of me. The bald man snaps in half like a deck chair as he grabs his throbbing penis. *Thanks, Dad!*

However, my fight is all in vain. The men begin barking at each other in a foreign language. I'm too high on adrenaline to try to work out what they are saying. Whatever was said, it clearly unites them. Slowly, the three of them surround me like a pack of wolves, desperate for a meal. Each man quickly secures one of my wriggling limbs.

"Help! Help!" I shriek again but I know it is useless. It is 1am. Nobody is going to leave the club for another three hours. Inside, the pounding music would have quickly drowned out my voice.

Like a rag doll, they bundle me into the boot of their car. Silence and darkness consumes me, and I'm left alone with my fear.

Chapter Three

MAYA'S POV:

A haunted chorus of female cries startles me awake. My head pounds and my mouth feels dry as I tear my gaze left and then right. *Fuck.*

My sick reality sinks in.

A rusty cage surrounds me, locking me into a tight rectangle of bars. In one corner, there is a dog water bowl, in the other corner, a bucket. On the outside of my confinement, hundreds of other cages loaded with women. Each woman cowers in their own little hell hole. My heart skips a beat and my stomach churns.

"What the fuck!" I yell before I can stop myself, "Let me out! Let me the fuck out!"

Frantically, I yank on the prison bars. I try every single one, searching for a weakness in the cage. A chain around my ankle tries to restrict me from moving. I fight back against it. The smell of faeces and ammonia climbs up my nose and dies there. The mournful song of sobs increases around me.

My chest heaves and my body aches. Exhausted, I fall backwards. My knees press against my chest, and I wrap my arms around myself protectively. Dried blood stains my skin and I nervously pick at it to inspect the wounds. I wince as the stinging quickly follows. My bruises have bruises.

"Stay quiet." A voice hisses.

In the cage beside me, a tiny looking lady in her late twenty's stares back. Sweat and tears drench her face, and her dirty blonde locks are matt. It looks as if she hasn't washed in weeks. Weakly, she offers me a smile. I do not return it.

"Stay quiet or they will hear you." She drops her smile. It is replaced with a grim line on her thin lips.

"Where are we?" I gawp, "What is this place?"

Despite being chained at the ankle, I manage to pull myself closer to the lady in the cage next to me. The saddest blue eyes watch me. Her clothes are ripped, and blood stained, and her ribs protrude from her chest. Her body lurches forward as she coughs. Splatters of blood fly from her lips and stains the tarmac floor in front of her. My eyes never leave her arms which are like bamboo sticks. *When was the last time she ate?*

"We are in a prison." She croaks.

"A prison?" I scowl. My fingers quickly jump into my bra to locate my stolen goods. *Gone.*

"Fuck." I hiss, "This isn't good."

Never before in my life have I been caught stealing. And now I find myself in prison! *What happened to having a fair trial? Pleading your case in front of a judge and a jury?* If given the chance, I will plead guilty by reason of insanity. *I can do a pretty good crazy impression.*

For the first time ever, my sarcastic thoughts do not make me feel any better. I am still stuck in jail.

Defeated, I scan the cage again searching for something I can use as a weapon if the men come back. My eyes settle on a pool of blood behind me. Startled, I check my body for open wounds, big enough to make that kind of puddle.

"It's not your blood." The lady whispers with a hoarse voice. Her miserable gaze never leaves me.

"Well, whose blood is it?" I frown.

"The girl before you. She left three hours ago." She answers with a tremble in her voice. My jaw hardens.

"Left to go where?"

A long, miserable silence floats between us.

"Heaven." The woman whimpers before flopping back into a pile of bones on the cold floor, "She didn't make the selection."

"The selection?" I frown. My blood chills. *What kind of prison is this?*

Suddenly, the sound of doors slamming echoes around the warehouse. The lady next to me throws her arms over her head and sobs. I scowl at her and edge forward in my cage, searching for the source of the bang. Two guards patrol around the warehouse. They each have huge batons sticking out of their black jumpsuits. I straighten my back defensively. Although my body is screaming for rest, I am more than prepared to continue the fight. No way in Hell will I end up the same way as the unfortunate lady before me. My Father trained me way too hard for that fate.

The two, huge men stalk each cage, greedily eyeing up the women. I squint to get a better look at them. The realisation quickly sinks in; *they are the assholes who kidnapped me!* My upper lip curls up in a snarl. A small sense of satisfaction washes through me as I admire their bruises and cuts. They advance closer. Now, they don't look anywhere near as powerful and intimidating as before. It is hard to be afraid of a wolf who is covered in his own blood.

A smile teases my lips. *Let that be a reminder of what is to come.*

In the dim lighting, I can just about see the plaster covering the bigger man's nose. His eye is swollen shut and his lip cut. The smaller one, with an eyebrow piercing, looks just as beaten with a swelling on his head.

"You should really rest for forty-eight hours after a head injury." I point out sarcastically when their eyes fix on me, "Just in case you have concussion."

The smaller man snarls. He quickly closes the distance between us and clutches at the bars of my cage. I refuse to cower away. They will not see my fear.

"Well, well, well." A thick Russian accent stumbles out of his crusty lips, "If it isn't for the little thief."

Another smile plays on my lips. I look at his watch and see it has been restored.

"I never did get your name, Handsome." I cock my head to the side, feigning bravery. Suddenly, he throws his fist into the cage bars. The sound echoes around the room and repeats over and over until it joins the soft chorus of sobs around me. The meathead hisses as the pain quickly floods through his hand. I bite my tongue to stifle a laugh.

"Don't let her tease you, Dima. She is a dirty little whore who will get what's coming to her." The larger one comforts his mini-me, *Dima*.

"Actually, I am not a whore. I never got to clarify that i-" I retort, holding my finger in the air.

"Silence!" The bigger one barks. I slump backwards and close my mouth.

"You might think that you are clever because you have witty comebacks. But look around you." He growls, "You are the one in Hell. Not us."

"It's a warehouse, not Hell." I mumble sarcastically under my breath. Luckily, he doesn't hear me so doesn't respond. However, he fumbles around in his pocket. A jingle echoes around the cage as he pulls out a large key chain. He squints as he tries to find the right key.

Fuck.

My heart skips a beat as I slowly shuffle backwards in my cage, away from the men. The chain on my ankle forces me still. I keep my head held high.

"What's wrong, Kitten? Lost your humour already?" Dima

mocks me before turning to his friend, "They always lose their humour. It's such a shame."

"Not me." I perk up happily, "I'll never shut up!"

My sarcastic beam earns another snarl from the larger man. He thrusts the key into the lock on my cage and swings the door open. I patiently wait for the opportunity to escape.

However, he does not unbuckle the chain around my ankle. Instead, he yanks me forward. I lurch towards him, trapped between my chained ankle and his grip. Dread starts to settle in my chest as I realise that I'm totally defenceless in this position.

Whilst the bigger one holds me by my shoulders, Dima grabs me by the hair and yanks my head back. A grunt leaves my lips when his hand strikes me across the face. I bite back the hiss and let the pain settle. He hits me again. And again.

"At least unchain me." I pant breathlessly, "For a fair fight. Unless you're afraid of getting your ass kicked by a girl? *Again*?"

The larger man brings his face closer to mine menacingly.

"Watch it, bitch." He growls. With a smile, I spit in his face. He drops me to the ground. Quickly, I catch myself on my hands before I can hit the floor ungracefully. In the awkward position, my chained ankle cries out in pain. *Fuck. That hurts!*

Suddenly, a boot lurches into my side. I cower away from it but there's not much I can do as the chain forces me still. A cry leaves my lips as the pain soars through my side. It feels as if someone has set my skin on fire, dipped me in petrol and then set me alight again. Dima lifts his foot over my head and gets ready to stomp down. I flinch and wait for the pain to come.

"Stop!" A roar echoes around the room. The sound bounces off all the walls and repeats over and over until it is barely a whisper. Dima quickly removes his foot from above my head. Both men fall into line.

I scramble backwards into my cage. Desperately, my fingers tug at the chain around my ankle in one last attempt to free myself. The pale skin now pulses different shades of purple and scarlet. I silently pray it will be okay to run on in case I get the opportunity to flee.

"Is it this one?" Another thick Russian accent rings around the room, "*She* is the one who hurt you?"

The man's face is slowly revealed as he stalks closer towards my cage. Wrinkles seep into his papery looking skin, and his eyes are low and heavy. Bags pull his face downwards as does his thin lips which are in a permanent scowl. He looks like someone has melted his face. With an amused twinkle in his dark eyes, he looks between me and his men.

"I apologise for my men's behaviour here." The boss snarls, "We do not hurt women at this stage in the selection. We can't have our buyer put off by bruises and broken bones. It will hide your natural beauty."

He scowls at his guards. Both of them cower away and avert their eyes. Yet the apology still doesn't feel genuine. The way his eyes latch on my body makes me shiver.

"If you unchain me, I will be able to give a fair fight if they did it again." I suggest unhelpfully. The man's lips curl into a smile and he nods his head slowly.

"Yes." He mutters, stroking his stubbly beard, "I suppose that would be fair."

Sinisterly, he twists towards his men and barks something in Russian. My stomach lurches as Dima advances towards me. Violently, he yanks at my ankle with the chain before unlocking it. I yelp in pain and resist the urge to kick him in the face. It will do no good. There are three of them, and one of me.

"Come." The Russian boss waves a hand at me nonchalantly. I freeze in my spot and shake my head.

"No."

"*No?*" He raises a curious eyebrow at me. His awfully wrinkled skin sticks out as he scowls.

"Where will we go?" I ask. Something inside of me tells me it is safer to remain here than be alone with the angry Russian crew.

"You are resisting? Bizarre. Are you not afraid of us?" He asks coldly. A grim expression seeps onto his face. It's a malicious, curious look. Perhaps one of amusement too.

I bite my lower lip nervously. The truth is that nobody will ever scare me as much as my Father does. This is my superpower. I shake my head once, then twice.

"No." I announce firmly. The Boss parts his lips and keeps my gaze. His eyes feel like they are undressing my soul, sifting through it like flicking through the pages of a book. I recognise the look. He is scouring for a weakness. Something he can use against me. It is my signature move.

"Let's go." He snaps, losing his humour quickly.

"I quite like my cage." I protest desperately. In the cage beside me, the blonde woman collapses to the floor with a thump. Her eyes roll to the back of her head as she slips into unconsciousness. Her cries no longer add to the miserable choir. I glance at her nervously.

"We can do this the easy way..." The Boss glares at me menacingly. Then he pulls a gun from his waist band and points it at my forehead.

"Or the hard way." He finishes his sentence. My jaw hardens as I reluctantly exit the cage. This isn't the first time I have been threatened with a gun. But I also don't want it to be the last time. I have so many more insecure men to piss off before I die.

"I choose the easy way." I smile at him, "You're in control here, Boss. Lead the way."

He snarls at my sarcastic comment, but he doesn't say anything. Aggressively, Dima grabs me by the arm and pulls me towards the door. This time, I do not resist.

A lump forms in my throat as I stagger through the warehouse. On either side, cages of women pile high. The smell of poo and wee grows stronger and stronger as we head towards the exit. All of the women cower away from us as we pass them. No one dares to make eye contact with the Russian Boss.

My jaw hardens and a slither of despair fills my chest.

Oh Maya, what have you gotten yourself into?

Chapter Four

ALESSIO'S POV:

"What the fuck!" I bellow. My hand crashes into the glass table, sending it flying across the room. It smashes into tiny pieces as it explodes against the wall.

"How did this happen?"

The heat oozes from my body and my fists tremble. *I need to hurt somebody, bad.* Unamused, my Brother watches me. His lips pull into a straight line as he leans back in his chair.

"Alessio." He tuts, "Instead of letting your famous anger get to you, perhaps we should find that Russian twat first and then break things after?"

My Brother has always been the more rational one. But this doesn't matter. I am in control. I am the king of the Italian mafia. And until the day where I am no longer in charge, we will do things my way.

"Mateo, how did this happen?" I seethe. He doesn't break my eye contact as I lean forward menacingly. We almost look like twins with our towering height and stocky builds. Like mine, his eyes swirl with violence in our dark orbs. Our skin is tanned and hair coal coloured. The main difference is, whereas his body is bare, mine is littered with tattoos. One tattoo for every life I've taken. My skin is one permanent canvas of ink.

Again, he ignores me. I grab his mug from the side and lob it over his head. It smashes and joins the glass table on the floor.

"Smashing my office up will not change the fact that fifty women have been snatched from our streets last night." Mateo huffs. He is right, breaking things will not bring those women back to safety. *But it sure feels fucking good.*

"We don't know how they got away with it." His face contorts into a grimace, "The Council will be here any minute now. We can discuss it further then."

As if on cue, my team file into the room. My Father set the Council up when he was in control of the Italian mafia. Ruling an empire is much easier if you have a group of men and women managing over certain sectors. We, the Council, control everything in Italy. The drug imports, stock shares, hell even how many loaves of bread will be put on display in the local bakery. The Italian mafia is ubiquitous.

Quickly, they all take their seats around the rectangular meeting table. Nobody dares to make a sound. Today is a day of mourning and punishment.

"Please enlighten me as to how Sasha Ovlov and his bandits managed to capture fifty women and children in one night?" I roar. My eyes snap to Angelo, my head of security. I raise an eyebrow expectantly.

His brown hair flops into his face as he stands up nervously. His shirt is creased and the bags under his eyes are heavy. Like the rest of his team in security, he would have gotten minimal sleep last night as they stalked the streets for the rival mafia.

"We have surveillance footage showing the attack but not much more than that, as of yet. It's as if they vanished off the face of the earth after they loaded them into cars." Angelo gawps. He waves his hands around frantically. *Desperately.* He knows better than to displease me. And boy has he fucking annoyed me today.

Opposite him, my head of foreign relations scoffs.

"I have reviewed the footage too." She interrupts, "It looks as if Sasha has sent his best men to do his dirty work. Dima and

Andrei plucked the women one by one with relatively minimal fuss. There was a third man, but I think he might be new. I have no information on him."

A frown stains my face.

"Why would he send his best men? He has dozens of ground men to do this type of risky work for him." I ask the question out loud, but I'm greeted with silence.

In the past, when other mafias kidnapped our women, they'd send disposable men to do the dirty work. Most of the time, I'd catch them. They'd be thrown into prison or killed. Sending their best men into my streets is equivalent to signing their death warrant. *So, why do it? What are the Russians planning?*

"Sir, I believe they might have been looking for something in particular. Or someone." Aria explains, "Their actions were bizarre. As you know, I've been tracking their movement across the globe. Usually, they snatch and dash. But last night…"

She trails off into silence, biting at her pen lid. Her blonde hair tumbles into her face but she quickly pins it back up into place. Her lips seal shut, telling me she has nothing more to say. I stew on the thought for a little longer.

What could Sasha Ovlov, the Russian Mafia King, want in a small town near Venice?

"Was there a specific type of woman they kidnapped?" My Brother frowns at the Council. At the furthest end of the table, Casper raises his hand timidly. Being the head of information means he must analyse trends and patterns in situations like these. I sit back in my chair, praying for good news.

"I'm afraid not. Blondes, brunettes, fat, slim, tall, short, old, young…" He begins but I quickly cut him off.

"Enough!" I snap, "We get the image."

My bones chill at the thought of it. When I came into power, I promised the citizens that the Russian mafia would no longer terrorise our streets. Or any other mafia for that matter. That our women and children would be safe. I have failed. And I don't do well with failure.

"What was the time of the attacks?" I seethe.

"Six pm on Friday until One am on Saturday morning." Angelo answers. This makes me frown.

"I don't understand." I mutter, "Why would they kidnap fifty women? They've never taken that many before. And why stop at fifty? Why stop at One am? They usually begin their attacks then. It just doesn't make sense."

The room hums with tension. To my left, Angelo shuffles uncomfortably in his seat. A year ago, his sister was one of the victims. She still hasn't been found. I let him simmer in shame and anger. As my head of security, he should have been able to prevent the attack.

"Give me the rest of the day." He finally finds his voice again, "I will find out more."

His eyes find mine and he offers me a reassuring smile. I do not send him one back. *Why would I reward failure?*

"Casper, you work with Angelo today." I bark at my head of information. He nods his head slowly and scribbles some tasks off of his to-do list. Whatever he had planned to do today can wait.

"As for Aria and Carlos, you shall find out everything there is to know about Sasha Ovlov. And I mean *everything*. I want to know what his mother's maiden name is, what he eats for breakfast. Fuck it, I want to know which position he sleeps at night. Am I understood?" I declare. Carlos, my head of finance, gives me a firm nod in agreement. I return the gesture before spinning around to the board.

Red string trails between the different faces. In the middle, Sasha's ugly face glares back at me. The string stretches out to different locations and different people involved in his various schemes. As of yet, we have no motive for his kidnappings. My best bet is selling the women to sex rings and underground services. As a mafia, my Council and I might kill and torture people, but rape and kidnapping? That's not power. That's being a cunt.

"That will be all." I declare. The Council scramble out of their seats and hurry to get on with their day. My Brother remains behind. He closes the door behind the last person before turning to face me. A permanent scowl stains his lips.

"Do you think Dad knows yet?" He grumbles. The anxiety in my chest speeds up. It's a breathless feeling, tight and sore. I repress the ugly feeling. Mafia kings do not get anxiety. Mafia kings do not get scared.

"I don't care." I lie before slumping back into the office chair. My bones ache as I finally will them to relax. Then I open the laptop and sign onto the system. A ring of a phone interrupts my silence. I look at Mateo expectantly. He sighs before answering the call.

"Hello, Mateo speaking. Who is this?" He grumbles as he exits the room to continue the conversation. My mouse hovers over the file of the CCTV footage from last night. I double click on it. The awful footage quickly pops up. Putting on the times two speed, I sit back in the chair and watch as the black BMW with scrubbed out number plates stalks around the town. Every now and then, one of the cars pull up to the curb. Each time, three men jump out and grab the unsuspecting woman. None of them fight back. *How could they?* The men are huge.

"It was the Americans." My Brother announces as he re-enters the room. He shoves the phone into his pocket and sighs, "The Russians are going to host a mass selling of the women. There are bidders competing for the prettiest woman."

Another wild scream escapes me. *Fucking Russians!*

I send another mug flying across the room. It doesn't soothe my anger. So, I reach over and grab the closest glass to me, preparing for it to meet the same fate as the other smashed goods. My Brother takes it out of my hands like a parent removing a dangerous object from their child's grasp. I grumble and cross my arms defiantly.

"Is there anything on there?" He ignores my outburst and crosses the room. I feel his presence behind me as he stares down at the computer screen. We both watch in silence. The world's worst film plays in front of us. My jaw hardens as yet another woman is bundled into the back of the car.

The footage then jumps to the next victim. It shows a tall woman in a strappy dress stumbling down the road. She stares aimlessly up at the sky, watching something the footage doesn't pick up. Without thinking, I slow the tape down. Her long tan legs take shaky steps as she tip toes around the stones and broken glass. I frown and zoom in on the computer. *Why isn't she wearing her shoes?*

Then her face is revealed. Her lips match the colour of her shoes, and she wears dark, smoky makeup. With round, plump lips and a sharp jawline, she is a stunner. Her eyebrows shape her face perfectly and her long, curly hair cascades down her back. I dislike her dress though. It barely covers anything. *Surely, she knew better than to wear such clothes and walk home alone, intoxicated?*

Then, she stuffs things down her bra. I scowl, an amused smile flickering to my lips. *What was that?*

"A thief." Mateo spits behind me. I raise a hand to tell him to stop talking. I don't care what she is. She is gorgeous.

Suddenly, the same black car pulls up beside her. My jaw hardens and I fall back in my seat. I wait for her inevitable easy capture, just like the others. The seconds tick by and yet the men haven't been able to catch her. Curiously, I pull the laptop closer to me. The woman fights back with extraordinary strength and precision. Despite three men towering over her, she doesn't back down. Aggressively, she swings her heel at one of their faces, leaving a nasty gash on his cheek, before turning around and kicking another one in the groin. I am mesmerised as she takes every opportunity to bring these men down. My heart thumps faster and louder in my chest. Even though I know the ending, it's like a movie I want to watch again. The way she moves, the way she fights, the way she oozes violence. I am captivated.

"What a little warrior." I hear myself sigh.

However, her fight doesn't last much longer. Soon, the three men coordinate their attacks. Her exhausted body is quickly overpowered and thrown into the boot of the car. My knuckles turn white as I grip the mouse harder and harder. Then, it breaks with a snap.

"Fuck!" I growl, throwing myself up from the chair. My hatred towards Sasha Ovlov doubles. Behind me, my Brother remains quiet. He knows when to step in and when to leave me alone.

Furious, I storm out of the office. I need to let off some steam before I can think rationally on how to kill this Russian prick.

Chapter Five

MAYA'S POV:

Limping through the winding corridors, my body cries out in pain. Each guard clings to either arm as if they do not trust me to walk nicely. As if I'd try to escape. *Maybe they have a point.*

"Where are we off to?" I chirp. The anxiety bubbles in my stomach, it makes me use humour as a defence mechanism. It was my Father's trick. *Your enemy will be intimidated by your lack of fear*, he taught, *It is the perfect opportunity to frighten them. Make them mess up. And then you win the fight.*

The Russian Boss leads us down another corridor. It smells of damp and mould down here and it is eerily quiet.

We stop outside a metal door. It reminds me of the ones I used to see on television on prison shows. The man in charge then pulls his own set of keys out of his pocket. He flicks through them, settling on a big gold one. He thrusts it into the keyhole and opens the door.

My heart leaps in my chest as I peer in. It is a similar layout to the cage, with a water bowl and a bucket. However, now I get a carboard box for a bed. Thankfully, there are no blood puddles in this room.

"This is where the troublemakers go." Dima grins before looking to his friend, "Isn't that right, Andrei?"

I silently note his name down too. If I escape, no *when* I escape, I will be ensuring that both these men will hang from their toes until they break, and then hang from their ankles until they also break. All the way up their bodies until they finally, and miserably, die an agonising death. The thought brings a smile to my lips.

"You shouldn't have." I say cheekily. Suddenly, Dima chucks me to the floor, and I hit it with a thud. He chuckles when I groan. They slowly exit the room. The fear grips me instantly.

"No, wait!" I gasp, jumping to my feet, "Am I going to be alone?"

The Boss smiles at me knowingly as if he can sense my fear.

"This is for your own good. You, my dear, will make me lots of money. So, it's better that you're alone where no one can hurt you." He grins, the ugly wrinkles jumping over one another as he does so. Before I can react, he slams the metal door in my face. I sprint towards him and grip at the small bars.

"Let me out of here, fucker!" I cry out desperately. My shoulders feel like they're going to pop out of my sockets as I yank on the bars violently.

"The name is Sasha, not *fucker*." His lips curl at the crude nickname. My face feels hot, and my chest tightens to the point it feels like it's going to explode. The anxiety melts away my humour and pride.

"Sasha, please! Take me back to the others. I swear you won't hear me! I'll be good I sw…" I ramble on but he raises his hand to silence me. My lips snap shut obediently.

"You have no bargaining power, little Maya." He chuckles. My blood scorches and my head snaps towards him. *How does he know my name?*

"Daughter of Chris Baker, yes?" He smiles. Behind him, Dima and Andrei flash their cocky grins. Each of the three faces soak up my shocked reaction. I nod numbly. *This isn't a random attack. They're trying to get to my Father.*

"Not so chatty now, are we?" Dima pipes up. I shoot him the middle finger.

"Whatever you and him are arguing about, I can assure you I have no part in it. I barely see my Father!" I hiss, knuckles turning white as I grip onto the bars harder, "Let me go!"

"You play a very key part, actually." Sasha raises an eyebrow mischievously.

"If you're trying to use me as blackmail, you have the wrong kid. He won't pay a penny for me." I scoff. The words sting as I speak them into existence. It is true. My Father loves my Brothers much more than me. They are stronger, bring him more pride. Whereas I am simply a pair of long legs who can thieve and escape without anyone noticing. The only thing my Father likes about me is the stolen goods.

"Your Father owes me quite a bit of money." Sasha looks down at his nails as if he is bored with the conversation. He bites at a cuticle and spits it out on the floor.

"Good for you." I murmur bitterly.

Suddenly, Sasha's hands shoot through the bars. His grip tightens around my hair, and he slams my face into the door. A cry of shock leaves my lips and I desperately scratch at his hand to stop his assault. He's much stronger.

"I take it *daddy* didn't teach you any manners growing up." He snarls, "That's something we're going to have to work on before I sell you on."

Despite his agonising grip, I don't let him feel my fear. I bare my teeth at him, "You can't sell me. I'm annoying. Trust me, I'll turn all the customers away."

My humour doesn't evoke the anger I want out of him. I want him to become furious. To open the door to teach me a lesson. At least that way I will not be alone.

"Then I guess I will just have to kill you." He seethes. He forces my face up against the bars and grabs the gun from his pocket. The barrel kisses my forehead. My teeth bare as the cold weapon presses against my skin.

"Then do it." I hiss. Our eyes never leave each other's, quietly daring the other person to make the first move. After what feels like an eternity, Sasha pulls back and releases his grip on me.

"I think I'll make you suffer first." He grins, taking a step back. Fear washes through me as the three men walk away. I stare out at the empty corridor. Looking left, then right, I desperately search for another person. But it is no use.

I am trapped with nothing but my memories. Maybe Dima and Andrei were right. This place is fucking Hell.

Chapter Six

ALESSIO'S POV:

A dull throbbing sensation taunts my fist as I land another punch into the punching bag. Luckily for me, the gym is empty. A chorus of slapping rings around me from my fists against the bag, alongside my rapidly beating heart. Low growls tumble from my lips. Each successful hit releases more and more anger.

My Father always told me that there are three ways to calm down. Through a fight, through a fuck, or through fitness. And since the first two are off the cards, the last must suffice for now. Another punch lands and I quickly dodge the bag as it swings back towards me. *Left, left right. Left, left right. Right, right, Left. Right, ri-*

"Alessio?" My Brother's voice rings through the gym. I watch as he saunters further into the room. He grabs my towel on the bench and lobs it at me.

"Look alive." He says grimly, "We have more information."

Hope fills me.

Quickly, I follow him out of the room. I try to remove as much sweat as possible and control my breathing. It doesn't really work. My heart still races and my body aches to continue the workout.

"Evening." I nod politely at my staff. They each repeat the phrase back to me, respectfully nodding their heads.

"We know where Sasha's prison is. The southern side of Russia, *Tuva* to be precise. It's hidden amongst the mountains." Angelo beams at me, trying to make up for his mistake. Again, I do not smile at him.

"How long will that take?"

"Five hours on the jets." He reads off the sheet of paper in front of his face. A trickling of hope flickers across everyone's expressions. However, I will not let my team celebrate until we have every last victim on that jet, on our way home.

"Is it difficult to get in?" I frown, crossing the room and falling into my seat. My Brother thrusts blueprints into my hands. I stare down at the sketched drawing and silently plan our routes.

"It is mostly unguarded on the outside. However, the numbers inside are less predictable." Mateo blows out a breath of despair. I run my fingers over the drawing of the building. It is huge. *How have we not found it before?*

"Anything else?" I cock an eyebrow up at my team. Casper leans forward in his seat. It groans underneath him as he shuffles uncomfortably.

"Yes," He says with a grim expression, "We should expect more than three hundred women there. Minimum. I've spoken to Aria, and we've figured out there are dozens of other women missing from their homes across the globe."

My pen snaps in my fingers as I grip onto it too tightly. The ink shoots out and coats my trousers. My eyes stay fixed on the blueprints. I don't doubt for a moment that the prison couldn't hold all these women. *Hell, it could put palaces to shame.*

"Right then. We better head off." I sigh, pushing myself to my feet. My Council all rise too. Just as I fold the blueprint in half, the office door swings open. My eyes tear up as a small, tan woman leaps into the room. Her eyes are dark, and hair dyed a vibrant red.

"Brothers!" She announces, opening her arms wide.

"Sophia." I say tightly, "What are you doing here? Why aren't you in the North? Is everything okay up there?"

My mind races with all the potential problems which could have occurred. *Gang wars? Large thieving rings? Financial ruin?*

I don't need any more on my plate, but a good king is always four steps ahead. She blushes and shakes her head in a no. Before she has the opportunity to speak, Mateo beats her to it.

"Nice of you to show up to the meeting earlier." He glares at her.

"What?" I snap, spinning around to them, "Why would you tell her? She doesn't need to know about it."

"Relax, Alessio." Sophia scolds me playfully, "I'm twenty-two now, I can hear about these things. Plus, it's not just your city and southern girls who have been snatched. I noticed a couple reports come into my office this morning too. Don't worry, I hid them from Father. That's why I'm here."

I visibly relax. *She is right*. She should be involved with all these conversations and action plans. But it doesn't stop the aching in my heart. When I look at her, I can still see the little sister who would beg us to play barbie dolls. Her head was always in the clouds, and she wore a permanent smile on her thin lips. Unlike me, she had a childhood free from mafia talk. I guess I still want to protect her.

"We're going to Russia." Mateo tells her sternly. The playful smile on her lips fade and she snaps into business mode. With one curt nod of her head, she's on board.

"I want a fucking army to join us." I snap, turning to the Council. Each member here has at least three hundred people working below them. If I ask for an army, I expect an army within a heartbeat.

"We set off in thirty minutes. Get the planes ready and bring extra weapons. Who knows what will greet us on the other side?" I check my watch as I bark out the orders, "We will bring six jets and three large planes. I want one of us on each of the jets. Sophia, you will go with Angelo as you're a latecomer."

She twists towards him with a coy smile. I don't miss the look they exchange. I'm not stupid, I can feel the connection the pair of them have. She will be safe with him; he'll protect her with his life. And if not, he'll have me to answer to.

"Mateo and I will cover the front," I explain, pointing to the blueprints, "Aria and Casper through the back. Angelo and Sophia, you will wait outside and be loading the women onto the planes. Carlos, you shall control military movement and reinforcements. Am I understood?"

I am greeted with a low murmur of approval from each member. Satisfied, I lead the way out the doors and towards the jets.

MAYA'S POV:

I startle from the light sleep I managed to force upon myself. The door to my prison cell slams open. Defensively, I shoot to my feet and hold my fists up. Sasha greets me with a disgusting grin.

"What do you want?" I spit.

"Your lessons in manners begin today." His eye twitches as he scans me up and down. Protecting my modesty, I try to pull the skimpy dress down further to cover more of my bare skin. It just tugs the top part lower. With a yelp, I pull it back up.

"But first." He grins, revealing some missing teeth. My eyes jump to it, and I visibly recoil from him.

"I am offering you an opportunity none of the other girls are being given." He tells me grimly, "You get a choice."

"A choice?"

"Yes. You get to decide your fate." He nods approvingly. Before I can react, he crosses the room towards me. His fingers curl their way back into my hair and he quickly pushes me to my knees. In this position, I can't fight back.

"Option one. You will marry me." He states, eyes never leaving mine. Bile rises in my throat and my body begins to tremble.

"As my bride, you will become my equal. And together, we will rule the world."

"I would rather die." I retort quickly. His hand connects with my cheek and the stinging brings a layer of tears to my eyes. As if spurred on by my pain, he strikes me again. This time, a solitary tear slips down my cheek. *Fucking traitor,* I tell it silently.

"The other option," His grin grows more perverse, "I will use you. Over and over again until I'm done with you. Then, I shall sell you onto the highest bidder who will also mutilate your body."

"And option three?" I try desperately.

"You die." He states simply. I push my luck, "And option four?"

Another hand whips me around the face. This time, it's hard enough for my jaw to click. The pain radiates up into my ear. He throws me to the floor. For a moment, the world is fuzzy. All I can hear is the blood rushing in my ears. His coffee and cigar breath swarms my senses as he grabs me by the hair and pulls me back into a sitting position.

"No fucking around, Maya." He seethes. I hold my hands up defensively. *He's going to have to hit a lot harder than that if he wants me to crack.* My Father trained me too well to give up this easily.

"Sorry, sorry." I whisper before catching his eyes again, "What was choice four again?"

Suddenly, I'm flying across the room. With a thud, I collapse in a heap. Pain scorches through me but I throw myself to my feet and raise my fists. My vision is hazy, but I can still make out a fat man in front of me with grey hairs on his balding head.

"Don't mock me, girl!" He spits. I feel as the spit particles hit me on the face. I resist the urge to gag. Slowly, my vision restores itself. I peer down at the keys in his pocket. *If I can just get close enough...*

"Don't mock me, girl!" I tease. He charges towards me, but I lose my nerve last minute and bolt to the side. He gives chase but I am much faster. Suddenly, he pulls out a knife. I freeze as he points it at me.

"You really want to be hurt, don't you?" He seethes. It's as if his eyes flicker red as he corners me.

"You won't kill me." I breathe out, "I'm too valuable as you've proven. Either as your wife, as a toy or as profit. I mean look at me."

I spin around to show off my body, "I will sell for millions."

He lurches for me and thrusts the knife in my face. This time I snatch the keys from his pocket, dodging the weapon. Before he can stop me, I'm bounding towards the door. I pull on the handle to open it, but it is locked. Desperately, I fumble through the keys trying to find the gold key from yesterday. But it's incredibly difficult to do as I also monitor his movements.

"To answer your bold statement." He flashes his ugly smile as he advances towards me, "You can still be my *toy* if you're dead."

Chapter Seven.

ALESSIO'S POV:

With a small thud, the jet finally lands. My watch tells me it's 5:08pm so we are ahead of schedule. *Finally, some good fucking news.*

Around me, the other planes quietly land. We are half a mile away from the prison and came in through a route where we wouldn't be spotted.

Quickly, I jump off the plane and meet with Mateo who already waits for me. We lead a group of men towards the prison. I clutch my gun tightly, aiming it at anything that moves.

"There is no one at the door?" I scowl as we advance closer. My Brother flicks his safety switch off and points it left.

"This is a very underground mission. I doubt Sasha was able to get that many people involved." He mutters grimly. I nod.

"On my count." I tell my men, "One, Two, *Three!*"

My foot boots the front door down, sending it flying backwards. Half of the team flank left, the other right. Another squadron quickly follows behind us. Whilst my men work on the downstairs rooms, I head straight for the stairs. My hunger to hurt Sasha increases. It's as if I can smell the dirty fucker up here.

I fire once into the guard on the stairs. Before he even realised that I was there, the bullet licked straight through his brain and out the other side.

Downstairs, a delicious chorus of flying bullets ring out. I smile. It's such a beautiful noise. Behind me, my Brother closely follows suit. We charge down the corridor, peering into the locked, single cell rooms, searching for victims. Mateo shoots the lock off of the door on the left. A tanned woman scurries out. Matted hair and blotchy faced, she throws herself into his arms. Quickly, he directs her down the stairs, to safety.

I stalk closer towards the end of the corridor.

Then, I hear a faint scream. The cry is muffled but it still forces me into action. Something primal rages through me as I race towards the sound. *I'm coming for you, Sasha.*

MAYA'S POV:

Gun shots ring through the building as Sasha parts my legs. I scream out, desperate for anyone to hear me. I can't tell who is shooting, but from Sasha's grim reaction, I can tell he is in trouble. My mind screams that it is my Brother and Father. That they are here to save me. *To rescue me!*

"Get the fuck off of me!" I yell. Filled with hope, I gain more strength to fight back. I buck my hips to try and throw him off but he's too heavy. My hands claw at his chest. I cry out as one of my nails snaps backwards.

Maliciously, he leans forward and presses the knife to my throat. Another terrified scream leaves my lips. His hand strikes me around the face and then covers my mouth.

"No use in screaming. They can't find us up here." Sasha grins cockily. Despite his confident words, his eye twitches and his gaze nervously flicks between me and the door. His knife slices my neck slowly and I cry out in agony. Below him, I writher and scream as hard as I can. My fists pound into his chest but he doesn't relent. Just as I think I'm done for, a bullet echoes through the room. The door swings open.

Sasha's head snaps upwards.

"*You!*" He gasps. Fear and horror melts onto his face. I use this opportunity to drive my elbow into his stomach. He lurches over, giving me the perfect opportunity to use his weight against him. I buck him to the side, so he falls left. From there, I snatch his knife away and press it to his throat. The rage and violence takes a hold of me before I can stop myself.

"You fucking asshole!" I shriek. A thin layer of blood trickles from my own wound. He cowers away from me, his mouth opening and closing like a fish. For a moment, I relish in the fear. I pull back and drive a foot into his groin area. He howls in pain and folds in half like a chair. I do not stop the assault. Repeatedly, I drive my foot into his body until I feel the bones snapping and the blood seeping through his clothes onto my toes. Weakly, he lays on the floor in a puddle of blood. I grab him by the shirt and yank him into a sitting position.

"How dare you think you can use me as bait?" I hiss at him, "I would rather die than be your wife or plaything."

I spit in his face. He recoils but doesn't lift his hands to wipe it away. My eyes bear into his. He needs to remember this face. The woman who lived. The woman who will get her revenge. I drop him to the floor, and he hits it with a thud.

"Fucking took your time." I complain before looking up.

However, I'm startled. Neither my Father nor Brother stand in the doorway. Instead, it is as if I've been rescued by a Greek God. He is as tall as the door frame, broad and beautiful. Tattoos kiss every inch of his huge arms, and his dark clothes clings to his chiselled body. I am left breathless as I look up at his handsome face. Raven coloured hair slicked back, dark eyes and round lips. I stumble over my words before remaining silent. His beautiful eyes gaze into mine. He also doesn't make any effort to talk.

Suddenly, a ring of bullets fly through the upper floor. My saviour reaches out and I quickly race towards him. He guides me out of the room and down the stairs, his hand on my lower back. If I wasn't so anxious, I might have enjoyed that possessive, warm touch.

Then, I stumble forward. Bile rises in my throat and my vision starts to grow hazy. Around me, the world seems to pump in tune to my heartbeat. Shakily, my fingers reach up and I touch the wound on my neck. I peer down at my fingers. *Blood*. The adrenaline dulls the pain, but my body betrays me. I fall.

Then, the world goes dark.

Chapter Eight

ALESSIO'S POV:

Fuck, she is stunning.

My heart *and* dick throbbed when i watched her fight Sasha. Like a true mafia queen, she fought back with a vengeance and violence others can only dream of.

Now, she sleeps on my lap. I don't know why but the idea of loading her onto one of the other planes whilst she is unconscious makes my blood boil. *No.* I want my little warrior here. Next to me. Where she belongs.

Gently, I run the alcohol wipes over her neck, cleaning the blood. I can't help but admire how beautiful she is. Long black eyelashes, pale skin with rosy cheeks, and full lips. My eyes linger on her lips for a little longer before I snap my head away.

Get it together, for fuck's sake, Alessio!

"How is she?" Sophia asks softly as she sits next to me. She grabs another wipe and slowly removes the dried blood from the woman's leg.

"The medic said she will be fine. She's lost enough blood to make her woozy but other than that, she will just need to rest." I hear my voice respond but it doesn't sound like me. Instead, the voice is chipped, nervous almost. I grab another wipe and begin removing the dirt from her cheeks.

"I heard Sasha got away." Sophia says. Her eyes flick between me and the woman on my lap, as if she is waiting for me to freak out.

"We will find him again." I grumble, "For now, the women are safe."

Mentally, I kick myself. I should have stayed and continued the fight with Sasha's men. But the overwhelming urge to protect this little fighter hit me. Even though she clearly can manage on her own, I had to make sure she made it onto the plane. And good thing I did too. The second her foot hit the final step, she collapsed in my arms.

My thumb gently rubs at some dirt below her eye. I tense up. Something protective grips my heart as I replay her words to Sasha *'I would rather die than be your wife or plaything.'*. I tremble as the violence seeps through me again. If Sasha thought he had an enemy of me before, he now had a fucking war coming his way. The little fighter in my lap is a ball of perfection. From the moment I saw her on the CCTV, to the way I saw her beat up the Russian Mafia boss... A mix of beauty, strength, and courage. Everything desirable. Everything I could want.

Her lips seem to swell under my touch as I wipe away some dried blood. They redden and respond to me. My jaw hardens as I avert my eyes. I must control myself. I am a gentleman. Fantasising over her is one thing, but having a physical reaction to her? *No.* That's too far. This woman is a victim, and my main priority is to nurse her back to health. Then, it's helping her out of whatever situation she landed herself in with Sasha.

After all, she is an Italian citizen. It is my duty to protect her.

"Angelo asked me out." My sister's small voice pulls me from my thoughts.

"On a date." She adds. She bites her lower lip nervously and doesn't make eye contact. A small smile teases my lips. *I knew it!* I knew they liked one another.

"What did you say?" I answer calmly. My little sister is like a deer in a field. Startles very easily. You must let her come to you and reveal things about her life. If you approach her, she will flee.

"I said yes. However..." She trails off into silence before finally peering up at me, "It's Thursday night. And I know you set me some extra tasks to complete by then. But I promise they will all be done, I sw-"

"Sophia." I cut her off, "Enjoy your night off. You haven't had one in over a year. I can grant you an evening off work. Angelo too. He's worked very hard to find the women."

Her eyes light up with hope.

"Oh, really?" She squeaks. She is in disbelief. Awkwardly, she pulls me into a side hug, avoiding the woman in my lap.

"You're old enough to make your own decisions. However, please just don't make a thing of screwing my Council members. I can't be arsed to hire HR when it all goes wrong." I smirk. She blushes and pulls away from the embrace.

"I promise I won't." She nods in agreement.

I peer down at the beauty in my lap and sigh. Sophia will find love in Angelo, I'm sure of it. My Brother always had a long-legged stunner on his arm. *And me?* I've married myself off to the business.

MAYA'S POV:

Ah, my fucking head!

It feels as though someone has shot me three times in the brain, pulled the bullets out and then fired another round. Weakly, I push myself into a sitting position. One hand grabs my thumping head and the other props me up. However, I am no longer greeted with a hard ground.

Startled, I jump off of the bed. It is huge, with large fluffy pillows and expensive looking sheets. A rouge coloured, satin throw crumples from where I slept on it. Around the room, rich looking oak furniture. A soft rug cuddles my toes. I stare down at my clean skin and my jaw drops. *Has someone cleaned me?*

"What the fuck?" I whisper in fear. Dread sinks further through me as I race towards the door. *I'm alone! I'm alone! Fuck. I'm going to die!*

Suddenly, a flush of a toilet pauses my racing thoughts. I freeze and stare expectantly at the door on the other side of the room. My fists clench, ready to fight my way out. A bright haired woman with a round face stumbles out of the bathroom. She wipes her wet hands on her jeans. Then, she startles when she sees me.

"Oh, hi!" She beams.

"Who the fuck are you? And where am I?" I hiss. The last couple hours are hazy in my mind, and I can't remember how I left the prison. A frightening thought enters my mind. *What If they have kidnapped me too?*

"I am Sophia." The woman says, her smile slowly fading, "You are in Rome."

"Rome?" I gawp.

"Yes," She says nervously, "We are the Italian mafia. We saved you from the prison in Russia. Do you not remember?"

"Russia?" My jaw falls open. Nervously, I start pacing around. *Yes, I remember the Russian men who kidnapped me. But were we really imprisoned in Russia? How did they get me all the way there without noticing?*

My memory seeps back in slowly as I desperately try to remember the last things before, I passed out. A beautiful, dark-haired man seems to haunt my memories. He and his impressed look as I beat Sasha up.

"I want to leave!" I demand. I scratch at the bandages around my arm. Sophia's face drains her colour slightly.

"Oh, you can't." She says with wide eyes, "You're still sick."

"I am not." I hiss. Like a caged animal, I feel threatened. I don't care who she is, I will claw the hair off her scalp if she tries to keep me locked in this room.

"If you want, you can take the bandages off? My Brother and I cleaned up most of the blood, but you can have a shower to get rid of the rest." She smiles, noticing my discomfort. She points towards the door where she came from. My eyes dart between her and the bathroom. With the door wide open, I can see the luxury bath. It is huge, like a hot tub, in the middle of the room. A soft looking towel drapes over the side. The room smells of lavender and makes me feel warm inside. Silently, It beckons me in.

My escape can wait, I tell myself, transfixed by the majestic tub. My Father and Brother wouldn't be looking for me yet, most likely. I have another couple hours to kill until the clubs open and I can go back to work to make up for the lack of stolen goods. There is no way that I will be able to return home without something for my Father. And I suppose I do need to freshen up. It is hard to flirt and thieve off of men if you smell like shit.

"I suppose I could have a bath?" I raise an eyebrow up at her. Satisfaction sinks through her expression. She bounces on the spot before quickly ushering me towards the bathroom. Eagerly, she turns the tap on and hangs the towel on the door handle.

"Only one condition." Sophia says, twisting around to me. I stumble backwards as she invades my personal space.

"I will wait in the bedroom and will sit with my back to you. But you must leave the door open." A blush coats her cheeks, "Nothing weird. It's just that my Brother wants to make sure you're safe. If the door is shut and you pass out in the bath, I won't be able to know."

I can't nod fast enough. Being alone in a strange place is my worst fear. Any company is quickly welcomed.

"Sure!" I chirp. She pours some pink liquid into the bath. It instantly pops and crackles, releasing a beautiful strawberry smell. I feel the water and turn the temperature up.

"That's too hot." Sophia scowls, reaching out to turn it down. I slap her hand away.

"No," I bark, "It's perfect."

"Please, you'll burn your skin off." Her eyes widen as she pleads with me. I shake my head once, then twice.

"I don't care. I will burn his touch off of me even if that means removing a couple layers of skin."

She doesn't protest any further. Instead, she turns on her heel and scurries out the bathroom, leaving the door wide open. I waste no time stripping down and climbing into the tub. Bubbles pop around me, and my body instantly thanks me for the relaxing massage. My head lulls back in bliss.

A low growl echoes through the other room. My eyes shoot open, and I stare into the bedroom. The

man from earlier stands, fists clenched, eyes dark.

"Brother! She's in the bath, Alessio! Leave!" Sophia squeaks in horror. She tries to push him out, but he doesn't budge.

It's him. The man who saved me. *Alessio.*

The bubbles protect my modesty and yet it feels like he can see straight through the bath walls. It's not a look of lust, It's a look of desperation. Subconsciously, I can feel the anger radiating off of him. Dishevelled hair, torn clothes, and a muddy face. He looks worse than me. And he definitely does not like my justification of the boiling water to Sophia.

"I'll be in my office when you are done." His jaw hardens as he averts his eyes. Just as quickly as he appears, he disappears again. A scowl coats my lips.

"What does he want with me?" I ask his sister, Sophia. Her lips pull into a thin line, and for once she doesn't smile.

"He's going to make you a deal." She whispers.

ILLEGAL ACTIVITIES

I sink further back into the bath and squeeze my eyes shut. I don't want any more choices. I don't want any more deals. Sasha ruined freedom of choice for me. My body pulses as the hot water scorches my skin. Another ten minutes and his touch shall be gone from me, I tell myself.

"I brought you some clean clothes, Maya." Sophia calls out. My gaze snaps towards her. She sits on the bed, back to me, folding some clothes into a neat pile.

"How do you know my name?"

"We know everyone's name. Every victim from the prison has been brought to the city to get better. Alessio has created programs to help everyone recover." Sophia answers. My heart does a little flip in my chest. *Handsome and caring?* Someone pinch me!

"We are a similar size." Sophia notes, holding up a black tank top with frills, "So you can borrow some of my clothes."

I scowl at the skimpy top and tight jeans she has laid out on the bed for me. I want to tell her that there's no need, that I will not be staying that long. I will finish my bath, tell the sexy man to fuck off with his deal, and then skip to the club to start work. I keep my lips shut as I look at the fluffy socks she places on top of the neat pile. They look so warm.

Okay, maybe I might steal her clothes. And then I will leave.

"Thanks." I mutter. I make quick work of scrubbing my body clean as the bath water turns an awful colour and the strawberry scent starts to fade. Standing up, I hose myself down with the detachable shower handle, before helping myself to the shampoo and conditioner on the side. In my defence, I don't know when I will have this kind of luxury available to me again. I will make every second count.

Towel wrapped around my body, I step into the bedroom. Sophia hears my footsteps and heads towards the chair in the corner of the room. She turns to face the wall and takes a seat. Suspiciously, I eye up the clothes on the bed before slowly putting them on.

"What's the link between you guys and Russia?" I ask thoughtfully, yanking a sock up my foot. My thoughts race with all the ways that Sasha is going to pay when I find him again. Only this time, It shall be on my terms. And I will have many more weapons.

Sophia sighs, "I can't talk about it."

"Sure, you can." I beam, "Open and close your mouth and let the words fall out."

She chuckles at me but remains quiet. I finish dressing myself before drying my hair the best I can with a towel. Sophia quickly links my arm when I drop the towel to the floor. She guides me out of the room, and suddenly I feel like a lamb to the slaughter.

This mansion is huge, with long winding halls and beautiful paintings on every available wall. It drips a wealth which I can only dream of. Sophia pauses outside a large door and knocks.

"Come in." Alessio booms. My heart jumps in my chest at the authoritative tone.

"I brought Maya." Sophia announces as she opens the door for me.

Nervously, I shuffle into the huge office room. Alessio leans forward in his seat and his suit strains against his large body. His dark eyes remain glued to me. I want to squirm under his gaze, but I don't give him the satisfaction. I'm sure, like all other mafia men, he will be arrogant and sinister the minute he opens his mouth.

"Thank you." He nods his head approvingly at his sister. She scurries out of the room. Her footsteps are audible for a couple moments longer before the silence hums between us.

"How are you feeling?" Alessio slumps back in his chair and shuts his laptop. Anxiously, I take a seat in front of him.

"Better." It is a one-word answer. Something tells me I should thank him for saving us. I should show a little gratitude. But I wasn't raised with manners. I was raised to survive.

"I believe Sasha is looking for you." He confesses with a scowl. He clears his throat and pulls the paperwork from a drawer beside him. Slowly, he thumbs through the sheets.

I remain silent as I watch him.

"You will stay here until I understand why." He sighs, peering back up at me. Alarmed, I shoot out of my chair.

"No." I say firmly, "I am leaving as soon as this conversation is over."

"No, you are not." He cocks his head to the side with a confused look, "Did you hear what I just said? Sasha is looking for you. If you leave, he will find you again."

"Then let him. Makes my revenge much easier." I fold my arms stroppily. Alessio scowls,

"I will not let you get caught by him again. It's my duty to protect Italian women."

"That's great…" I say sarcastically, "for your ego. However, I can look after myself."

He groans and adjusts himself in his seat.

"Sasha is very mad with your Father. I bel-"

"What?" I snap, "How do you know that?"

His eyes widen in shock as I openly argue with him.

"You have no right to snoop into my life!" I shake my head angrily, "Fine, thank you for taking us out of there. But I can assure you, I have it from here."

The anger vibrates through me. I am fucking sick of being a thing for men to pass around. Always trapped in the shadows of another man's demands. My body turns to head towards the door to leave but I'm quickly stopped. As if he teleported, Alessio appears in front of me. One of his hands grip my arm and he holds me still. His touch sends shivers through my traitorous body. I bite my lower lip to stop my racing thoughts.

"Feisty Maya." He whispers so quietly I almost don't hear it. Then he speaks a little louder, "I will not let you leave this house."

"Watch me." I hiss. Pathetically, I try to pull my arm away from his grip, but he doesn't let go.

"Can you not see a fair and good deal when it presents itself to you?"

"I will not live here under your roof, Alessio." I tell him with a scowl. Something in his face flickers when I say his name.

"Why not?" He tries.

"Because I can handle myself."

"Where will you go?" He continues the assault of questions. My heart races in my chest and the anger rises and rises. The last few days have been too much. Kidnapped by the Russian mafia, only to be kidnapped again by the Italian mafia. All whilst my Father and Brothers are oblivious and make no effort to help me. *Fucking men!*

"Home." I spit. His eyes darken.

"You will not leave."

"I fucking shall." I keep his eye contact, daring him to look away first. A small twitch of his lips makes my heart flip inside my chest. I scan his beautiful face. Then it drops slightly in despair.

"Let me help you." He croaks, "Just until I can figure out what Sasha's next plans are."

I bite my lower lip nervously. On the one hand, I want to leave. *Need* to leave. I must return to work and steal a lot of stuff. Father would be furious if I returned home empty handed, kidnapping or no kidnapping. We don't do excuses. We do success.

On the other hand, Alessio is right. Sasha will come find me again. My Father owes him a lot of money and I had bested him. He is the type of man who would not stop until he got what he wanted. Perhaps it is safer to plan my own revenge on him in the comfort of safety. And luxury.

"Fine." I spit, "I will stay. But not because I'm afraid of him, but because I like your bath."

It is a lame argument, and it makes the sinfully attractive man in front of me smile. He releases a sigh of relief and nods.

"Okay." He smiles, releasing my arm from his grip. My skin moans out from the lack of contact. As if he also feels the withdrawal, his fingers stroke my face gently. I freeze under his soft touch and resist the urge to cuddle further into his hand. He offers me a softness and calmness. I crave more.

"Get some more rest." He whispers. He is very close to me right now. *Too close.* My eyes flicker up to his lips as they move. I long to feel them against my own. *Would he be a soft kisses or more violent and possessive?* I pray for the second option.

"I don't want to be alone quite yet." I hear myself respond. The sound is small, timid. *It's fucking pathetic.* But it is out there now. I cringe and avert my eyes.

"Sleep here." He says softly, pointing toward the two-seater armchair in the corner of the room. Greedily, I eye up the comfortable looking thing.

"Okay." I say nervously. It is better than being alone, locked away in that room, with nothing but my thoughts and memories.

As soon as I sit down on the scarlet-coloured sofa, my body groans in approval. I swing my legs around and lay down. He takes off his suit jacket and lays it over my body. The gesture is so endearing. A small blush kisses my cheeks.

I know I shouldn't trust him. I can't trust him. He is a man, and he has power. The two worst things in history. But when I peer up into his genuinely caring eyes, my concerns are hushed.

"Pinkie promise you won't leave me alone whilst I sleep?" I stick out my pinkie finger.

"What's a pinkie promise?" He frowns. I grab his unwilling pinkie finger and link it with mine.

"It's a promise, but even more certain." I tell him before yawning. He smiles down at me and nods his head, "Of course, Maya. I pinkie promise that I will stay here."

Chapter Nine

MAYA'S POV:

Groggily, my eyes flutter open. The sound of frantic typing pulls me from my deep sleep. I peer up at Alessio. He bashes at the keyboard, eyebrows burrowed together. A grim line rests on his lips and he shakes his head disapprovingly at something. Then his eyes catch my gaze. Instantly, he softens.

"Morning." He smiles. I push myself into a sitting position, keeping his jacket wrapped around me. He leans forward at his desk and clicks a button on his telephone.

"Bring it up, please." He says before lifting his finger off of it, "I've ordered you some dinner. Hope that's okay?"

Approvingly, my stomach growls. I could have bitten his hand off right there for some grub. A knock at the door follows moments later. An older looking lady dressed in white hands me a plate with a bowl over the top. I quickly pull the food to my lap and remove the lid. The smell of fish and chips attacks my senses.

"Freshly battered cod, with homegrown potato chips, and peas. With a garlic mayonnaise side." The lady nods her head before handing me a pair of cutlery. I quickly tuck in.

"Thank you." I say between mouthfuls. A large smile pulls at the lady's face.

"Thank you, Mary." Alessio says politely. She sends him a wink before exiting the room.

"Did you not get anything?" I frown up at Alessio. He watches me with an amused smile. Slowly, he shakes his head.

"Maya, it's three in the morning. I've already eaten." He says.

"What!" I gawp, "You should have woken me up. I'm sorry!"

Guilt eats away at me as i realise how kind this man truly is. *First, he saves me. Then, he gives me a place to stay and food to eat, for free. And now, he stayed awake all night to fulfil my silly pinkie promise.*

"No, no it's fine. I had to work anyways." He shrugs before leaning back in his chair. He looks so handsome in his devilish attire with dishevelled hair. My fingers itch to touch the raven coloured strands. I finish off the plate and let it rest on the arm of the chair. Despite being asleep for how long, I stifle a yawn.

"We should go to bed." I say before blushing, "I mean, like separately of course. Like, let's go to sleep."

"You've slept quite a lot." He grins before crossing the room toward me.

"I've kept you up." I whisper, "You need to sleep."

He takes a seat on the chair next to me and undoes his tie. I watch with greedy eyes as he slowly undresses to become more comfortable.

"And you need to feel safe. I'd stay up all night if I have to." He smiles. It reaches his eyes and melts me into a pool of hormones.

"I feel safe." I confess without thinking. Mentally, I kick myself. I shouldn't be creating connections with him. A long and comfortable silence drifts between us. I hate it.

"Maya." He grumbles, looking lost for a second, "why do you not want to be alone?"

I tense up.

"I- uh," I stumble over my words. I avert my eyes and try to think of a lie.

"And I want the truth." He whispers sensing my plan. I gulp and nervously play with my fingers. My lips slam shut, and I try to wait him out. He doesn't relent and instead places one of his hands over my fingers reassuringly. I peer up at him and his eyes almost soften. My mouth becomes dry.

"Growing up, If I was naughty, my Father would lock me in a room alone." I mumble, "In the dark, alone, for days at a time sometimes. When you're alone, you have nothing other than bad thoughts. And *memories*."

Beside me, Alessio flinches. His touch becomes more rigid, and I can feel the slight tremble in his hands.

"I understand." He nods his head slowly, "And at night? Where do you usually sleep?"

Another blush coats my cheeks. I peer down at our hands entwined together. Usually, if a stranger touches me, I'd attack. Like a hungry lioness defending her territory, they would quickly become my prey. But now, I welcome his comforting touch.

"I sleep in my Brother's room. Bunk beds." I whisper, embarrassed. I have never told anyone that story before. I can fight, I can steal, I can lie. I just cannot be isolated. It's pathetic.

"Would you like to stay in my room tonight?" He asks. My eyes shoot up in shock and I begin to shake my head. No. I *shouldn't*. We shouldn't be bonding. In a couple days, I will leave. I don't need to create attachments here.

"I will even sleep on the floor." He whispers, "If it makes you feel safe, I'm more than happy."

Another wave of guilt flows through me.

"I'm not going to kick you out of your bed, Alessio." I stare at him, shocked that he would suggest such a thing.

"Okay." He ponders on my answer, "Separate sides of the bed. I promise I won't try anything."

His thumb gently traces over my knuckles. Another blush coats my cheeks. I almost wish he would try something. I have never laid eyes on such a compassionate and handsome man before. Something twists in my stomach.

"Okay." I smile at him, "Thank you."

His bedroom is huge. It can fit my entire living room and dining room in here, and still have enough space for a bed. In the middle of the room, a majestic, queens sized bed, surrounded by expensive furniture; fit for a King. *Or an Italian mafia boss.*

"I have a shirt you could sleep in if you'd prefer?" He offers me, heading towards his oak chest of drawers.

"Please." I take a grey shirt from him.

"You can get changed in the bathroom. It's just through that door. There are spare toothbrushes too under the sink."

I head towards where he points me and quickly get dressed. The soft material brushes against my thighs and hangs loose. I bring it to my nose and sniff. *It smells like him too.* Oak and vanilla. Mixed with a musky, delicious violence. My new favourite smell.

As I exit the bathroom, his eyes are instantly on me. He takes a sharp intake of breath as his eyes roams up my body. I shiver under his approving gaze.

"Come." He whispers, patting the bed beside him. I slowly stalk towards the soft looking spot. My eyes are fixed on his naked torso. Muscles bulge around those black slithering tattoos. I itch to touch them. To *taste* them. He wears a loose pair of black pants. My eyes widen as I look at his huge bulge. Another blush stains my face as I quickly avert his eyes. A smirk on his face tells me he noticed my eyeline.

I jump into bed and pull the covers up to my chin before I can embarrass myself any further. He folds the corner of the page of the book he is holding. Then he puts it on the side before getting comfortable in bed.

"There is a celebration tomorrow night." He says, turning to face me. My heart races one hundred miles an hour at how close we are.

"Right." I mumble, half listening.

"To celebrate the freedom of the women. Sophia arranged it." He sighs, "Would you like to go with me?"

I freeze. Like a fish out of water, I open and shut my mouth. I must look like an idiot as my mind races for an answer.

"I mean you don't have to, of course. I just thought It would be ni-" He panics. A look of despair and then humiliation crosses his expression. I watch as he mentally kicks himself for suggesting such a thing.

"Alessio," I interrupt him, "I would love to go."

Instinctively, my hand shoots out to his chest to steady his ramblings, but I quickly regret it. His eyes darken and he freezes under my touch. I pull away. And then regret that too, missing the touch of his warm, hard chest.

"You are so beautiful." He murmurs. My heart flips in my chest as I shuffle closer to him. I don't know why I do it but It's like a magnet between us. I'm drawn closer. His arm reaches out and he pulls me up against him. The breath in my lungs vanishes. His hold is protective. I blush.

"I mean it." He whispers, bringing his other hand to move some hair from my face. His fingers remain on my cheek a little longer. He tilts my chin upwards, and I'm forced to keep his gaze. I squeeze my legs shut and wish the throbbing away.

Slowly, he moves his head towards me. My tongue darts out to wet my lips. *I should move away. I should pull away.* But I stay still, silently begging for more. Then his lips touch mine. It starts of soft, gentle. And then a delicious violence seeps into the kiss. My fingers jump to his chest, tightly holding onto him as if he will disappear if I let go. His hand on my back slips down to my bum. He squeezes and I moan into the kiss.

"Fuck." He groans, rolling on top of me. My legs wrap around his back desperately. The shirt rides up and his hand slips up towards my breast. His thumb flicks over my nipple and I can't help the moan which slips through my lips. A delicious need floods through me. He continues his assault on my breast as he trails kisses down my face, to my neck. I wince as his lips find the cut. Startled, he pulls back.

Even in the dark, I can see the desire in his eyes. I feel it pulsing off of him, mixing in with that beautiful woody smell. I reach up to pull him back into a kiss, but he remains frozen.

"I shouldn't have done that." He whispers, voice small. Humiliation floods through me.

"What? Why? Is it me?"

"No, God no!" He shakes his head and falls onto the bed beside me in despair, "This is so wrong of me. You're healing. You've just had an awful trauma. I'm supposed to help you, not try and bed you."

My cheeks turn scarlet. He seems so genuine.

"I want it." I say before I can stop myself, "Don't make the decision for me. I am not a victim, Alessio. Don't treat me like one."

He shakes his head and puts some more distance between us. I resist the urge to scoot closer.

"I would be taking advantage of you." He whispers, voice hoarse.

"You wouldn't!" I protest, reaching out for him. He allows my touch but doesn't return it. My body still screams with need. I desperately try to turn it off but how can I when I have him this close to me?

Defeated, I pull back and wrap my arms around my body protectively.

"Fine." I whisper, turning my back to him. The humiliation is too much. I am a grown woman. If I want to have mind-blowing sex with a Greek god, then I should be able to. And if he believes that I would give up the chase because of a couple words, he is wrong. A small smile creeps to my lips as I slowly stick my bum out. He grunts.

"Night, Alessio." I whisper coyly.

Once my racing heart calms down, I drift off to sleep, thinking of all the ways I can torment him until he gives me what I want until I eventually leave for my revenge on Sasha.

Namely, I want him.

Chapter Ten

ALESSIO'S POV:

My fingers drum against the desk impatiently. I barely got any sleep last night. All I could do is think about the beautiful woman beside me. And her fucking ass grinding into me. A heat flushes through my body just thinking about it.

I can't act on it. I *won't* act on it. It's an abuse of power. What if she only wants to have sex with me out of guilt for everything that I've given her? *No.* I could never forgive myself if that happens. I don't do good things for a reward. Good things should be done because they are fucking good. Not because they promise sex after.

"I have bad news." My Brother pulls me from my thoughts. He marches into the office and quickly takes his seat.

"Course you do." I mutter, running a hand through my hair.

"It's about Maya." He bares his teeth. My curiosity is piqued.

Mateo hands me a piece of paper. On it, there is a screenshot of a text message.

"It's in Russian." I frown at him, "What does it say?"

"Aria translated it. Sasha sent this message out to lots of high-ranking people. It's him ordering people to find her and turn her in to him." He winces, "And that he is going to marry her."

My blood boils.

"He has also put hits out on our heads." Mateo sighs. If possible, the violence in my system rises.

"Then we will go to war with the Russians." I spit bluntly. Mateo's eyebrows almost touch as he scowls.

"Brother." He starts but I cut him off.

"No, we will fucking destroy every last one of them. What other option do we have?"

"We have two more options, actually." My Brother's jaw hardens. I sit back in my chair and urge him to continue.

"Option one, we hand the girl over. It removes the hit from our heads." He explains. A menacing growl escapes my lips.

"Don't ever fucking suggest that again." I warn him. He nods in understanding. It's not an option he would consider either, but it is an option that must be mentioned.

"Option two, you marry the girl." He confesses. My jaw drops.

"What?" I hiss.

"Think about it, Alessio." He explains, "You cannot marry another woman's wife. Plus, if the people this message was sent to see that you've married her, they wouldn't dare try and take her from you. And it must be you. She must be a mafia bride."

"Not happening." I shake my head in despair, "She'd never agree to it."

"We cannot go to war with the Russians over her." He sighs, "It's too costly. It's too risky. You understand that, right?"

I grunt in agreement, but the plan doesn't leave my mind. I barely managed to convince her to stay in the mansion for a couple days! As if my stubborn, strong-willed little Maya would agree to marriage. It's pretty fucking permanent for a woman who loves control and freedom.

"Plus, think about the appearance of it. You stole Sasha Ovlov's bride. That's pretty fucking big. If that doesn't send the other countries scuttering away, I don't know what will." He adds. A growl ripples through me.

"Fuck!" I howl, slamming a fist into the table.

As much as I hate to say it, my Brother is right. Maya will become a mafia bride. Whether that's with Sasha, or with me. And I hope to God that she picks me.

MAYA'S POV:

Sophia skips ahead of me in the garden. She leaps from stone to stone across the pond. I walk around the edge, enamoured by all the different sweet smells and colours.

"Do you have any siblings?" She asks, readying herself for a big jump.

"Yes." I tell her, "three Brothers. Cole, Ben, and James."

"You'll know my pain of having Brothers then." She smirks before taking the leap. She wobbles on the next steppingstone but quickly steadies herself.

"What are they like?" She asks.

I pause and think about my Brothers. *Would they be worried about me? Would they have tried to find me when I didn't return home with stolen goods? Perhaps they have a search team scouring the globe for me right now?*

Of course not!

We were raised to quickly forget one another if we were ever split up. Family only means something if everyone is profiting.

And in my family, you only profit if you provide. And me? Right now? I am not providing.

"Cole is the eldest." I tell her, "He is lovely. Very caring, affectionate even."

My heart pangs. *Cole*. Oh, how I miss him. Being seven years older than me, I always looked up to him as a Father figure throughout my childhood. If I needed money, he supplied it. If I was hungry, he would feed me. Not once would he complain.

"James is next. A trickster. If there was a prank to be pulled, James would pull it." I smile fondly at the memory of him. My smile falls quickly. Past tense.

I haven't seen James in years. One day, he took off and never returned home. The only thing that reassures me that he is still alive is the constant stream of money in the joint bank account. When I'd ask about him, Cole would tell me he was on a very large business trip. That he was doing us a huge favour and I should be grateful, not sad, that he's gone. Even now, I'm not sure whether Cole was lying or not.

"Ben is... well how can I describe Ben?" I scoff, scowling at the ground, "Ben was very good at his job, let's say."

"What job is that?" Sophia frowns as she takes the last leap across the pond.

"Stealing." I smile.

"He is a thief!" She startles and shakes her head disapprovingly. My lips snap shut, and I avert my eyes. *She clearly doesn't know very much about me.*

"*Was.*" I mutter, "Ben is no longer with us."

"Oh, how horrible! What happened?" Sophia gawps as she joins me back on the path. My lips remain shut, and I shake my head. I don't want to remember. I don't owe her any more information about me.

Understanding my silence, she nods her head slowly.

"Why don't we go back inside and get ready for the celebration?" She offers with a smile. Thankful for the conversation change, I nod my head. Something inside of me almost longs for the celebration tonight. At least this way, I will be reunited with Alessio.

Chapter Eleven

MAYA'S POV:

I borrowed one of Sophia's dresses for the celebration. A long, black silk dress, with a slit at the thigh. It is low cut and compliments my bust perfectly. Scarlet heels match my dark, smoky makeup and a small silver necklace rests around my neck, covering the small, scabbing wound. Sophia gave me her straighteners too, so my long, curly hair became even longer as it sashayed by my hips. And she gave me a silver clip to push back the hair on my left side, revealing beautiful, long earrings. They tickle my cheek if I turn my head too fast, and they jingle as I walk. But they are perfect.

"You look beautiful!" She clasps her hands together as I turn to show her my finished look. I blush and bite my lower lip nervously. I need to look stunning. Rejection isn't something I'm familiar with. The only man I've ever wanted has pushed me away. And he is going to regret that decision.

"Thank you. You look even better." I respond sweetly looking at her blood-red dress with frills. It matches her wavy, red hair and makes her look like a danger sign. *Well, she is the friendliest danger sign I've ever met!*

"Oh, I know." She waves her hand around teasingly.

A small chuckle falls from my lips. I never had friends growing up. Especially not friends with girls. My Father had me stealing from a very young age, which made the other children wary of me. Wherever I went, something would go missing. And then when I became a better and more discreet thief, it was too late to make friends. My Father purposely isolated me. He told me that friends and relationships outside family would ruin the dynamic. Family should come first and last. Nothing else should be on the list.

And yet, as I stand here, staring at myself in the long mirror with Sophia, I can't help but long for friends. Loneliness is my best and only friend. Things must change.

A knock at the door pulls me from my thoughts.

"Are you decent?" Alessio's low voice calls out. The sound sends shivers through me. *What will he think about my outfit? Will he love it? Will he rip it off me?* I squeeze my legs shut.

"Yes!" Sophia chirps before throwing the door open.

My heart almost leaps from my chest as I look at the sinfully handsome man in front of me. With his dark suit clinging to each of his muscles, and the white shirt underneath contrasting his tan skin, my legs almost give away. A sultry smile teases my lips as he scans my outfit.

"M-maya," He stutters, "You look fantastic."

His compliment makes my mouth dry. Nervously, I bob my head to thank him. His darkening eyes never leave my body. My floral perfume, which I borrowed from Sophia, quickly merges with his musky scent as he takes me by the arm. It is a smell I don't think I'll ever forget. It is perfect. I want to bottle it up and take it home with me when I eventually leave.

This thought, for the first time, makes my stomach churn uneasily. Leaving is the last thing on my mind right now. Tonight, I will just enjoy my time at the celebration. *Perhaps I can pretend it is one of my Saturday night freedom fantasies?* Tonight, I am a free woman, attending a Ball just because I fucking can!

"Come on then guys, the party won't start itself!" Sophia breaks the tension in the room, skipping out the door happily.

"I guess we better follow." Alessio smiles as he leads me out of the room.

"So, you like the dress?" I ask with a raised eyebrow. His jaw slackens and he shakes his head in disbelief.

"Maya," He says with a dreamy look in his eyes, "I love the dress. You look stunning in it."

I feel my face flush with heat at his compliment. I look down at the stairs to hide my expression. But I feel the way his body trembles as he chuckles.

"Have I told you how beautiful you look when you blush?" He grins.

"No." I squeak.

Keep your cool, Maya, for everyone's sake! My cheeks turn a brighter shade of scarlet as I think about how much I'm stumbling over my words and making a fool of myself. *Relax*, I tell myself. Tonight, you are a free woman, on a date. *A date!* My first date ever!

Alessio's arm around mine stiffens as we advance down the stairs towards the huge dining hall. His hard demeanour quickly returns when we show our faces. Multiple people greet him, smiling and congratulating him on his success. Not for a moment does he let down his guard, nor does he let go of my arm. His face is permanently twisted into a fake smile. He pulls me towards someone else.

The man is just as handsome as Alessio, just shorter in stature and clean of tattoos. He grins as we make our way over to him.

"Maya." He smiles, pulling me into a hug. Shocked, I let him embrace me, but I don't let go of Alessio.

"This is my Brother, Mateo." Alessio says tightly, "He doesn't understand personal boundaries."

A smile teases my lips at his jealousy.

"Nice to meet you." I say politely.

Mateo exchanges a look with Alessio. I can't decipher it, but it leaves Alessio feeling stiff. He shakes his head no to an unspoken question. I frown.

"Very well." Mateo grunts, "I will get us a drink."

He disappears into the crowd of expensively dressed people. Alessio's face remains in a scowl. I step in front of him.

"What's wrong?" I whisper. He scans my face for something but then sighs and shakes his head. After a long pause, he changes the subject.

"You really are stunning, Maya." He says, gently placing a hand to the small of my back. His touch sends shivers through me.

"Thanks. I'd say you might make top five men in this room." I tease him, looking around at the other guests, "Wait, maybe top ten."

A low chuckle leaves his lips as he pulls me closer. I can't help but stare at those lips. The same ones which made me feel all types of ways last night. Shakily, he takes a deep breath as he notices my gaze. His face is conflicted with emotion. I send him a seductive wink.

"Behave." He growls.

"Or what?" I retort quickly. My fingers trail up his arm. Longing dances in his eyes.

"Why don't you just kiss me?" I bat my eyelashes at him. His gaze jumps down to my lips, and they remain locked on me.

"No, I can't." He whispers.

"Why not? You want me, I want you. Unless there's some jealous ex-girlfriend I need to be worried about?" I mock him. His grip on my back tightens.

"I don't date." He mutters between bared teeth. His eyes still remain locked on my lips. For some unknown reason, it feels like my heart deflates in my chest. It's not as if I want him to be my boyfriend. I just want his body. *So why am I so disappointed with his answer?*

"I mean," He splutters, "Because of work. I don't usually have the time."

"Oh." I say lamely.

"Here you go." Mateo's voice rings through the awkward silence. He thrusts the pink glass into my hand and I'm happy to gulp it down. The fruity, alcoholic taste swarms my senses. I welcome the warm feeling in my stomach.

"Thanks." I breathe out before placing my empty glass on the table next to us. Mateo's eyes widen in shock but a look of amusement flickers across his lips. The Brothers begin talking about some business things, but I zone out. I honestly couldn't care less about mafia talk.

Uninterested, my eyes scan the expensive looking guests. I itch to get to work on these mobsters. The amount of money I would be able to steal within an hour…

"I'm just going to-" I say pointing into the crowd. Mateo shrugs me off but Alessio's eyes never leave me. A look of concern splashes across his face but his Brother quickly gains his attention back. With one final look, he leaves me to my own devices.

I head towards the bar area to get myself another drink.

"Double vodka and lemonade please." I tell the small woman behind the bar. She nods her head obediently and begins making my drink. I twist around and stare out at everybody. There must be at least one hundred people and the party has only just begun. My eyes dance between the watches, the phones and wallet shaped dents in trousers. Instinct drives me forward, but reason forces me to stay put.

I don't think Alessio would take too kindly to me robbing his friends.

"Hello there, beautiful lady." A male voice grabs my attention. I twist to look at a sheepish looking man with beautiful blonde locks. His dimples jump out as he smiles.

"I'm Casper." He outstretches his hand. My eyes lock onto the rings on his finger. That hand alone would settle my Father's debt I'm sure of it. I shake his hand, resisting the urge to slip one of the rings off.

"Maya." I offer politely. Behind me, my drink is ready.

"Let me." Casper says, rummaging around in his pocket. He pulls out a Versace wallet and then a black card before tapping it on the card machine.

"Thanks." I say awkwardly. My plan was to simply slip into the crowd before the lady asked me to pay. *This works too.*

I take a large sip of the drink before returning my gaze to the nervous blonde in front of me.

"Why are you here tonight?" I start conversation. He sends me a playful wink.

"Working." He beams. I raise an eyebrow and turn to face him a little more.

"Oh, yeah?"

"Yeah." He agrees, "I'm head of information on the Sasha case."

My jaw slackens. Like a schoolboy, he grins at me with a childish twinkle in his eye. My smile grows wider at the realisation that this man can help me find Sasha when I eventually leave this place. My dream for revenge suddenly becomes much more real.

"Do you know where he is?" I ask. Casper's lips thin slightly and he casts a nervous glance around him.

"I'm not to talk about it." He answers cryptically. My head tilts sideways and I give him a long, sultry smile.

"Why not? I can keep a secret."

My fingers itch for revenge against Sasha. There's even a slight tremble in my body of hope and anticipation for his downfall.

"I'm afraid I'm sworn to secrecy." He holds his hand up like a boy scout.

"Oh, it's classified?" I raise an eyebrow, "How dangerous. You must be fearless."

He is instantly swooned by my charms. A blush creeps onto his cheeks.

"I guess." He agrees with me. *Barf*.

"So, let's say, you were trying to track him down. How would you do it? Surely, you can tell me that." I wink at him. He leans on the bar beside me and smiles.

"I suppose I can tell you how to do that." He says proudly, "If it's just the theory of it, not telling you any actual information."

Hope swarms through me. I nod excitedly. He leans in closer.

"Well, first-" He begins but is quickly cut off.

"Casper! May I talk to you for a second?" Mateo appears out of nowhere. The hope in my chest fizzles out. I look at him in despair.

"Is it your mission to stop everyone from talking to me, tonight?" I hiss. A boyish grin flicks onto his lips.

"No Maya." Mateo grins, "You can speak to whoever you want."

A huff falls past my lips, and I cross my arms bitterly.

"Am I in trouble?" Casper frowns at Mateo. Mateo's smile never leaves his face. However, it does twitch into something more menacing when he looks at Casper. I glare between the two men.

"No." Mateo says tightly. Then, he brings his lips to Casper's ear and whispers something. I scowl at the rude gesture. After a couple moments, Mateo pulls away and gives me a smile. Beside him, Casper trembles. His body becomes rigid, and he loses a couple shades of colour.

"I must go. There's something I need to do. I mean. *Bathroom!* I need to go to the bathroom." Casper stumbles over his words before scurrying off. Horrified, I glare at Mateo.

"What did you say to him?" I gawp. I resist the urge to swat him in the chest. He has just scared off an opportunity to find Sasha.

"Nothing." He answers with a shrug of his shoulders. I shake my head in disbelief.

"Doesn't seem like nothing. The boy looks like he's seen a ghost."

"Drop it, Maya." He tells me before snapping at the bartender to make him a drink. I bring my glass to my lips as I sulk.

"Are you alright?" Alessio asks as he joins us. He quickly picks up on my frustration.

"No." I respond bitterly, "Your Brother has just been very rude."

Alessio's eyes darken as he looks at his Brother. If looks could kill, Alessio would be a fantastic hitman right now.

"Why?" He seethes, "What did he tell you?"

My eyes widen.

"Tell me?" I frown, "No. I mean he just scared off my friend."

"Friend!" Mateo scoffs as he brings the beer glass to his lips. He sips at it with a twinkle in his eyes.

"Casper?" Alessio chuckles, "Casper isn't your friend."

"What is wrong with you two?" I hear myself say, "Why are you acting so strange? Am I not allowed to talk to people here? Is that it? Am I to be a prisoner until I'm allowed to leave?"

I feel the temper rise in my chest. I feel cheated of my revenge. Cheated of my night of freedom.

"Casper wanted to be a little bit more than your friend, Maya." Alessio lowers his voice. I raise my eyebrows at him in disbelief.

"So? Is that a crime?" I spit. My arms cross over my chest defensively. He can't refuse me *and* refuse others to have me too! It simply isn't fair.

"When it comes to you, Maya. Yes, it is." He mutters bitterly. My heart flips in my chest.

"How dare you!" I seethe at him before twisting on my heel and storming off. I can't be near him right now. Just like every other man in my life, his ego and possessiveness is worth more than my feelings. I will not stand for it.

"Where are you going?" He calls out after me.

"I'm going home." I spit. He quickly catches up with me. His hand shoots out and he spins me round to face him.

"You're staying." He growls, "Please, Maya. Don't be stupid. Stay where you are safe."

"Stupid!" A scoff leaves my lips, "You have such a way with words. Do you know that?"

"God, woman! Stop being so stubborn and just let me help you!"

I pull myself free of his grip and my lips seal into a tight line. Childishly, I turn my head away from him so I can't see him.

"Sasha has upped the stakes on you. There are actual hitmen and bounty hunters out there right now searching for you. He has told everyone that you are going to be his wife." He hisses.

"What?" I gawp. It doesn't make sense. *Why is he so hell bent on having me back? All because of a little bruised ego? Just because of my Father?*

"You will never be safe, Maya." He whispers. His voice is hoarse and painful. A redness seeps into his face as he winds himself up.

"Is that why you won't sleep with me? Because I am to be his wife?" I hear myself ask the question before I can stop myself.

"Maya!" He booms. Around us, the room falls silent, and every pair of eyes jump to us. I feel the anger pulsing off of him. He grabs me by the arm and pulls me out of the room. I yelp in surprise and stumble behind him.

"This isn't about sex, right now. This is about your fucking life." He hisses.

"I am not going to be your little prisoner for the rest of my life, Alessio! I am not afraid of him!" I spit back, pushing him in the chest. He doesn't move an inch.

"You can't leave!" His eyes are wide. Genuine fear seeps through his expression. I shake my head.

"Yes, I can."

"No, Maya." He grabs me by either arm and holds me firm, "You will die. If not, worse. You don't know what those men are like."

"Yes, I do!" I protest, "Yes, I fucking do, Alessio! Why? Because I have been surrounded by men like that my entire life. My dad, my Brothers, him and now you! You will not take my freedom away!"

He visibly flinches and releases me.

"Is that what you think? That I'm like them?" He whispers. A pain tugs at my heart. My words are cruel and partly untrue when it comes to him. In the handful of days that I've known him, he's been nothing but gentle and caring. Truthfully, he is miles from the other men. I just need to hurt his feelings enough to be free.

"There is one way that you can be free." He mutters quietly, "Free *and* safe."

"What is it?" I snap.

"It's quite a high price though." He stalls. My temper only rises.

"Oh, for fucks sake, Alessio. Spit it out! What is it? How can I be free?" I cry out furiously.

A long silence drifts between us before he sighs. His firm grip on my arms grow much softer. He almost deflates in front of me.

"Marry me." He whispers.

Chapter Twelve

MAYA'S POV:

My jaw drops.

"Excuse me?" My cheeks flush red.

"Marry me." He repeats, his eyes hard. This time, he sounds much more certain.

"You didn't even want to fucking kiss me half an hour ago." I scoff.

Adrenaline courses through my veins. *Marriage is pretty fucking permanent.* As if a big mobster leader like Alessio would want his *wife* returning back to a normal life, living in a dingy house, robbing people. I'd become a trophy wife and like hell would I allow that. *This is the complete opposite of freedom*! The polar opposite to escaping controlling men! I'd be selling my freedom.

"Maya, think about it. Your safety will be ensured, and you will be able to leave the house. It just makes sense." He persuades, his hands acting things out dramatically in the air. I give him the middle finger, but he just snatches my hand in his and continues,

"No one would dare to touch you if they knew you were mine."

"*Yours*?" I spit with disgust, pulling my hand out of his. *What a misogynistic pig!* And to think I desired him more than anything in the world an hour ago. His eyes widen,

"I didn't mean it like that!"

"Then how did you mean it?"

I throw my hand to my hips and glare at him. He shakes his head quickly,

"Maya don't be so stubborn. This is the best option for us."

"What are you getting out of it then?" I spit but he falls silent. This increases my anger.

"What is it, Alessio? Fame that you stole Sasha's fiancée? Is it power? What the hell could you possibly want to do with this marriage! What are you not telling me?"

"Maya, you're overreacting." He rolls his eyes.

"Overreacting! My life is on the fucking line because of what my Father did, and now my only option is to marry into your family to protect myself?" I shriek, "This is *not* overreacting!"

He nods slowly, understanding my distress.

"I will not marry you." I seethe.

"No, Maya." His eyes widen, "You have to. You'll die otherwise."

"Good." I spit. His lip twitches menacingly.

"Don't say that." He scowls, "Never say that. I will not let you throw away the opportunity of safety!"

"And I will not let you use me as a puppet in the mafia war!" I retort quickly.

"You will marry me!" He panics, growing more and more distressed. My hand shoots out and smacks him around the face. It makes a satisfying noise but the stinging feeling after removes any satisfaction. I try to smack him again, but he catches my open palm.

"Hit me once, I understand. But a second time? You're playing with fire." He growls. A red mark slowly appears on his face. This brings a smile to my lips. It quickly falls.

"I'm going home, Alessio." I seethe.

"You are not." He grips onto me tighter, "Forty-eight hours! Just give yourself forty-eight hours to decide. I promise that if you still want to leave after that time is up, I will let you. Hell, I'll even pack your bags for you."

My eyebrows burrow together on my forehead. My heart races one hundred miles an hour in my chest, and my clothes stick to my skin from the sweat. He has a point. If I leave now, I will die. Sasha or whoever else my Father has pissed off, will be looking for me. And though I can handle myself in a club, It is significantly harder to remain alive whilst in the middle of a mafia war. With forty-eight more hours in safety under my belt, I will be able to make a plan.

"Promise?" I say nervously. I scan him to see if he is telling me the truth. He stinks his pinkie finger out at me.

"Pinkie promise." He tells me. I keep his eye contact for a moment, debating whether I should trust him. A genuine, fearful look lingers in those beautifully dark eyes. Then I take his pinkie with my own.

"Fine." I mutter, "But only forty-eight hours and then I'm gone."

ALESSIO'S POV:

Her temper is exhilarating. I shouldn't be so excited by her ability to fight back, but for some reason I am. Her stubbornness on the other hand, *devastating*.

She glares at me with fury.

"I am not some pretty, little housewife, Alessio. I will not marry you." She spits. My mouth ovals.

She's frightened! Her words cut through me deeper than I thought they would. My little Maya is so unpredictable and independent- *there is no way she would have accepted my offer easily.* I expected a war. Perhaps worse than the Russians.

But if she tries to leave, I don't know what I will do. This longing in my heart to protect her is much stronger than any other emotion I've ever felt. If she leaves, she will be committing suicide. If she leaves, I think she will kill me too. *A murder-suicide.* I wince.

"So, the problem is with the connotations of being a wife to a mafia mobster? Rather than an issue with marrying me?" I hear myself speak the words out loud and it burns. *How can I sound so desperate?*

Because you want to protect this girl, The voice in my head suggests. *Because you have inexplicable feelings for her which you've never had for anyone before.*

After a long, tiring debate, she finally agrees to take forty-eight hours to decide her next move. A small smile pulls at my lips. *So, there is some reason in that explosive little brain of hers.*

She lets me take her hand but the look of disgust on her face doesn't leave. It's a small victory. One I shall cherish for the rest of my life.

She pulls me close and brings her lips menacingly close to my ear.

"I hate you, Alessio. I hate you so much right now. You are just like the rest of them. You are just using me." She hisses before pulling away. Suddenly, she twists on her heel and half runs up the stairs. It's like another slap to the face. It stings at my heart and feels as though someone has stabbed me repeatedly.

I itch to follow after her. I let out a sigh of relief as she storms up the stairs rather than out the house. Her enticing hips sway as she runs, silently pulling me closer. But I don't follow her. I must respect her choice to be alone. Even if it means her being in distress about that too.

"I'm taking she didn't take the news well?" Mateo grins looking at the burning mark on my cheek. I grumble as I rub it better.

"I knew she wouldn't take it well." I grunt, "She hasn't decided yet. I gave her forty-eight hours to come to a decision."

His lips pull into a straight line, and he nods his head slowly.

"She has a mean right hook, I see." He cracks a small smile. I'm not sure whether it's from relief or delirium, but I can't help the smirk which coats my lips. *My feisty, little Maya.* Never backing down from a fight. A stubbornness I love and loathe at the same time.

"Speak to Angelo. I want extra security around the house. She gave me her word, we even pinkie promised, but I recon she'll try and escape." I run a hand through my hair.

"Pinkie promise, Brother? You made a pinkie promise?" His face lights up in amusement and he blows out a breath, "You've got it bad for the fighter."

I don't deny it. *How can I?* The little siren haunts my every thought.

Suddenly, an angry storm of red floods my vision.

"How dare you!" Sophia shrieks as she descends down the stairs quickly. She waves her arms around in my face aggressively.

"I refuse to believe that marriage is the only option! Have you even thought about her feelings?" My little sister yells at me. Mateo's grin only grows as he enjoys my misery.

"Sophia." I murmur, shaking my head, "I have no choice."

"No choice!" She scoffs in delirium, "She's on the phone to her Brother crying."

"What?" I snap, "She has a phone?"

Sophia freezes and a guilty look washes through her face.

"I gave her my phone." She confesses. My jaw hardens and I shake my head at her.

"Why?" I growl, "There will be people hacking her family lines as we talk."

"Relax, Brother." Mateo steps in and places a hand on my chest. It doesn't calm me. *Is no one taking her safety seriously other than me?* If anything happens to that girl under the foolery of my siblings, I'll have them both begging for mercy. Mercy which I wouldn't supply. Siblings or not.

"*Relax!*" I scoff in disgust before breaking free of his hand. My legs force me up the stairs towards my room. *Who do they think they are? Making rules without my permission? Allowing such stupidity into my home? I'll teach them a lesson-*

I stumble to a halt as I hear a sniffle. My hand removes itself from my door handle and I stand still. Maya is on the other side of the door, crying. My mouth becomes dry.

"No, Cole, you don't understand. I'm fine." She says, pausing to hear what he has to say before continuing, "Alessio is lovely to me, I promise. I'm just upset with the whole situation."

Her voice seems a little pitched as if she is nervous to talk about me. I know I should walk away and give her privacy, but my feet remain glued to the floor. *It's my fucking house after all.*

"He rescued me from Sasha. Then he fed and clothed me and kept a roof over my head. All for free. I'm safe here." She murmurs and I feel a glimmer of hope seep into my heart. *Maybe she will stay here and marry me? Maybe she will choose reason?*

"It's a shame I have to escape." She whispers and my blood becomes cold. A stinging swamps my heart. *I knew it.* My feisty little Maya would never submit to any man.

"Why? Because he wants to marry me, Cole, that's why!" She explodes. I wonder what Cole is saying to her on the other end. I keep my ear pressed to the door, eager to hear her thought processes.

"No. Sasha is after me. I need you to come meet me, please. I can't do this alone and I don't want to marry either man." She goes silent for a bit and then I hear her hiccup a cry, shattering my heart.

"Cole please. I can't- I must leave."

I want to go in and comfort her. To hold her close and tell her everything will be fine- but I don't move. It's like my own personal hell loop as I listen to the woman I care about, cry about not wanting to be near me.

"Fine," She suddenly snaps, "If you won't help me, I will escape alone. I thought you'd be on my side! I will not marry a man out of fear for my safety. You should know me better than that. I will not be a housewife like mum, Cole."

My ears prick. So that's why she won't marry. *Is she afraid of turning into her mother?*

"I will see you in the early hours of the morning." She announces and I quickly flee my hiding spot.

Early hours of the morning, she says. *Not happening.*

I storm into my office, the anger coursing through me. *Why can't she just let me help her? Why is she so afraid of marrying me and staying safe?* My hands shake with anger as I pick up the phone.

"Angelo? Send me all the information on Chris Baker and his wife." I snap, before hanging up.

I need to know who I'm up against if I am to convince Maya to stay.

Chapter Thirteen

ALESSIO'S POV:

Impatiently, my fingers drum against the desk as I wait for Angelo's email. I check my watch. It's been ten minutes. What is taking him so long? I expected to have read the folder by now. My fingers itch as I go to pick up the phone to call him again.

Ding.

I've never moved faster in my life to open an email.

"Nothing?" I scowl. *This cannot be!* I scan through the document on Chris Baker and the only thing I find is that he married a woman called Lisa. *That must be Maya's mum.* But there is no criminal history, nor are there any children listed. *What the fuck?*

My palms grow sweaty as I pull up the search base and type in 'Maya Baker'. *Nothing.* Fury races through me. *Who the fuck do I have staying in my house? Who have I let into my home?*

"Angelo?" I bark down the phone, "Dig deeper into Maya. There are no records of her. Or someone has wiped them clean. Find out which."

"You got it." He answers. I hear him frantically typing away on the computer. I end the call and call my Brother.

"Get here, now." I say sternly. Mateo grunts on the other end of the phone but doesn't answer. A couple minutes later, he's standing at the doorway to my office. He rests one leg up against the wall behind him and folds his arms.

"It's Maya." I seethe, running a hand through my hair.

"Did she agree to marry you?" My Brother scowls. A scoff falls past my lips. I shake my head twice.

"No," I sigh, "But, little Maya isn't who she says she is."

"What do you mean?" Mateo quickly takes a seat in front of me.

"Her file. It's empty." I tell him, pushing the computer screen towards him to have a look.

"I don't understand." He frowns, "We had all the women screened before coming here. So, we know where they're from and how we can help them more. She would have had a file then."

"Well, it's not here now." I grunt. A scowl kisses my lips as my thoughts run wild.

Who does Maya and her family know that is powerful enough to wipe my records? Perhaps her Father severed ties when he realised that she was gone. To keep himself safe. My fingers clench into fists. *Did her Father give up this easily to protect himself?* My anger towards him doubles.

Another ding rings through the room. I yank the screen back to me and open the email from Angelo. My body trembles as I look at his findings.

"It's worse than I thought." I hiss, "The parents have different names. Fake names."

A strange wash of emotion flows through me. *Was she going to keep this from me? Did she not trust me with this information?* This kind of thing could have quickened the process of finding Sasha or anyone else who wants her dead!

I keep scrolling down the page.

"Her Father, Charles, was an abusive drunk and gambler." I read out, "Trained in the special forces. Quit when wife fell pregnant. Diagnosed with PTSD later on... Where is she?"

I click control and F to bring up the 'find' button. Quickly, I type in her name. The document jumps down to another section.

"Here we go." I say, slight satisfaction washing through me, "They have four children together. Cole, James, Ben, and Maya Carter."

"Why change the parents' names if only to keep the children's the same?" My Brother rightly points out. I scan the document for a year of birth, or any indication of when they changed their names, but it comes up void.

"Maybe whoever they were running from didn't know they had children?" I speculate, "It says here that there is a warrant out for the arrest of Charles Carter. Fucking hell, it's for nearly everything. Fraud, robbery, battery and assault, murder, attempted murder."

Mateo blows out a breath of shock. His face contorts into an ugly scowl,

"We are housing the daughter of a high-class criminal, who is also a criminal? Great."

"Don't judge yet." I snap before I can stop myself, "You and I both know the unfortunate circumstances of growing up in a family like that. You don't disobey family. You simply follow the lead of the strongest person there. My money is on her doing the same."

My lips pull into a grim line as I continue flicking through the document.

"Who are you running from?" I whisper to myself. A strange protectiveness waves through me. On the one hand, I don't know the woman who is in my room. On the other hand, I long to get to know her. To help her. To protect her from whatever threat hunted her and her family down. She is like a drug to my starved mind.

"It just doesn't make sense. You said her dad was in debt to Sasha, so he knew the family recently. Do you think he could have helped them change identity?" Mateo suggests. I look at my Brother as I ponder on the idea. It is very possible. Sasha Ovlov is notorious for his illegal activities. He can quite easily make an entire family disappear.

"What would he get in return? Just money? Surely, he would have known the debt the family was in prior." I protest. Mateo sighs and shrugs,

"It's not like Sasha would be opposed to ruining a family. I think he may actually enjoy prying on families who cannot pay him back. It means that they owe him a favour. He'll be able to cash in at any time. And unfortunately, Maya seems to be the prize he wants."

A low growl escapes my lips. My blood boils at the idea of Maya and Sasha marrying one another. As much as she doesn't know it yet, she is mine. *Mine.*

"We could pay Sasha off for them?" I suggest, hope brimming to the surface. My face falls quickly as I argue against myself, "But it's no longer about money, is it? It's about pride. Ego. She escaped him; she beat him up. He's now put a number on her head, he won't be able to remove it without looking weak. Like he couldn't catch her."

My Brother nods slowly.

"She won't ever be free." He whispers, "But I don't blame her for not wanting to marry you. She has been passed between men her entire life. I mean, you've got the file. How would you feel? She's frightened, Alessio. You can't blame the poor girl."

My Brother is right, but the feeling of possessiveness doesn't leave my body. I know she is scared. I know she feels helpless. But I can help her. I will help her. Unless she escapes.

"She's going to escape tonight." I confess as I shut the computer down. A small twitch flickers across his lips.

"Maybe she is the woman for you. A fucking handful and will always keep you on your toes." He makes light of the situation. I scowl at him and shake my head. But, yet again, my Brother is most likely right.

Maya is the woman for me. If it hadn't been for the unfortunate circumstances of forcing her to marry me, I know deep down I would have pursued her in a better way. She is everything I have ever wanted.

MAYA'S POV:

With a shriek, I throw the phone across the room. It bounces off the bed and lands on the floor. Violence courses through my body.

Who does Cole think he is? I've been kidnapped by the mafia thanks to my Father, and my only option is to marry another mafia boss! Regardless of how attracted I am to him; he will *not* be my new captor. In fact, when I leave, I'm leaving for good. I will never be around another man again. I swear by it.

I just want to be free. *Is that too much to ask for?* But no, my Brother will not come and help me escape. He told me *"You'd be safer there than here."*. I scoffed at his ignorance and spat some pretty nasty things down the phone.

Yes, I'd be safe from my Father. Yes, I'd be safe from Sasha. Yes, I'd be safe from whoever is hunting dad down but…

My pride. I want to be free. I need to be free. I'm sick of being stuck under men and their violence, and I sure as hell will not stick around to be the happy housewife of another man in power. No, it won't happen.

I march around the room, looking for anything sharp as a weapon. I just need something deadly enough to protect me until I reach my home in Venice. From there, I will sleep with a gun every night. I scramble back towards the phone and play some music.

My fear of being alone is unpredictable. Sometimes, I can deal with it. Other times, it's too much. I spoke to a therapist once, before I robbed her. She told me that I can only deal with being alone if I am the one to isolate myself. If someone else isolates me, that's when the problems begin. She is right. But right now, the silence and loneliness is overpowering.

I click shuffle on Sophia's playlist on Spotify. 'My Immortal' by Evanescence begins playing.

My heart lurches in my chest. I haven't heard this song in years. My Mother used to love Evanescence. She would play it all the time as she cleaned the house. It was the first thing you'd hear on a Monday morning and the last thing on a Sunday night. You couldn't get away from the depressing words and sad melody. Until one particularly rough night between her and my Father. I do not know the actual events which occurred. All I know is that from that moment forward, my Mother would never make another noise again. No more music. No more laughter. It was as if someone had flipped a switch. My Mother had become a zombie. A slave to my Father.

I pull my knees to my chest on the bed. My head rests on them and I let the sob wrack through my body. I have no plan. It is physical suicide if I decide to leave tonight. But it is mental suicide to remain here. *Which is worse? Which is better to sacrifice?*

My Brother had told me *"this is your chance to start again."* But I can't help the bitterness. *Start again for the third time?* I don't want another new life. I want to be free. For the first time in my life, I almost longed to be alone and away from everyone else. I asked Cole if my Father was concerned about where I was. The answer was painful to hear. My Father hadn't even noticed. He continued his daily activities as if I was still there. It makes me feel sick.

Even if I was still with Sasha, being tortured and raped, my Father wouldn't have batted an eyelid. I would have paid for his crimes. And he wouldn't have cared.

It was a lesson he taught us from a young age. But to see it in action... *Fuck*, it stung. My Brother had promised me that he would come get me when it is safe. When I am married, he means. Despair fills me. I don't have a choice.

"Maya?" I hear Alessio's voice at the door. I freeze, not answering him.

"Maya, can I come in?" He tries again. My voice is snatched from me. I have no control over my body. Just another thing I'm losing control of.

He opens the door slowly and peers around it. A red mark still stains his face from earlier and his eyes seem lower, sadder.

"I know you said you hate me and that you don't want to see me but…" He starts, dropping his head miserably. A lump forms in my throat.

"You can come in." I hear myself say. The sound is distant, helpless. His gaze shoots back up to me and a quizzical look stains his face. But he doesn't protest. He scurries into the room and takes a seat on the end of the bed.

A solitary tear falls down my face.

"Please, don't cry." He whispers and holds a hand out to wipe my tear away. I flinch and pull away from him. He drops his hand to his lap. A pained look flickers across his face and some guilt pools in my stomach. I push the feeling away. I am well within my right to hate everyone right now.

"I suppose you are here to make me change my mind." I whisper. A numbness floats through me and I avert my eyes.

"No." He says timidly, "I'm here to see if you're hungry."

My head snaps up as I try to see whether he's being sarcastic. A look of genuine concern crosses his face.

"They are serving dinner downstairs. Would you like to join me?"

As if on cue, my stomach growls. I bite my lower lip nervously. I am hungry. But I don't want to be around any of them right now.

"We don't even have to talk. Just come and eat." He pleads. When his eyes meet mine, I almost forget how to breathe. Those dark orbs are wide yet gentle. A funny feeling swamps my stomach.

Even when we are arguing, he is taking care of me.

"Okay." I tell him quietly. Another rumble of my stomach pulls me to my feet. He leads the way.

When we re-enter the room, there are dozens of round tables. At least ten people sit around each table and they all tuck into a delicious roast. I quickly take my seat next to Alessio.

"Here is your phone." I say to Sophia handing it to her. She smiles sweetly at me. Thankfully, she doesn't comment on the chipped screen. Another wave of guilt floods through me. *I'll fix that when I get money,* I think nervously.

"Thank you," She says, "How is Cole?"

I don't answer her. Instead, I nod my head slowly and reach for my glass of wine. The liquid soothes the anxiety in my stomach. Beside me, Alessio stiffens. Everyone begins eating in silence before Mateo finally breaks the silence.

"How rude of us." He says, turning to look at me, "We haven't introduced you to the Council."

I want to tell him that I don't plan on sticking around long enough to care. But I don't. Instead, I look at him expectantly.

"This is Angelo, head of security." He points to a large, blonde man in his late twenties. He nods his head politely in my direction and I offer him a small smile. Beside him, Sophia's eyes twinkle as she looks at him happily.

"Then there is Carlos who is head of finance, Aria who is head of foreign relations and finally Casper who is head of information, though I'm not sure where he is now." Mateo says. His eyes twinkle as he mentions Casper. I instantly know he is lying.

I cast my gaze over the other two Council members. Aria has slicked back hair, in a neat looking bun and minimal makeup. She is naturally very pretty and thin. Having said that, she also oozes a sense of power. Beside her, Carlos waves his hand at me. He is the smallest man at the table, with big, round glasses and a boyish smile. Perhaps in his late thirties, Carlos's hair is greying, and the wrinkles are starting to stain his darker complexion.

"Nice to meet you." I say politely.

"So, Maya, where are you from?" Aria starts polite conversation. I hesitate and bring the glass of wine to my lips. I always feel uneasy lying about my past but at this table with a bunch of power people, I cannot risk the potential threat. I learnt pretty quickly that lying needs to be second nature around dangerous people.

"Originally, I'm from Rome." I answer her before popping a potato into my mouth. I take my time to chew it, trying to look distracted to avoid any more questions. Alessio's grip seems to tighten on his wine glass, and he doesn't look my way.

"So, you are a local?" Carlos smiles, "You'll fit right in then."

My lips thin out as I look around at the table. I become very aware that everyone knows about the marriage proposal. A blush licks my cheeks, and a nervousness fills my stomach.

As a little girl, I dreamt of marrying the man of my dreams. A tall, happy man with lots of love to give. I'd marry for love, not money, not power. It would be the happiest day of my life when he proposed. After that, I'd never have another sad day again. Yet, as I sit at this table, a slight shiver wracking through my body, I feel sick. Within a week, I've had two marriage proposal. Neither man is in love with me, nor do I love them. As usual, my dreams have been snatched from me.

I look at Angelo and Sophia who seem to be whispering to each other. A happy look stains across her face and she can't stop smiling. In response, he sends her a cheeky wink and says something else. A giggle left her lips this time. *That* is what I want. That kind of happiness.

Alessio places a hand on my thigh. The touch is warm and protective. My traitorous body instantly relaxes under him and itches to scoot closer. Eager to distract myself, I take another gulp of wine.

"What do you do for a job?" Carlos asks me. My mouth dries and I almost choke on a breath. *Can I really confess to being a thief against a group of men and women who aim to solve crime on the Italian streets?* I think back to Sophia's utter disgust when finding out my Brother was a thief.

"Let's stop with the interrogation. She's had a very long week." Alessio comes to my rescue. I send him a small thank you smile before averting my eyes again. He squeezes my leg. His touch, once protective and reassuring, now feels completely different. My body reacts to him. I squeeze my legs shut to stop the throbbing, but it just squeezes his hand further into me. *Traitorous body!*

Shocked, his gaze snaps to me and he raises an eyebrow. Desire and confusion dances through him. I bite my lower lip nervously and keep his gaze. Something in my heart flips when he looks at me. A warm feeling fills me, and I can't help the smile on my lips. He catches every movement with his greedy eyes. I watch as his Adam's apple bobs when he gulps. I squeeze my legs tighter together, the desire growing stronger and stronger.

"I'm actually quite tired." I lie. I turn back to the table and offer them a small smile, "I think I'm going to head to bed early."

"I'll walk you to the room." Alessio says hurriedly. He pushes himself back from the table as I stand up.

"Night." Sophia beams up at me with a little wave. The others say their polite goodbyes too. Almost frantically, Alessio guides me out of the room.

"You can stay with Sophia tonight, if you'd like?" He offers politely, "I know that we are not exactly on talking terms."

The throbbing between my legs suggests otherwise. Maybe it's the alcohol, or maybe I'm cursed, but my body can't stay away from him. I gently press against him as we walk. His arm slithers around my waist.

"If it is okay with you, I'd like to stay with you?" I ask him. Shock crosses his mind, but he quickly nods his head in agreement.

"Yes, of course."

"But don't feel like you have to come up to bed now. Please, go and enjoy the party." I squeak as we walk into his bedroom. The longing doesn't die down, and if anything increases the closer, we get to his bed.

"I don't like those things anyways." He gives me a winning smile and it almost melts me on the spot, "Would you like another shirt to sleep in?"

My heart flutters in my chest.

"Sure." I whisper.

Again, a look of shock crosses his face. It's as if he doesn't believe my change of attitude.

Unfortunately, Cole is right. I would not get very far if I escaped. My best bet is to put my name down on a stupid piece of paper and then flee. But as Alessio advances towards me with a black shirt in hand, my breath is snatched. As he hands it to me, our fingers touch. The feeling is magnetic. I almost beg him for more

"I'm going to take a shower." I blush and quickly rush past him. I don't fully close the door so that I'm not technically alone in the room, but I close it enough that he can't see my body.

I catch my reflection in the mirror as I turn on the shower. Red cheeks and swollen lips. My pupils are dilated, and I have a crazed, hungry look on my face. I shake my head and quickly strip down.

I need a cold shower to rid me of these thoughts. The water splashes down on my skin and I shiver. It doesn't help the burning desire. I pull the shower head from the side and rinse my hair. Then I move it under my arms and down my body, trying to cool down my burning skin. But the cold water on my hot skin ignites the flames more.

I imagine the cold water is Alessio's touch. In my fantasy, he holds an ice cube and traces it down me. It swirls at my nipple and makes my legs weak. I can't resist any more. My fingers jump to my clit. I have to release the tension before I do something I regret. *Shagging the enemy.*

At first, it's light and gentle but I quickly pick the pace up. I lower the shower head to my clit and let the water flick against it. A moan escapes my lips before I can help it. My other hand slams over my mouth but I don't stop. *Can't* stop.

I am so close. I imagine it's his fingers rubbing me as his cock slides in and out. Another muffled cry leaves my lips as the tension builds and builds.

"Alessio." I whimper quietly.

A growl forces my eyes to open. In front of me, Alessio stands, rock hard. His greedy eyes watch me fuck myself with his shower head. Humiliation fills me quickly. Fuck. *Did he hear that?*

"Does it feel good?" He grunts before tearing the shower door open. More heat flushes through me. I scramble to put the shower head back, but his hand stops me.

"I didn't say stop." He growls. Another wave of heat. I almost cum on the spot from his authoritative tone. Quicky, I return the shower head to my clit. Alessio reaches around me and twists the dial. Suddenly, the water comes out faster. My legs give way, but he holds me upright. Greedily, he takes in the sight before he kisses me. My mind becomes blurred as I focus on kissing back, holding the shower head, and trying to breathe. I choose his lips over oxygen.

"Fuck." I moan into his mouth as I feel myself edge closer. Suddenly, his fingers replace the water's touch. I cry out in pleasure. They are fast, frantic. He pushes me closer and closer to the edge.

"Alessio!" I whimper, "I'm close!"

"Cum for me, Maya." He instructs before plunging two fingers into me. My hands wrap around his neck, trying to keep myself from collapsing. With the mix of his fingers on my clit and inside of me at the same time, slamming against my g-spot, I fall over the edge very quickly.

"Oh God!" I cry out as I ride the high.

"Good girl." He growls into my ear. He doesn't stop playing with me and before I know it, I'm falling over the edge again. My grip around him tightens as another long moan escapes my lips. My head lulls forward and my entire body shakes.

"Alessio." I whimper. He removes his hands from me and wraps them around my back. His lips return to mine. I struggle to control my breathing as I match his frantic kiss. My fingers trail down his naked body. I feel up his broad shoulders, rock hard abs, and tease lower to his cock. His hands grab mine before I can get what I want.

"Maya." He groans. The noise sends more desire through me. I am ready to go again. I need him. My fingers try to break free from his grip, but he doesn't relent.

"No." He whispers against my lips. I pull back from him, confused. The longing still stains his face, but another look joins it. My eyes widen,

"Please."

"No. I will not sleep with you until you've made your mind up." He tells me. His voice is strained and painful. A lump forms in my throat.

"Alessio, I'm staying." I tell him. Shock jumps to his face, then confusion then desire.

"Promise? You're not just saying that?"

"I pinkie promise, Alessio." I tell him, thrusting my pinkie finger out at him. He looks at it warily.

"But I heard you talking to Cole. You said you were going to escape." He whispers. I pull back out of his touch.

"You listened to my private phone call?" I gawp at him.

"No, I mean yes. I didn't mean to. I just overheard." He splutters over his words. A scoff tumbles from my lips as I push him away from me. I point a threatening finger at him.

"How dare you, Alessio. Is this what married life will be like with you? A constant invasion of privacy and a lack of trust!" I growl. He looks hurts as he stumbles backwards.

"Maya, I'm sorry. I just want wh-"

"You just want what's best for me, right? Is that what you were going to say? Because you, a big strong man, knows exactly what is right and what is wrong? Oh, you must help the damsel in distress." I spit, glaring at him menacingly. I storm past him and wrap the towel around my naked body. I refuse to let my eyes wander from his face. My body still thumps with desire even if I am furious with him.

"Why are you fighting with me on this? Just let me help you!" He follows after me. He wraps his own towel around his waist. My greedy eyes soak up the water droplets trickling down his tattooed chest. I avert my eyes quickly.

"I don't need your help. I don't need anyone's help." I hiss. *The only help I need from you is sexual help,* I add in my head, *And even then, you fucking ruined it by being a possessive, mafia asshole.*

"Yes, you do." He retorts. My body screams as it agrees with him.

With a huff, I shove past him and climb into bed. I pull the covers up to my chin and keep my back to him. A long silence pools between us. My heart still races from the come down and my body hums with desire. I drown out those traitorous symptoms.

The bed dips as he slides in beside me.

"Goodnight, Maya." He whispers turning the light off.

I don't repeat it back to him. *I hope he has a miserable night.*

Chapter Fourteen

MAYA'S POV:

"Get dressed." A voice pulls me from my sleep. Groggily, I turn over and peer up at Alessio. He is already dressed in a devilish suit which strains against his muscles. My tongue darts out and coats my bottom lip.

"I'm taking you on a tour of the house." He states. I glare up at him and pull a pillow over my face. I have no plans today other than to mourn my freedom. No one is going to interfere. And besides, I am not talking to him.

"Maya." He grumbles, "I know you're being stubborn and petty but-"

"I have a right to be petty and stubborn!" I half shriek. Suddenly, he yanks the pillow away from me. The covers quickly follow. A cold breeze has me shooting to my feet.

"Okay, Okay, I'm up!" I huff before storming to the bathroom. On the toilet seat, fresh clothes sit. A note on top of them gains my attention. *Love, Sophia. X*

With a sigh, I pull on the outfit. As usual, Sophia has gifted me tight jeans and a tank top. This black, ribbed top is very low cut and my breasts threatened to spill out of it. My lips pull into a grim line.

"Are you ready?" Alessio calls out to me. I quickly run my fingers through my hair, trying to make myself look a little more presentable. My brain may dislike him very much right now, but my body has other plans.

"Coming." I murmur bitterly as I stalk back into the room. A blush kisses my skin as his gaze roams up and down me approvingly. His jaw hardens and he quickly averts his eyes.

"First things first," He says as he leads me down the hall and towards an elevator, "The basement."

"Basement?" I gawp, quickly catching up, "How many floors does this place have?"

A feeling of ignorance floats through me. I have been here almost three days and I haven't explored further than the bedroom, dining hall and part of the garden. Even then, I have spent most my time in bed.

"Five." Alessio smiles proudly. Something in his expression shifts as he gently takes my hand. I let him take it. A strange feeling in me screams to get closer to him. I push it down.

The elevator grumbles as it opens. We both step in. Alessio leans towards the keypad and presses the 0 button. It dings as the doors close.

"How long have you lived here for?" I make polite conversation. He smiles and squeezes my hand a little tighter.

"Three years. I've only just finished building it. Took me a while."

My lips pull into an O shape as I nod my head slowly.

"It is my dream home." He tells me, "Each floor has a different purpose, but all in all, it's my place to live. You wouldn't have seen when we landed, but we are in a town. Every other house round here is either a Council member's house, or a hotel for the homeless or needy."

"Wow." I breathe out. *He is so generous.*

Growing up, when my Father told us stories about the mafia, he depicted them as an evil, powerful bunch. Ugly, perverted men who murdered because they could. But talking to Alessio, learning about his kindness and generosity, my head feels muddled.

The elevator doors groan again as they open. The smell of chlorine instantly hits me.

"A pool?" I gawp in disbelief. A huge, 50 metre pool stares back at me, with a jacuzzi to the side. Despite being underground, it is surprisingly light and airy in here. Alessio stays quiet. A smile licks his lips as he watches me.

"What's through that door?" I point towards a wooden door on the other side of the pool. A nervous smile crosses his face.

"The gym."

"There's a gym through there? Alessio, how big is your house?" I blurt. A slither of me is jealous. My family struggled to survive, to eat and there are men like Alessio with an Olympic sized pool in their basement. I repress the jealous thought.

"You're *rich* rich then." I say, nudging him teasingly. His dimples jump out of his face when he smiles. It takes my breath away.

"Perhaps." He whispers before leading me back into the elevator. He presses the number 3.

"Floor one is the kitchen, dining room and ball room. Floor two have the bedrooms and living rooms." He explains, "But you've seen them so we can skip over that part of the tour."

I am mesmerised by his modesty. Despite all this wealth, he still appears so down to earth and humble. He uses his money for the good. He rescues those in need and helps them flourish. A backwards Robbin Hood, with all of the good qualities.

The elevator doors open again. I peer out at the long corridor. Either side, there are doors leading to different rooms.

"Offices are on floor three." He tells me, "They're boring. You'll never have a need to come up here."

Before we can explore, he hits the next button up. The elevator door's grind shut, and we begin moving up again.

"Floor four..." He says before pausing. I look at him with a curious look. He doesn't finish his sentence. Instead, he lets the floor itself do the talking.

"Alessio." I breathe out in shock as I stumble into the biggest library I have ever seen. There are books everywhere, towering high on different shelves. Small writing tells you exactly which section is which. Excitedly, I roam the shelves.

"Sometimes I like coming and just reading in here. It is like a pause from the world." He whispers. A dreamy look flickers across his face. My eyes catch a book *Frankenstein* by Mary Shelly. I almost squeal in excitement.

"I haven't read this book since I was at school!" I gasp, running over to it and taking it off the shelf. My fingers flick through the pages, admiring the dark print. Small white letters stare up at me.

"Is this?" I gawp.

"A limited edition with a signature from Mary herself? Yes." He answers my unspoken question. Like a child in a sweet shop, I stare around in awe. I pull the book to my chest and hug it.

"Come on, I have two more things to show you. Bring the book." He smiles, holding his hand out. I quickly take it and let him lead me back into the elevator. We go up another floor.

"This is the cinema room." He announces. At least thirty rows of seats sat in this room, with a huge flat screen television at the front. On each side, popcorn, and cotton candy machines. My jaw drops.

"Of course, you have a fucking cinema in your home." I scoff.

"Would you believe me if I told you I don't use it much?" He raises an eyebrow at me, "I bought it so I can give large presentations in here. It just so happens that Sophia loves watching movies too."

I nod slowly. Mentally, I make a note to drag Sophia in here with me.

"And now for my favourite room." Alessio whispers as he leads me out the cinema room and up the stairs. The smell of lavender and fresh air instantly hits me. We are on the roof, surrounded by beautiful plants and flowers. It's like a portable version of the garden below. In the middle, a swinging chair rests. I hurry towards it and place my book on the table next to it. The sun is only just starting to rise and now I understand why he dragged me out of bed for this.

Up ahead, a flock of birds fly over us. A group of beautiful sea gulls, flying in perfect formation. Today, no bird trails behind. A happy smile appears on my lips.

"Birds." I sigh. Alessio takes a seat next to me and pulls the fluffy blanket over our bodies. I shuffle closer to him and rest a head on his shoulder. He slowly swings the chair.

"Birds." He agrees.

"It's beautiful up here, Alessio. I can see why you like it." I peer up at him. He has a dreamy look on his face. Then he looks at me. For a second, I'm hooked. Those delicious eyes flicker with a longing, and I welcome it. Our argument the night before fazes into nothing but a distant hum. Today is a new day.

Slowly, he brings his lips down on mine. It feels different to our usual kiss. There is no violence or burning franticness. Just a passion. His thumb tilts my head up to get a better position and I moan into the kiss. My fingers fist his shirt and I pull him closer. He quickens the kiss, and our usual franticness increases.

A ring of a phone makes me jolt. With a grunt, Alessio pulls away.

"What?" He barks into the phone. I am still breathless, drunk on his kiss. Immediately, his warm and gentle expression hardens.

"Yes. Yes. I'm coming now." He snaps before ending the calls. He looks over at me with a sheepish and irritated look.

"I have to go. It's work." He sighs, tearing his gaze between the phone and me. It's like he is debating whether he will go to work.

"It's fine." I smile, "I mean, I understand."

"Thank you." He whispers, bringing his lips to my forehead. A flutter echoes through me and a blush covers my cheeks.

"Shall I send Sophia up so that you are not alone?" He raises an eyebrow at me as he stands up. A stronger blush covers my cheeks. *He remembered.*

"No, thank you." I pick up my book and wave it around, "I have a distraction."

"Okay." He nods. I can see that he is forcing a smile to his lips but something that was said on the phone has bugged him. He twists on his feet and makes his way down the stairs. I watch him sadly. Then, he quickly spins around.

"Will you accompany me to dinner tonight, Maya?" He calls out. I can't help the smile which jumps to my lips.

"Of course, I will." I grin. This time, a genuine smile flickers onto his lips. I watch as his dimples jump out and the thin lines around his eyes curve. He is unlike any other man I have ever seen before.

"I will see you then." He nods before disappearing out of sight.

I open the first page of the book and sigh. The rising sun is slowly heating up the roof top, but I snuggle into my blanket more for extra heat. My eyes scan the beautiful fields which stretch for miles around the town.

A sarcastic thought teases my mind: *I suppose I could marry into a worse off family.*

ALESSIO'S POV:

As I barge into the meeting room, my Council all tear their eyes towards me nervously. Mateo looks at me with a grim look.

"Where have you been?" He hisses, "The meeting was supposed to start ten minutes ago."

"I was giving Maya a tour of the house, if you don't mind." I retort bitterly. My heart constricts as I remember how beautiful and peaceful, she seems on that swing, clutching onto my book. Her face had lit up when I introduced her to my sweet haven. It makes me long for her even more.

"Maya, your *wife*?" He raises an eyebrow expectantly. I feel my face pale.

"Perhaps." I sigh, "I'm going to get a certain answer tonight at dinner."

The silence in the air is palpable. Arranged marriages are the kind of thing we seek to eradicate. Choice and freedom are the two things we fought for daily. And now, we are introducing it into our own ranks. It doesn't sit well with anyone.

Aria stands and advances towards the projector. She connects her laptop to the huge board behind her before turning back to everyone with a serious look on her face.

"Sasha fled the mountains when we raided, we know that much for sure." She begins, showing a slide of his prison. I tense up at the image. *My beautiful Maya was in there.*

"But now there is no sight of him. Dima and Andrei are missing too." Aria flicks the side to mug shots of each of the men. My fingers itch.

"They have stopped snatching girls from the streets, so we know of. There have been no new reports anywhere in the world of mass kidnappings. They are remaining under the radar." Carlos adds. Aria nods her head at him.

"And we cannot trace the email to a location." She sighs, "But looking at the email and phone recipient list of the message he sent out about taking Maya back, we have a rough idea who is now our enemy."

"But he has been so secretive about everything else. Why leave an email and phone trace?" I frown, chewing on my pen, "Any credit card use or CCTV activity?"

Angelo shakes his head.

"No. Nothing anywhere. My best guess is he had a private jet waiting for him and has paid off people to wipe camera footage."

A growl escapes my lips. *The smart bastard.*

"But there is some good news." Aria chirps, "We are on the email list, undercover. Which means he may send more messages to his hitmen, and he is bound to slip up if he's under pressure. He has no access to card, only cash. And he didn't have much time to flee. Hopefully, we can wait him out."

"I don't want to wait him out. I want to find him immediately!" I growl and slam the table. *Is this a joke to them?* Aria flinches.

"Brother, Sasha has thought all of this through." Mateo interrupts my rage, "Maya is at risk from more than just Sasha. We must be on the lookout for spies, hitmen and more. I fear Sasha will create a distraction. And we cannot afford to make any mistakes, and this is why we must let him make them instead."

Curse Mateo's reasoning skills.

"Fine." I grumble, looking back to Aria. She smiles and continues, "We can track the recipients' movements though. This means we can pay our little friends some visits and find out if they are hearing anything more from Sasha."

The next slide reveals the names of the men on the email list. Each name and face burns into the back of my mind like ink into paper. One of those fuckers would be out to hurt Maya. Ten different names. Ten different threats.

"Have we done background checks on them? Who is the one we should be most worried about?" I scowl, looking over to Angelo again. He looks down to his document pile and slides them over to me, "Meet Bradley Piper. An American mafia hitman, apparently the best money can buy."

A lump in my throat stops me from talking. I don't know what

I would do if I lost her. Hell, I've only had her three days but that feels like a lifetime. Whether out of greed and longing for her, or altruistic goodness of protecting Italian women from other mafias, I'm not sure. All I know is that she will never be unprotected.

"Remember, Brother, you having Maya means you are in a position of power. Of bargaining." Sophia begins, "These ten threats will not be as powerful as you, even with their armies behind them. You have taken Sasha Ovlov's bride and made her your own. This is a brilliant opportunity to showcase your power to the world. Think of all the opportunities which will follow."

I purse my lips.

"Not to mention the Americans." Mateo suggests, "Remember, they won't deal with us unless you have an heir. Family means everything to them. They need to know business with us won't end with you, and then me, and then Sophia. You need a wife. You need a child."

My head hurts from all the information. Just yesterday I found out I must marry Maya, and now they are mentioning children. No way would Maya agree to that either. She'll rip my fucking balls off!

"Yes, yes, I get it. She will be my wife." I declare. *Though she will hate me for it*, I add silently in my head.

Everyone around me nods with approval.

"Is there anything else?" I ask. Nobody answers. I sit up straighter at the desk, "Okay great. Please keep working on it and come back to me with any results. In the meanwhile, I'd like the findings written up in a report."

"I'll do it." Casper offers, not meeting my eyes. I smile proudly. *Good, he should be scared after he approached at my girl like that.*

"Fine." I grunt, "You may all leave."

The room fizzles out and I'm left to my thoughts. I take another look at the PowerPoint and at the documents Angelo gave me.

Bradley Piper.

His toothless grin smiles at me, an ugly scar sitting just above his lips, running from his eyebrow to below his nose. I look at the document which shows me a list of places he's been in the last couple days, and then the predicted places he will visit.

Perhaps I should pay Bradley a little visit tomorrow to announce that he has an attack on my wife's head, and this could cause major issues.

Namely, issues with his life.

Chapter Fifteen

MAYA'S POV:

On the swing chair, sleep takes me in and out of consciousness. I'm surrounded by snacks, books, and pillows. It's my own little fort. A safe place.

"Maya?" A voice interrupts my peace, "Have you been up here all day?"

Groggily, I shuffle to the side as Alessio sits next to me. A frown slithers onto my face.

"All day? What time is it?"

"It's seven o clock, dear." He chuckles. A guilty smile coats my lips as I pull my legs to my chest.

"It really is lovely up here." I sigh, "And I've already finished the book."

"Well, it's a good thing we have a library downstairs, isn't it?" He smirks. My heart does a flip. *We* have a library. Not *I* have a library.

"Are you hungry?" He raises an eyebrow as he stands up from the chair. I almost scurry to my feet in agreement. I have binged on sweets and crisps today. I long for something a little more substantial.

"Of course, I am."

A goofy grin covers his face when I answer him. Gently, he takes me by the arm and leads me down to the dining hall.

The huge hall has been emptied. In the middle, a fully set-up table for two. A long candle burns in the middle and a vase of roses rests beside it. My breath is taken away as we slowly approach the beautiful table.

Alessio holds the chair out for me. I blush and take a seat.

"Thank you." I say quietly. He quickly joins me at the table before reaching over and holding my hand. His touch is like fire as it sparks up my body.

"Would you like some wine?" A male waiter, dressed in a smart suit, raises an eyebrow at me.

"Yes please!" I say as I push my glass toward him. He scowls and I immediately cringe. *Am I supposed to touch the glass or let him, do it?* I do not know date etiquette. His lips pull into a fake smile as he begins pouring the wine.

"Dinner tonight is roast beef with rosemary potatoes and steamed, fresh vegetables." The server announces proudly, and I feel myself grin. I *love* roast beef.

"Cool, thanks." I smile. The server looks at me again with slight disgust. He pours Alessio's drink and then scurries off without so much of a look back at me. *Snob*!

My attention returns to the handsome man in front of me. An amused expression kisses his face as he watches me. I feel my cheeks turn a couple shades of red under his gaze.

"How was work today?" I ask politely, trying to divert his attention.

"It's done. That's all that matters." He answers cryptically. I watch as he reaches for his wine and takes a large swig. I copy him. The bitter grapes quickly taunt my senses. I resist the urge to gag on the oil-tank flavoured stuff. *Do they not have any cheap bottles from a local corner shop?*

"We need to talk about the marriage proposal." Alessio says with a nervous look in his eyes. I take another sip of wine, trying to repress the lump in my throat.

"What about it?" I whisper.

"Will you do it? Will you marry me? I need an answer for certain." He raises an eyebrow. My lip's part and I feel my face fall. This is not the type of proposal every little girl dreams of.

"I'm sorry that this isn't the ideal situation, Maya. But I honestly believe this is what is best for you." He says kindly as his thumb strokes my hand. It soothes me a little but the knot in my stomach doesn't leave.

"Have you found Sasha yet?" I peer up at him sadly. His lips pull into a thin line. He clears his throat and shakes his head.

"No, we are still looking into it. It's hard to find a man who really doesn't want to be found."

"But if you find him, I won't have to marry you. Right?" I ask him hopefully. His jaw hardens and his expression stiffens. A long silence drifts between us.

"It's not just about Sasha." He finally says, "You've always had a target on your head, Maya. Your Father has made sure of that. Sure, it's Sasha this time, but who knows who is next? You'll never be safe unless you have my last name."

"You don't know my Father nor my family. We will be fine." I protest defensively. But it's useless. I can argue back all I want, through as many insults around as I can possibly think of. It doesn't change the truth. I am a walking target.

"Fine." I hiss after a pause, "But I will not be a stay-at-home wife. I will be free and not chained to you."

"What do you mean?" He scowls at me, "You will be free for the most part. Sure, you'll have to play the part in public but behind closed doors, you don't even have to look at me if you don't want."

"So, I must live here? There is no way around it?" I ask. He shakes his head.

ILLEGAL ACTIVITIES

"You must live with me, Maya. If the enemy catches drift that this is a fake marriage, they will be more likely to come for you because they'll assume I don't care that much."

"And do you?" I hear myself whisper, "Do you care?"

He looks at me for a long moment, shock in his eyes. My mouth dries and my heart races in my chest.

"Maya," He says, "Of course I care for you. I wouldn't be doing this if I didn't."

His words, though clear, feels cryptic. I itch to ask him why. *Why me? What do I have that he wants? What will he get out of this?*

"As my wife, you will be my equal." He tells me. I trust that he is telling the truth but the nagging at my heart still doesn't fade. Sasha also told me that. *Perhaps these mafia men do not know the definition of equal?*

"And free?" I raise an eyebrow.

"And free." He confirms.

I nod my head to show him I understand. The doubts still pull at me. A fake marriage. An arranged marriage. Just like my parents. And look how they turned out. My mother cries herself to sleep as my Father fucks any woman who gives consent. And even that last bit can be quite hazy. I feel myself pale slightly.

"Fine." I hear my voice grow hoarse, "I will marry you under those conditions."

Hope fills his face, and he nods quickly.

"Good." He says, "We will be married tomorrow afternoon."

"So soon?" I hear myself squeak. My voice is small, timid, afraid. A part of me slowly dies.

"The sooner we are married, the sooner you're safe." He tells me, "It will be a quiet ceremony, only a small amount of people will be present. Sophia will prepare everything; she loves designing these kind of things."

AMELIA BROWN

He reaches for my hand, but I pull away and sit back in my seat. Defensively, I wrap my arms around my body. I don't even feel angry anymore. My rage towards my Father and the men in my life has dissipated. Instead, a numbness takes over me.

I am completely and utterly helpless.

Chapter Sixteen

ALESSIO'S POV:

"He's in there." Mateo announces, before kicking down the door of the club.

My target sits in the purple Boothe, surrounded by two barely dressed women. *It's 10am and he's already drinking.* In the club, it's dark and stinks of cheap perfume. I turn my nose up and get a better look at the man I came here for. His eyes are wide and lustful as he stares at the dancers in front of him.

I advance towards him. They all feel my presence as their heads snap in my direction.

"Get out." I bark and immediately, everyone scurries from the room. The sound of heels on tiled floor echoes around the club for a couple moments. And then silence.

"Bradley Piper." I look at my target menacingly. A slightly shiver wracks through him but he controls it.

"Yes?" He raises an eyebrow.

"You have a hit on my fiancée, Maya Baker." I announce, "Tell me what your instructions are."

A sinister look coats the man's face as he sits back in his chair. He gives me a toothless grin, "And why should I tell you?"

The anger and impatience rises through me. *I have 9 other fuckers to deal with today, I can't be dealing with interruptions.* Before he can react, I grab him by the head and smash it into the table. A howl of pain escapes his lips.

"Because I'll fucking kill you if not." I growl, watching the blood stream from his broken nose. His hands flail around in fear. They attempt to contain the blood. I bang his head against the table again.

"I'm waiting." I hiss. A sob of fear tumbles from his lips.

"Alright! Alright!" He exclaims, "Sasha Ovlov wants us to kidnap her from inside the Italian's house…"

He pauses and looks between me and Mateo. He makes an 'O' shape with his mouth as he realises who he is talking to. More fear pools into his pale face.

"How?" Mateo barks beside me. He fumbles with the weapon in his pocket menacingly. Bradley's eyes catch the threat.

"I- I don't know!" He lies. I grab his arm and pull him to the floor, twisting it until it makes a satisfying crunch. Mateo pulls the gun out and presses it to his head.

"Yes, you do." I seethe.

"Okay, okay!" Bradley shrieks, "There is no way to do it. It's anyway we can enter and get her."

"How much is the reward?" I boom, twisting his broken arm more to inflict more torture on the man below me.

"F-five million!" He cries out, the tears flowing down his cheeks. My temper doubles, "You will not touch her. And you will spread the word that no one will be coming near my house nor my wife, understand?"

Bradley nods frantically, whimpering in pain.

"Good." I mutter before letting him fall to the ground in a heap of bones.

"And we can also trust that the American mafia will side with us on this matter of importance?" Mateo declares, "There should be an understanding that men should not touch another's wife, yes?"

Bradley's eyes widened, "I can't promise that! You know I can't. I'm just a hitman I have nothing to do with the American mafia..."

My foot bounces into his chest three times. Bradley wails in pain and snaps in half protectively, protecting his stomach.

"I can try." He whimpers, "I will try!"

"You will not *try*. You will ensure it." I growl.

"You need to speak to my boss; he can ensure it!" Bradley sobs. He no longer oozes any sense of danger or power as he cowers away from me. My lips thin. *I'd rather not speak to Vincent Trench if I can help it.* I do not trust him nor the way he runs his business. We use each other for trade and security but there is a mutual distrust lurking around.

I look to Mateo whose eyes tell me the same answer.

"You will run back to your boss and tell him we would like to talk." I hiss, picking Bradley up by his collar. He flinches. *This is the man who is supposedly the best hitman?*

"O-okay." He stutters. I keep him in the air for a moment before throwing him to the floor. *He gets the message.* Without even looking back, Bradley scurries out of the club to deliver our message.

"I don't like this." Mateo groans with a bitter look. I nod my head in agreement. Dealing with Vincent will be unpleasant. He won't trust us until I have an heir to take over. And I won't trust him until he is dead.

"Neither do I." I mutter, "But we can strike a deal with him for the protection of Maya and finding Sasha."

∞∞∞

It doesn't take long for Vincent to contact us. He has been itching to make a deal with us for the last couple years now. We hold power that he longs to access.

I shuffle in my seat as the call connects. In the meeting room, my Council and I surround the large monitor. Vincent's face appears on the screen. His pale features contrast the lines in his face which have developed over the years due to stress. He has thin papery lips but big dark eyes which give him a look of superiority.

"Vincent." I politely nod and Vincent's smile, if possible, grows larger.

"Ah, Alessio! It's been such a long time." He announces, his voice rumbling through the tv speakers. His eyes fix on Aria, "Aria, my lovely. How have you been?"

Aria smiles politely, tucking a loose blonde hair behind her ear, "I've been good thank you, we need to meet up some point in this week to talk about the shipments."

He nods at my head of communications.

"Anything for you, my dear." He tells her. Aria doesn't flinch or seem uncomfortable. She is used to weird mafia men making moves on her. It is her job to trick them into trusting her, and therefore me. She has been slowly working on Vincent and the American mafia. *It is clearly working.*

"Vincent, Sasha Ovlov has a hit on my Wife's head, Maya Baker." I get straight to the point.

"I see." He says, "Wife or fiancée? The last time we spoke you were single?"

He raises a confused eyebrow as he tries to read me. I remain inscrutable.

"She will be my wife in two hours' time." I tell him, "I hope you can appreciate why I wanted secrecy in my relationship.

You know how hard it is trying to find love when others are involved."

Vincent nods understandingly. He brings his fingers to his cheek and leans on them.

"Congratulations, Alessio." He tells me, but his voice sounds anything but celebratory. I do not smile back at him. A small grunt passes through my lips instead.

"One of your hitmen, amongst other people in your mob have been bribed by Sasha to take her from me."

"That is not good at all." He agrees with me, "I will ensure nothing bad happens to your wife from anyone from my side."

Hope stirs inside of my chest. Perhaps Maya will be safe after all. But can I really trust a man who built his empire on backstabbing others? I look to my Brother and then look away. We are no better than Vincent.

"Only If..." Vincent smirks. My jaw hardens. *Conditions.* There are always fucking conditions.

"Only if I get to meet you and your wife. I would like to see that she is happy with you. After all, she is also promised to Sasha. You know how I only work with trustworthy family businesses. I do not want to pour money into a broken marriage. Into a broken mafia mob." He explains.

I nod my head even if my brain is screaming at me. The hypocrisy jumps from the screen. Vincent is the most disloyal man I have ever met. He has had four different wives in the last two years alone.

"My wife shall not be meeting anyone." I tell him sternly. Maya will snap if I ask any more of her. Not to mention how furious she would be if I put her in a room full of mafia men. Beside me, Mateo glares at me. He silently pleads for me to be quiet, but I can't. For Maya's sake.

"You see, Alessio. There is a lot of money going for Maya. I do not wish to see this opportunity disappear in an unhappy marriage." Vincent protests.

"Sasha is your problem too, Vincent. Girls from your country are disappearing too. If I remember correctly, it was my side who saved them from an untimely death. We must work together to stop him from carrying out these brutal attacks." I threaten him, leaning forward in my seat. His lips thin and the smile fades.

"I'd be more than happy to work together to locate Sasha. But my request remains. I want to meet the wife of my mafia ally." He hisses. I resist the urge to tell him we will never be true allies. There will always be a wall of distrust between us.

"And how do I know that this isn't a ploy to lead me and my wife to you, for you to kidnap her?" I retort, my fists clenching. Vincent nods.

"I would not be so stupid, Alessio. My loyalties have always been to you, not the Russians."

A sinister silence drifts around the room. I can feel my Brother's silent pleads grow stronger.

"Fine," I relent, "but the meeting shall take place here."

Vincent's smile grows into an ugly grimace.

"Brilliant!" He clasps his hands together, "I look forward to meeting the newly wedded couple. In the meantime, I shall dig deeper into the issues on my side regarding my men attacking your home."

The words are snatched from my lips. Instead, I nod at him before hanging up the call. My mind races with too many emotions. The main one is fear.

Not because of Vincent, nor even Sasha to an extent.

But I fear for my own safety when I tell Maya the bad news.

Chapter Seventeen

MAYA'S POV:

Bittersweet. It feels bittersweet.

The elegant dress which curves down my body in beautiful white flowers is stunning. Behind me, the dress trails out for what feels like miles. My hair has been delicately braided out of my face and the veil finishes off the look. I look stunning.

And yet I am ten minutes away from selling my soul to another Mafia devil.

"It's good isn't it!" Sophia breathes out lovingly as she feels the material of my dress. I bob my head in agreement, afraid that If I speak, I will cry. She wears a long, lilac dress with small poofy sleeves. It contrasts against her hair. I can't decide whether I like it or not. Either way, I will not comment.

I bring the glass of prosecco to my lips and chug the rest of the liquid. She offers me her arm and I slowly take it. Despair fills me. I will be given away by a complete stranger. It doesn't sit right within in my stomach.

"It will all be fine." Sophia whispers as we ascend to the top level of the mansion. My old dreams of a beach wedding, surrounded by hundreds of people, have been ruined. The reality is a roof top, secret wedding.

"There is someone I want you to meet before we go up." Sophia says, pulling away from me. The nerves fill my stomach as I hear the low murmur of guests upstairs.

"Who?"

"Me." My Brother's voice takes me surprise. My heart almost leaps from my chest and the tears steam up in my eyes.

"Cole!" I breathe out in shock. He pulls me into an embrace.

"It's okay, Maya. Don't be sad. I'm here." He whispers, rubbing my back soothingly. My breathing is erratic, and I can feel the tears threatening to spill.

"Don't cry, you'll ruin your makeup!" Sophia squeaks, "We spent so long on that, come on!"

Shakily, I bring my fingers to my eyes and stop the tears from spilling down my face.

"H-How? How are you here?" I stumble over my words. Cole pulls away from me but keeps a gentle hand on my arm.

"Alessio invited me. I'm here to give you away." He says sadly. A strained look burns into his expression. It mirrors mine.

"But I can't stay for long, Maya. Father doesn't know where I am. I told him I was sorting some business out in the city. He'll get suspicious if I'm gone for long." My Brother tells me. My heart constricts in my chest, and I slowly shake my head. My fingers grip onto his suit harder.

"No. No! Cole, please don't leave me here alone!" I whimper.

"Maya, calm down." He scolds me, "You are safer here. I cannot protect you in the same way Alessio can."

It hurts him to admit it, I can see it in his face. His own eyes sparkle with tears. Averting his gaze, he tries to control himself. We are stronger than this. We have had over twenty years emotion training from our dearest Father. Tears are not our thing.

"We need to start soon." Sophia whispers gently. She rubs my back soothingly. I peer up at the roof top. I can just about make out rows of strangers waiting to watch the ceremony, each in dresses and suits much more expensive than my Father's house.

"Okay, let's do this." I release a shaky breath.

Cole takes me by the arm and slowly leads me up the steps. Every step I take feels like a new elastic band around my heart. It hurts to breathe, and I want the world to swallow me up in the ground.

An organ begins playing in the background. My grip around Cole tightens as every face turns to look at us. The red carpet below us sticks to my feet and I feel silly. Like a child playing dress up. I am not meant for this life.

Then, my eyes find him. Alessio watches me, mouth slightly agape. As usual, his face is inscrutable but some intense emotion flickers across his face. Nervously, I lick my lips and my mouth becomes dry under his gaze.

Cole brings me to the front of the altar before pulling me into one final embrace.

"Be strong for me, Maya." He whispers in my ear. I bob my head but do not answer him. I can't. A sob tickles the back of my throat. My Brother gives my arms one last squeeze before taking his seat at the front. There, he uncomfortably shuffles in his seat as his eyes dance around at all the rich, mafia members. I watch as he eyes up the wallet shaped dents in pockets. He licks his lips.

"You look stunning." Alessio brings my attention back to him. A blush teases my cheeks and I avert my eyes. *He has to say that. It's all for show*, I tell myself.

"I mean it, Maya." He whispers, taking a step closer. I feel his warm breath on my skin, and it sends shivers through me. His eyes darken.

"You are the most beautiful woman I've ever seen." He compliments me. Again, another blush teases my lips. I smile at him. It comes out weaker that I mean it to.

"We are joined here today to witness the union of two souls." The priest begins. I zone out of the vows. If I listen to his long speech about loving one another, it might become real. I don't want it to be real. Alessio takes my hands in his. It's almost as if he sends some courage through me.

"Do you, Alessio Morisso, take Maya Baker to be your lawfully wedded wife?" The man in white robes asks Alessio. Alessio never removes his eyes from my face.

"I do." He answers firmly. My heart flips in my chest.

"And do you, Maya Baker, take Alessio Morisso to be your lawfully wedded husband?" The priest turns to me. My mouth dries and a lump forms in my throat. Alessio shuffles nervously in front of me.

"I do." I finally say the two cursed words. A look of relief sinks through him and he releases a sigh. I do not relax. If anything, I become more rigid. I have just signed my life away to another man. I have broken my promise to myself.

"You may now kiss the bride." The priest declares. Nervously, I gulp. Alessio brings his hand to my face and tilts my jaw upwards. His burning gaze stare down at my lips. My tongue darts out and wets them in anticipation. Then, he kisses me. Our first kiss as a wedded couple. The fireworks are unlike anything I have ever felt before. It is a powerful kiss, possessive. *Perfect*.

Around us, the audience erupts into claps and cheers. I feel woozy as Alessio pulls away from me. If anything, I itch to pull him back to me. It's as if when our bodies touch, the world around me disappears. It is a feeling I can get lost in.

My *husband* stares down at me with a hungry look in his eyes.

"How are you feeling?" He whispers, keeping his voice low. The audience slowly dissipates around us, the crowd of people flooding towards the dining hall for the after party.

"Fine." I answer him breathlessly. He pulls me into an embrace, and I unwillingly relax in his touch. I can't help but think about how perfectly I fit here in his arms. The hug is strong yet kind. It is not for show. It's to help me. He gives me a quiet strength to continue.

Slowly, I pull back and avert my gaze. I look into the dispersing crowd for my Brother, but he's gone. A sad feeling hums through me. *When will I see him again? Will I see him again?*

Alessio takes me by the hand and leads me into the dining hall. Many guests come up to us to congratulate us. I play the happy wife well. Big smiles, kind eyes, soft words. Lying comes naturally to a someone who participated in illegal activities longer than she's kept a name.

I look at the name tag on the table at the front of the hall. *Mr and Mrs Morisso.* A lump forms in the back of my throat. *My third new name.* Perhaps this one I can keep for longer than the last two combined.

"Thank you for my Brother." I whisper to Alessio as we take a seat. He bobs his head in acknowledgement.

"I didn't want him to miss your wedding." He smiles sadly at me.

"*Our* wedding." I correct him, and his eyes twinkle. He hands me my glass of prosecco and gently dings it against his own glass. We both take a large gulp of the alcohol, eyes never leaving each other's. Then, his gaze travels lower down me. A dark look twinkles in his eyes as he appreciates my wedding dress. A pool of heat floods through me.

He pulls my chair closer to him. I shiver as he brings his lips to my ear.

"How about we leave the ceremony early?" He whispers, his voice laced with promise. My face flushes a deep scarlet colour.

"Alessio!" I gasp as his hand rests on my upper thigh. My body screams for more. I desperately want to leave the ceremony.

"What about keeping up the appearance?" I whisper harshly. His face hardens. I watch greedily as his Adam's apple bobs.

"Fine, we will stay here for a bit." He tells me with a strained look. Then, his hand slips up my dress. When his warm touch rests against my thigh, I am sure I might combust on the spot.

"Alessio." I breathe out warningly, "Not here."

It's a lie. I desperately want it here. I want him everywhere.

He senses my desire as his hand dips lower and rests over my mound. The heat and wetness pools in my panties. I try to cross my legs to contain the heat, but his hand forces my legs apart. A gasp escapes my lips. Nervously, I look around at the table.

Alessio and I sit on our own table, looking out to everyone else. Two metres away, another table full of Alessio's Council sit. We are far enough that no one can see his wandering fingers, but close enough that it is obvious what is going on if they look hard enough.

"Are you sure about that?" He groans, "Because your body is telling me otherwise."

A helpless whimper slips past my lips as I feel his thumb on my clit through my panties. I shuffle as close as I can to him, desperate for more. A huge smirk rests on his lips.

"Good girl." He tells me, voice deep and dangerous. Then, he slips his hand under my knickers. He wastes no time pressing two fingers to my clit. On cue, my body lurches forward. One of my hands grip his thigh threateningly and the other holds tightly onto the chair.

This man will be the death of me.

"Please." I whimper but I don't know what I'm pleading for. *Do I want him to continue?* To make me cum with his skilful fingers. *Or do I choose pride?* Do I really need this entire room of people watching me cum? Yes. *No!* Yes...

"Stop thinking so much and enjoy it." He growls. The vibrations give me my answer. I do want it. I want it so bad!

Obediently, I spread my legs. He groans in approval. One finger slips inside of me. My mouth becomes an 'O' shape, but I slam it shut. He picks up the pace and curls his finger. My heart races in my chest as I feel myself stumble closer to the edge.

"Alessio!" I hiss as I watch someone approach the table. He pulls out of me but never removes his touch on my clit. I tremble as he plays with my bundle of nerves.

"Congratulations." Mateo bows his head as he approaches. Humiliation stains my cheeks as a squeak falls past my lips. I avert my gaze and stare down at the table instead.

Mateo raises an eyebrow at me before looking at his Brother.

"We need to have a chat later." He says grimly. Alessio nods at him.

"I will find you." He tells him. Mateo sighs and agrees. Whatever is troubling him seems to have visibly shaken him up. He twists on his foot and storms off, back to his table.

My fingers jump to the tablecloth, and I squeeze as Alessio slips two fingers inside of me. I can't figure out how he manages to finger fuck me like this so discreetly. The rest of his body is rigid and upright. His gaze falls onto me. My breathing becomes uneasy.

"Cum for me, Maya." He growls, "Cum for me in front of all these people."

His scandalous words send me over the edge. A strangled moan tumbles out as I ride the high. My body buckles on the seat and I tremble. He holds me still as the pleasure fills me. Finally, I come down from the high and my head lulls forward.

"Good girl." He tells me before bringing his fingers to his lips. He discreetly tastes me in front of a whole room of people. My stomach flips at this dangerously delicious man.

Chapter Eighteen

MAYA'S POV:

"Great party, eh?" Sophia smiles over at me, "Are you having fun?"

Genuine concern crosses her face. I can tell from the bags under her eyes that all this wedding planning has stressed her out. Bless her. She really wants to make this as enjoyable as an arranged wedding can be.

"Yes, it's been lovely. Thank you." I respond politely. Alessio and I joined the large Council table half an hour ago. It has been nonstop talk about business. My body is still throbbing from my come down. All I want is to take Alessio upstairs and consummate the marriage. *Great sex is the only upside of the marriage.*

"Vincent will be coming down tomorrow." Mateo tells Alessio. Alessio stiffens and his eyes dart over to me. I catch his guilty look before he can look away.

"Who is Vincent?" I frown. The table hums to a silence. Anxiety creeps up in my stomach. *What are they not telling me?*

"Who is he?" I try again. Alessio's jaw hardens, and he glares at his Brother. When his gaze falls back on me a sheepish smile coats his lips.

"The American mafia boss. We are looking to go into business with them." He tells me. His hand jumps out and squeezes my hand, but I pull away, "So why the guilty look in my direction? What do I have to do with it? Is it linked to Sasha?"

"Darling, we will discuss this tomorrow." Alessio says before draining the remainder of his wine, "Let's just enjoy tonight."

"Well, what is it about?" I scowl. I will not let him avoid the conversation. Especially if I'm involved.

"I won't drop it until you tell me."

Alessio sighs. He dabs his lips with the napkin in his lap.

"Anyone? Is anyone going to tell me?" I hiss, shooting my eyes across the table, "Sophia? Casper?"

"Why are you asking him?" Alessio responds with jealousy. A scoff passes my lips. How can he be avoiding me like this, and yet still be jealous? Fearfully, Casper averts his eyes. I glare at my husband. *What has he said to Casper to make him avoid me? Will married life be a constant sense of loneliness and forced ignorance?*

"Tell me!" I growl.

"Calm down, Maya. You're working yourself up. It's not a big deal." Mateo blows out a breath. My eyes squint at him and my lip twitches. I sit forward in my chair menacingly, "What are you hiding from me?"

"You are now a Morisso, Maya. With this name, comes a couple responsibilities." Alessio says nervously, "One, as you'll know, is playing the part of wife. This means you will have to accompany me to some meetings."

"No." I respond sternly. I sit back in my chair and cross my arms. I don't even care if I look like a sulking child- I will not be getting involved with any mafia business.

"Yes." Alessio hisses.

I shake my head, "No. Not happening."

"Maya, please don't be silly. This is only a small request." Mateo tries to reason with me. I ignore him. Instead, I tear my gaze towards my furious husband. He is not used to being answered back to. Nor is he not used to not getting his own way. *Well, fuck him.* He has now met his match.

"You said I would be an equal, not a mafia bride." I spit.

"And you will be." He responds quickly. I shake my head in disbelief,

"No, I will not. I have no say in this. You kept it from me, hid it from me. You haven't asked my permission! That's me being an inferior, not equal!"

"Maya, calm down." Sophia squeaks beside me. Everyone on the table notices Alessio's eyes darkening and jaw hardening. But I'm too far gone in anger. I knew I couldn't trust any mafia men! He has me in a binding contract now, I have no more freedom. I can't believe I fell for it. Frustrated, I grab my napkin and throw it at Alessio. It lamely hits his chest and falls to the floor.

"Maya!" Sophia squeals. All eyes are on us. I throw myself to my feet.

"Fuck you!" I tell him angrily before storming off. I don't even care for the dozens of concerned eyes glued to the back of my head as I disappear out of the hall. I don't make it far. Suddenly, someone grabs my arm and yanks me around.

"Ow!" I squeal, trying to pull back. Menacingly, Alessio glares down at me.

"What the fuck was that about?" He growls, "Throwing things at your husband? Swearing at him?"

"Oh, so we are already playing the husband card!" I scoff in disbelief, "Sorry, Sir. I'll get back in the fucking kitchen and serve you, shall I?"

"Knock it off, Maya." He lowers his voice threateningly. He takes a step forward and I take one backwards. My back hits the wall but I don't back down. I keep his gaze and I remain firm.

"Or what?" I hiss.

"What have I done wrong to you?" His eyes suddenly become sad, "I have tried to do nothing but good for you. I saved you, gave you a place to stay, you a way to be safe. Everything I have done has been for you. All I am asking is for you to attend a couple stupid meetings."

My heart flips in my chest and guilt oozes through me. I lower my eyes guiltily. *He has a point.* I have behaved like a brat. Worse than that. An ungrateful brat. All because of my stubbornness to avoid mafia men. I peer back up at him. His dark eyes relax when our eyes meet. He reaches a hand out and strokes my arm gently. Even when I'm in the wrong he is being caring and gentle. More guilt pangs at my chest. Perhaps I am too harsh to judge Alessio in the same category as Sasha and my Father.

"I am sorry." I whisper. The word is foreign to me. In my world, you do not apologise. You fight.

"I will attend the meeting with you. And I will make it up to you for embarrassing you out there." I add quietly. Alessio looks shocked for a second. He definitely assumed I was going to keep protesting.

"Thank you." He nods his head gratefully. I stand on my tip toes and place a small kiss to his lips. As I pull back, his hands lock on my hips. He deepens the kiss and I'm immediately drunk on him. My body reacts to him as if he's flicked a switch.

"Alessio, Maya, will you be returning?" I hear Sophia's voice behind us. Alessio pulls away for a split second.

"No." He growls before scooping me up. I've never seen him move so fast as he charges up the stairs. I wrap my legs around him to stay steady. My lips trail kisses all down his cheek and his neck. Below me, I feel his hard member jumping out in approval. My body trembles.

"Alessio." I whimper.

"Maya." He responds in a deep growl. It only spurs me on more.

Finally, we make it to the room. He throws me to the bed and quickly rids himself of his suit. My body longs for him. We can have gentle, caring sex another day. Today, I need him bad. Hard and fast.

"Please, Alessio." I moan, pulling him close. My head lulls to the left when he grabs my breasts through my wedding dress. I catch us in the floor, length mirror. My heart flutters as I watch him drop to his knees. His face disappears up my dress and it's not long until I feel his fingers rip my knickers away. They snap and fall to the floor. His tongue is on my clit within seconds.

"Fuck!" I cry out, my back arching. I can't take my eyes off the mirror. I'm glued to how hot he is. He suddenly plunges two fingers into me as his tongue assaults my clit. I squirm around in pleasure.

"Alessio, I need you inside of me!" I hear myself beg. He removes himself from under my dress. A wicked grin kisses his lips. It's sinful and sexy.

Without warning, he plunges inside of me. My body lurches upwards in pleasure. A long moan falls from my lips as my fingers wrap around his huge muscles. He matches my desperation and slams into me, over and over.

"Alessio, oh my God!" I cry out. His fingers slide up under my dress and start playing with my clit. It is all too much.

"I'm close!" I tell him. He grunts in approval and picks up his pace. Suddenly, my body convulses under him as I cum. He quickly falls over the edge after me. We cling onto each other desperately, riding out our highs. My body shakes as he gives a couple last thrusts. A lazy smile coats my lips.

Yes. I think I am right. This may be the best part of our marriage.

Chapter Nineteen

ALESSIO'S POV:

The table trembles as Maya bounces her leg nervously into it. I place a reassuring hand on her knee, and she stops. Then, she begins bouncing the other leg.

"It's going to be okay." I tell her softly. Her once warm eyes turn cold.

"Is it?" She hisses, "Is it all going to be okay, Alessio?"

I bite back a growl. My little Maya will always fight back with me. It's something I love and hate at the same time.

My eyes scan the dining hall which has plenty of tables and chairs. The meeting with Vincent is scheduled for today. Hopefully, it is short and quick. I look back to Maya who gulps down more wine. There are bags under her eyes from where she hadn't slept last night. I felt her shuffling and rolling around uncomfortably all night. The meeting with Vincent frightened her. I squeeze her leg again. This time, she offers me a small smile. I quietly tell her it's going to be okay. She nods and takes a deep breath in.

"Alessio!" A voice booms behind us. I jump up and plaster a fake grin to my lips. Vincent sashays into the room, arms wide. He has a small army of people behind him all scurrying after the fifty-year-old man. I shake his hand and nod my head.

"Hello, Vincent. How was your journey here?" I say politely. Vincent's crooked teeth shine through as he smiles at me.

"Shit." He answers crudely. A deep chuckle leaves him. He holds his round belly as he laughs at his own joke. I resist the urge to roll my eyes. Vincent's eyes scan the room behind me before they settle on something.

"Ah," He mutters heading towards Maya. Something protective swims through me. I follow him closely behind. Defensively, she rises to her feet. Vincent holds his arms open to embrace her and I watch as she pales.

"No." I tell him sternly, stepping in front of my wife. Vincent's eyes widen. He looks between me and Maya suspiciously and I can tell he is embarrassed. I recon he is not used to being turned down. But I don't fucking care. He will not touch my wife. She is mine.

"My bad," Vincent says slowly, raising his hands up, "I should know better than to touch another man's wife."

"You should." I confirm.

Vincent steps away from Maya and I feel the rage slowly leave my body. Her small hand rests against my back. When I turn to look at her, she gives me a grateful smile. Right now, she seems so small. My feisty little warrior has a frightened look in those dark eyes. For once, she has no sarcastic comment to make.

"How was the wedding?" Vincent smiles but it doesn't reach his eyes. He takes his place across the table from Maya and me. I quickly sit next to Maya and pull her chair closer. It is silly but I desperately want her close to me. The urge to protect her, to make her happy flows through me.

"It was lovely, actually." Maya responds. It surprises me that she answers him, but I don't show it.

"Yes, it was." I smile at her, "A lovely private ceremony."

She blushes and averts her gaze. My hand returns to her thigh, and I give it another squeeze. Though this time, it isn't for reassurance. It is a reminder of what I did that night. My body flushes with heat and I long to do it again. I quickly grab my wine to soothe the burning desire in me. Maya copies.

Opposite us, Vincent frowns.

"Vincent!" Mateo grins as he walks into the room. Vincent stands up and embraces my Brother. They talk about business and take their seats back at the table.

"So, tell me more about this problem with the Russians." Vincent returns his gaze to me. Maya stiffens beside me. My eyes flicker between her and Vincent nervously.

"The man in control, Sasha Ovlov, as you'll be aware, has been kidnapping women and selling them to global, sex rings." I remind him, "He captured well over three hundred women within a month. Though, they are all free now."

Vincent's lips pull into a straight line. His eyes never leave Maya's cowering face. She stares at the table with hatred. It hurts me to see her reliving the traumatic experiences of that prison. My fingers itch to hurt Sasha even more.

"And what did he do to you, pretty?" Sasha asks her. My jaw clenches and I give him a warning look.

"What are you playing at?" I hiss, "She's gone through enough. You have all the information you need."

"Alessio, it's fine." Maya pipes up. Shocked, my head snaps over to her. She shuffles uncomfortably in her seat for a moment before playing with my fingers in her lap.

"He and his men beat me up. Then they took me to a private room where Sasha undressed me. He was going to take advantage of me if it hadn't had been for Alessio and his army." She squeaks. I can't look at her. My eyes remain firmly ahead, fixed on Vincent. His face is inscrutable. All I need is one flicker of enjoyment of the story, and I'll throw him across the fucking room. American boss or not. No one will mess with my wife.

"Understood." Vincent said grimly. He shakes his head and finally he shows emotion. Pure disgust ripples through him.

"He's an awful man for that. And I promise, we will find him, and he will be punished." He assures us. Mateo's face lights up.

"So, you will work with us?" He asks hopefully. Vincent nods his head slowly.

"Yes, I will." He announces looking between Maya and me, "Anyone can see that this isn't an arranged marriage. You care for her too much. This is love. And therefore, the Americans will back you in the war."

My heart flips as he answers. In this moment, I don't even care about the fucking war. My eyes jump to maya. She peers up at me nervously and bites her lower lip. I can't take my eyes away from that beautiful little face. The thought of losing her to Sasha makes my blood boil and heart hurt. I want to pull her closer and protect her from the world. Not that she needs my help. Feisty little Maya could survive on her own. But I don't want her to. I want her to stay with me.

Maybe Vincent is right. Perhaps this is what love feels like. And from the look in her eyes, I can tell she is thinking the same thing.

Chapter Twenty

ALESSIO'S POV:

"He's *there*?" I spit, frowning as I look at the report before my eyes. Angelo smugly grins, "I know, who would have thought?"

I stare down at the hideous warehouse in the picture. *As if Sasha could be hiding there, of all places?*

"Okay, perfect. Get the team together, we will leave at lunch time." I demand. Angelo bows his head respectively and then quickly leaves the room. I follow him out of the room and almost sprint into my bedroom.

Still asleep, Maya curls up in our bed. It's 9am and I know if she had her way, she'd sleep until noon.

"Maya." I whisper, giving her a little nudge. She is so pretty when she sleeps. I can't help the swooning in my heart. She doesn't respond. I place a kiss on her forehead. This time, she grumbles.

"Alessio?"

Slowly, her eyes open. A groggy look still kisses her face as she scowls up at me. I smile down at my gorgeous wife.

"We've found him." I beam proudly, "We've found Sasha."

She shoots up in the bed and rubs her eyes.

"What? Where?" She gasps.

"He is in a warehouse near the place you guys were kept." I say and the thought of reminding her of this place stabs me in the heart. Maya's small little features light up, "Cool, when are we going?"

A lump forms in my throat.

"You're not coming, Maya. It's too dangerous." I say quietly, rubbing her arms. She scowls at me, shaking her head, "Yes, I am. I deserve revenge too, Alessio."

"I know, my love. I will bring him back here for you." I promise her. Despair fills her. She purses her lips and shakes her head. I can see the rage bubbling inside of her.

"Please, Maya. It's too dangerous. What if we are outnumbered and then you get taken from me? Just please stay." I beg her. Her eyes grow watery, and she looks away from me, not wanting to cry in my presence. Her misery is like a knife to the heart.

"It's okay, my beautiful Maya. I promise you will get you revenge on him." I tell her for certain.

"Who is going?" She whispers. Her fingers wrap in my shirt, and she pulls me closer. I wrap my arms protectively around her. She sighs into me.

"Everyone in the Council." I answer, stroking her hair. Her little voice squeaks out, "I'll be alone?"

"I could get Sophia to stay with you?" I suggest and she shakes her head again, pressing it against my chest. I feel my chest grow wet with her tears and it hurts my heart. She doesn't let me hear her sobs though. I can't imagine what she is going through right now. Not only will she be forced to face her fear of being alone, but she is also not allowed to find the man who tortured her.

My fingers begin to tremble, upset at her distress.

"It's okay." I whisper, kissing her head. She peers up at me, her big sad eyes gazing into mine, "Can't you stay with me?"

"I can't do that, Maya. I'm the boss." I mutter quietly. Her sad eyes grow more pained as she looks away.

"You and Sophia will stay here. I promise I'll be back before dinner." I whisper into her hair. Her grip on me grows tighter.

"Please stay safe, Alessio." She whimpers. For the first time, I feel my little warrior cry. It shakes her whole body and stains my chest. I hold her tightly and pray she will be strong.

"I promise." I tell her confidently. Slowly, she peels herself away from me. Her face is red and tear-stained.

"Okay." She sniffles and wipes her nose on the back of her arm. Then, she peers up at me with more strength.

"Get that fucker." She demands.

I salute her, "Got it, Captain."

MAYA'S POV:

"We're going to have a great day." Sophia chirps, throwing the curtains open. I roll over in bed, hiding my face from the light with a groan.

"Come on, up you get." She demands, strutting over to the bed, and pulling the covers off.

"No." I complain but Sophia grabs me by the arm, "Get up and get dressed. We are going to have fun."

She's surprisingly strong for someone her size and she yanks me to my feet. Unwillingly, I head over to the wardrobe and settle on Sophia's dark jeans and a white plain shirt.

"What are we even doing today?" I ask, rubbing the sleep from my eyes. My plan had been to sleep away the misery of being left out of Sasha's capture. I want all the energy I can muster for his punishment.

Sophia's little face lights up.

"We are going to do some cooking." She tells me.

"Cooking?" I frown. *This doesn't sound like fun.*

"Well, baking. Let's make some cookies or something." She corrects herself before walking towards the door. I follow her aimlessly, knowing there is no use in fighting this. I recon Sophia is the kind of girl who would scream the house down to get what she wants. She is very much like me. Just slightly crazier.

"Miss Sophia." The old cook gasps as we enter the kitchen. The larger lady holds her heart in shock of our unannounced arrival.

"We've come to bake." Sophia beams. The lady shakes her head with a smile. She wipes her hands on her apron and pulls Sophia into a hug.

"I didn't realise you were back, my dear." She says gently. The wrinkles in her skin pull upwards as she beams down at Sophia. Her eyes twinkle with pure joy. The smile is contagious. I feel my own lips pull upwards.

"Yes, Ma'am." Sophia nods happily, returning the embrace. The Chef pulls away and returns to her dough. She throws more flour onto the bread she is kneading.

"What are you going to bake?" The lady raises an eyebrow.

"Cookies." Sophia nods her head, "Chocolate chip cookies."

My stomach growls in approval.

"And do you know how to make them?" The lady smiles at us. We must look like two mischievous children, looking to make a mess. Blankly, I look at Sophia and she looks at me. Both of us are clueless. Sophia's phone rings. Once and then twice. She ignores it and puts it on silent, too transfixed by the cookie conversation.

"I take that as a no." The lady grins. She picks up her dough and wraps cling film around it. Then she wipes her hands on her apron again.

"Okay, first let's gather the ingredients." She takes control of the situation. After a long struggle of Sophia and I digging down the endless cupboards, we finally had our ingredients all laid out in front of us on the large counter.

I scan the huge kitchen. It is probably the size of my entire house. White cupboards cling to every wall, creating an endless trail of kitchen space. The marble counters are beautiful too with their black swirly patterns. A breathless sigh falls from my lips. At home, I was never a big fan of cooking. But with a kitchen like this, I could get used to it.

"First, preheat the oven to 180 degrees." The chef says. Excitedly, Sophia skips over to the oven. I look down at her name badge. *Mrs Figgio.*

"You can call me Mary." The Chef catches my gaze. A blush coats my cheeks and I bob my head.

"I'm Maya." I say politely, extending out my hand. She glares down at it and instead pulls me into an embrace. The smell of vanilla fills my nostrils as her arms clamp around me. Oddly enough, the hug feels good. It's protective, motherly almost.

"Awe, come on, Ma'am. I'm going to get jealous." Sophia whines playfully behind us. Mary pulls back from me and tugs at my cheeks. I can feel the flour residue stick to my skin.

"I know who you are, dear." Mary smiles at me, "You're the lass who has made my Alessio very happy."

"Your Alessio?" I find myself asking. Mary beams and nods her head.

"Mary has been here since we were kids." Sophia explains as she jumps onto the counter. She pulls grapes from the fruit bowl next to her and slowly fills her stomach with them.

"She does it all. Chef, nanny, person who will play toys with you. Of course, that was when we were little. Now, all she does is give great advice." Sophia winks at her mischievously.

"And helps you bake apparently." Mary rolls her eyes sarcastically, "Okay, let's get on with it then, girls. Alessio will have my head on a plate if I don't have dinner ready for everyone by the time they return."

Another smile flickers across my lips. I can't help but feel mesmerised by this lovely lady. I try to imagine a young Alessio pulling at her apron, asking to play games with her. Or him baking with her in his toddler years. Perhaps he came to her for help when he became a teenager? Maybe he came to her recently about the situation between me and him? I can only dream of what it would be like to have someone like Mary in my life growing up. Perhaps I'd have more direction. Perhaps I would be smarter, more successful. I would not be a petty thief. Nor would I be on the run from mafia men.

"Sophia?" I ask as she combines some of the dry ingredients in a bowl, as per Mary's instructions. She hums to show she is listening.

"Where is your mother and Father?" I query, the curiosity getting the better of me. Both her and Mary stiffen. They exchange a small look with one another. It piques my curiosity more.

"My mother is no longer with us." Sophia says slowly. Her eyes now remain fixed on the bowl. Mary slides another bowl towards her with measured ingredients already poured into it. Sophia takes it and begins whisking away.

"And my Father lives with me. Though I am not to talk about him whilst in this house." She confesses. My lips curl into an 'O' shape and I guiltily avert my eyes. Her excitement slowly fades as she thinks back to her parents. My stomach churns anxiously. *Why is she not allowed to talk about her Father? Is it one of Alessio's rules? What had he done to deserve isolation from his sons?*

"I'm sorry, I shouldn't have asked." I apologise quickly.

"No," Sophia cheers up, "I know everything about you and your parents. It's only fair you know something about mine."

I know she is trying to soothe my guilt, but I can help a wince. *What does she know about me and my parents? How would she know? And how much does she know?*

Suddenly, the doorbell rings. Sophia's head snaps towards it and she scowls,

ILLEGAL ACTIVITIES

"Are we expecting anyone, Mary?"

Chapter Twenty-One

ALESSIO'S POV:

The flight feels like an eternity. My leg jumps up and down anxiously and my body trembles. I can't wait to get my hands on that slimy little fucker.

"Should only be two more hours." Aria offers as she bites into her apple. I nod and look out of the window. *How will I react when I come face to face with the man who's hurt Maya and put a hit on her?* I'd fucking kill him, most likely. But not before Maya gets her own revenge.

My phone rings, pulling me out of my thoughts.

"Shouldn't you have that off? Doesn't it interfere with signals or something?" Casper frowns at me. I glare at him before answering the call. He looks away timidly.

"Alessio?" A frantic voice calls out. My heart flutters at Vincent's voice.

"Vincent? What is it?"

"Maya is in trouble." He warns me. The world around me blurs and my heartbeat pounds louder in my ears.

"What do you mean?" I spit down the phone. I swear to God if he's lying or trying to freak me out.

"It's a diversion. There is no one in the warehouse!" Vincent panics, "We're here now. I think It's a trap. Sasha must be going to your house!"

Frantically, I throw myself to my feet.

"Fuck!" I shriek, "Turn this fucking plane around, now!"

My heart races in my chest and my mouth feels dry.

"Brother, it's going to be okay." Mateo tries to calm me, but I can't hear it. I storm out of the main seating area into the private room in the back. The plane lurches as it spins around. To let off steam, I release a load of punches into the sofa cushions. My body shakes with fear and rage.

How could this happen? How could we be so stupid? How would Sasha know our plans? A shiver wracks through me.

Do we have an imposter amongst the Council?

MAYA'S POV:

"No, I don't believe so." Mary scowls. She heads for the front door, and I nosily follow her. *Perhaps it's Alessio already?* It had only been a couple of hours though. I frown. *He can't be back yet, can he?*

Sophia races in front of the lady.

"I've got it, Ma'am." She calls out respectively. Sophia stands on her tip toes and peers through the peep hole in the door. Suddenly, she throws herself backwards in shock. Her hand covers her mouth, and she stares at us.

"Fuck!" She cries out quietly. Quickly, she grabs me and Mary and yanks us towards the kitchen again. She bolts the door behind her and hurries back over to us.

"Who is it?" I panic. Sophia is much paler now.

"It's Sasha!" She gawps. My heart drops in my chest.

"What?" I hiss, "No, no it can't be!"

Without warning, a large crash rings around the house. It is followed by thumping as the front door tries to withstand his assault. Sophia frantically types at her phone. It rings and then immediately goes through.

"Alessio!" She cries out, "He's here, he's here!"

I can't hear what is being said on the other side. My breathing is erratic, and my stomach is uneasy.

"I'm sorry, my phone was off!" Sophia protests, "How far away are you?"

"He won't get through the kitchen door." Mary tells me, wrapping an arm around my shivering body. The fear is intermingled with rage. I want my revenge on this asshole, but I'm supposed to be the predator in the scenario. Not the prey.

"Let me in, my lovely." Sasha's sing song voice rings through the door. It is followed by a pounding. I bounce in action.

"Where are the knives?" I hiss, rummaging around the drawers. Mary quickly assists me. I pull open a large draw and pull out the meat knife. I hand out the weapons to the women.

"Fifteen minutes? Okay, okay, we can try and hold him off for that long." Sophia pants down the phone. Hope starts to brim inside of me. Alessio would be here soon. He will help us.

"Maya, my beauty, open the door." Sasha calls out again. A horrible shiver harasses my spine.

"Of course, I won't let them fucking take her." Sophia spits down the phone. She eyes up her huge knife.

"Is there any way out?" I turn to Mary with wide eyes. Guilt floods through me. These two women might be harmed just from defending me. I won't let them get hurt because of me.

"No." Mary says grimly. The old lady doesn't show any expression of fear. An inscrutable look crosses her face.

"I will not let you go." She tells me firmly, "You have married Alessio. You are my daughter in law now. And I fight for family."

My heart constricts even more at the lady's kindness.

"Thank you, Mary." I whisper fearfully.

Suddenly, there is another bang at the door. The wood bursts open and Sasha's ugly face peers through. I break into action. I slice at his hand pulling at the wood. He hisses in pain and tries to grab me. I dodge him and keep slicing. Sophia joins me. We play a twisted game of whack a mole.

"Alessio will be home very fucking soon, Sasha!" Sophia spits, "You'll be torn limb from fucking limb!"

"Not if I get to you first." Sasha retorts. Behind him, I hear the cackles of Dima and Andrei. My blood boils and I stab the door. Sasha jumps backwards. My knife misses him by a centimetre. Suddenly, the door jolts as the three men kick at it.

"Get back!" Sophia hisses to me. I stumble backwards but hold my knife up protectively. I will not be taken from this place. From Alessio. This is my home now, and I will not let them hurt me nor my new family.

Dima lifts the door from the frames and removes it. Sasha cackles as he takes a menacing step forward.

"Get out! Get the fuck out!" Sophia snarls, she raises her knife higher. Andrei advances towards her. She slices at him but he's bigger. They take turns to throw punches at each other.

Sasha reaches out for me, and I stumble backwards in shock. Suddenly, Mary throws herself in front of me. She raises her knife to Sasha.

"Back off, boy." She hisses. Sasha's awful grin grows as he looks at the little old lady. My heart flips in my chest. I try to pull Mary back, but she doesn't move. For a small woman, she sure is strong. Sasha raises his hand to hit Mary, but I throw my knife out in defence. It slices into his arm.

"Right, that's it. Enough fucking around!" Sasha howls. He grabs Mary and chucks her to the ground.

"No!" I cry out as she hits the floor with a thud. Her response time isn't quick enough to soften her fall. Just as I go to help her, Sasha grabs my hand. I turn to face him and throw my head into his nose. A satisfying snap echoes through the room.

"You fucking bitch!" He growls before landing a punch to my face. And then a second. Then a third. And a fourth. My vision is hazy and the sound around me drifts into the hum of my heartbeat and blood flow. Everything hurts. My head lulls to the side and I watch as Dima and Andrei point guns at Sophia and Mary.

Mary cowers on the floor, her hands covering her head. Sophia stays on her knees, glaring into the barrel. Her eyes jump over to me, and something twinkles in her eyes. She's planning something. My lip's part to say something but Sasha lands another punch to my face.

"Did you really think you could escape me like that?" He growls, pulling me up by the shirt. I hang weakly in his arms. At some point my fingers releases the knife in exhaustion.

"Yes." I respond sarcastically. Blood trickles down Sasha's face from his broken nose. I smile at it.

"You have a little something." I say, touching my own nose. An evil grin coats his lips. Then the anger gets the better of him. He tries to throw another punch at me, but I dodge it. My leg swipes under his, knocking him over. Next to me, Sophia quickly grabs the gun off Dima and shoots him in the stomach before aiming at Andrei. Shocked, Andrei, holds the gun in the air and backs away from Mary. I force my foot as hard as I can into Sasha's crotch. He shoots upwards in pain.

A gun shot rings around the room. And then another. My head snatches in the direction. Sophia drops her knees. She clutches her bleeding stomach. Her lips curl into an 'o' shape and her eyes become watery.

"Fuck, Sophia!" I cry out. Her whole body spasms as she drops to the floor. I lurch in her direction, but Sasha already has me locked in his firm grip.

"Look!" He roars, grabbing my head, "Look what you have fucking done! You have killed each and every person here!"

I shake my head as the tears fall down. Mary twitches in a heap of frail bones. Beside her, Sophia's stomach spurts with blood. She quickly pales and her eyes flutter open and shut. Dima and Andrei both pant as they clutch their own blood wounds. They all lose blood rapidly.

"Boss." Dima croaks, "Help us."

Sasha shakes his head and spins me back around.

"This could have been avoided." He growls, grabbing me by the throat. He drags me out of the room. I kick my legs about frantically but I'm exhausted. He's much stronger than me.

Chapter Twenty-Two

ALESSIO'S POV:

I'm off the plane before the engines stop. My heart drops as I race up the path and spot the broken door. Everything hurts as I burst in. Then, my eyes spot them.

Sasha limps as he pulls Maya towards the door by her neck. Her eyes flutter open and shut as she chokes on her breathing. She is black and blue with bruises, and she trembles in fear. I see red. Suddenly, I'm charging at them.

My fist collides with Sasha's face. He stumbles and drops Maya. I quickly catch her and soften her landing.

"Alessio!" She cries out in shock, "You're here! Oh my God, you're here."

The relief floods through her facial expression but then it becomes despair again.

"Sophia!" She squeaks pointing to the kitchen. Angelo races past me. As does Casper and Aria. I hear Angelo's strangled sob and it strikes me straight in the heart. *My sister... what's happened to my sister?* I push my concern to the side momentarily. First, I will deal with Sasha. And then I'll join the others with my sister.

I gently put Maya to the floor and advance towards Sasha. He clumsily tries to get off the ground. I drive another foot into his stomach, enjoying the grunt of pain which escapes his lips.

"How *fucking* dare you!" I growl menacingly. I pull my gun out and aim it at his head.

"Alessio, please." He tries to beg. I land another foot in his stomach. His body convulses and he begins to cough up blood. Maya appears beside me. She places one hand on my back and uses the other to take the weapon from my fingers. I gladly let her.

Sasha's eyes widen as he looks between us in fear.

"No." He whispers, "No, this isn't you, Maya. You won't kill me. Otherwise, you'll become just like your Fath-"

Bang! Bang! Bang! Maya fires multiple rounds into Sasha before he can even finish his sentence. One in the penis, one in the leg, then arm. She aims for all the painful spots, like a true little warrior. I blow out a breath of shock.

Maya watches as he convulses and withers in agony. Her face is hard and inscrutable. Finally, Sasha takes his last breaths.

Suddenly, she throws herself into my arms. I hold onto her tightly. A tear slips down my cheek.

"Alessio!" She whispers.

"Maya." I half-sob.

"I thought I was gone then. I thought I lost you." She whimpers into my shoulder. I feel my shirt grow wet and my stomach churns in agony. My brave little Maya.

"I thought I lost you too." I confess, "Maya, I love you so much. I didn't realise it fully until today. I can't lose you. I just can't."

Slowly, she pulls back and peers up at me. Her tear-stricken and red-nosed face watches me. For a moment, I flush with humiliation. I have never said those three words before. *I love you.* Never, I wouldn't dare. And yet here I am, pouring my heart out to a woman I've known for a week. The most intense week of my life.

Maya pales and bites her lower lip nervously. It makes my heart drop in my chest. *Does she not feel the same way?*

"She's going to be fine!" I hear Angelo call out into the hallway.

I sigh in relief, knowing my sister is going to make it. I turn my attention back to my wife. She reaches up and touches my face.

"Alessio," She whispers, "I love you too."

The words squeeze my heart. I could have fallen to my knees and worshipped her there and then.

"Does this mean you'll stay here?" I whisper nervously. Surely, now that the main threat is gone, she can leave. There is no reason for her to remain *'captive'* here, in her words.

"Don't be silly, Alessio." She shakes her head with a small smile, "Of course I'll stay here with you. This is my home."

It's as if the breath has been stolen from my lungs. I nod my head slowly, in understanding. The smile doesn't leave my lips. I don't know if I'll ever be able to be sad again after this moment. And for the first time in my whole, miserable life, I feel happy.

Chapter Twenty-three

2 weeks in the future

MAYA'S POV:

A small, grey pebbled lane leads Sophia and I into the bumbling market stools. We walk in a comfortable silence, clutching bags of clothes and useless items. I use all my energy to immerse myself in the unfamiliar surroundings around me. Sophia had practically dragged me out of bed this morning to help her do some shopping. Though I wasn't particularly too upset with the proposition, I had been locked inside those four walls for weeks without seeing the outside world. At the mere mention of reality, I was up and dressed.

To the left of me, fair-haired siblings giggle as they race past us, weaving in and out of the crowds, playing some racing car game. Behind, their mother hurries after them in fear of losing them to the mass of people. Her sweet perfume sweeps past us as she disappears into the crowd. I smile at them, wondering what it would have been like to grow up with my siblings in normal circumstances. Where we could have played and fought like normal children, experienced the loving embrace of our parents like normal children, had a childhood without fear and loss, like normal children. But my Father didn't raise us to be normal. He raised us to be strong. I blink back the threatening tears and cast my attention towards the food stalls.

My belly growls in approval. I excitedly eye them up. A dark green box with a big metal bowl full of steaming walnuts has me stumbling towards it. I lick my lips, but Sophia has other plans.

She grabs me by the arm.

"Come on. Down here!"

She tugs me out of the food court and towards the clothes stands. Here, people from many different backgrounds, call out for your attention. They throw different things in the air: blankets, t-shirts, pack of cards. Anything and everything is on sale. I'm enticed by a velvety purple stand with beautiful gold silk hanging from the four corners of the gazebo. It reminds me of Aladdin's carpet. A dark-skinned lady wearing a bright pink dress offers me a magnificent smile.

"Hello, dear." She says, waving her hand over her stand, "Do you fancy anything? Take your time, take your pick!"

My eyes light up as I peer down at the beautiful jewellery on display. All fakes, of course. I'd know if they were real. She has rings, bracelets, necklaces, anklets, earrings, in every shape and colour. A gorgeous lavender smell wafts from this stand too. Like a piece of rope, slithering around my body, the smell yanks me closer and closer. Then my eyes land on the prettiest, gold bracelet I've ever seen. Fine fibres of gold weaves in and out in a beautiful, plaited pattern, twisting towards a beautiful emerald jewel. The green shines in the stunning sunshine, like a leaf out of the garden of Eden. I blink rapidly and raise it higher to see whether it's real or not. The edges are hard and stiff, and it doesn't shine a multi-coloured patten when raised into light. A smile licks my lips. It's real!

"How much for this?"

"500." The lady offers, "But for you, I'd do it for 350 euros."

My lips pull into a frown. And she was paying real prices for it too.

Longingly, I peer down at the beauty. I have no money on me; I refused all of Alessio's, and there is no way I'd ask Sophia to purchase this for me. Yet the bracelet seems to mould into my skin like it was made for me. Something burns inside of me to take it, to *steal* it. My entire life had been gearing up for moment like this. The quick slip into a pocket, or an innocent distraction as I disappear into the bumbling crowd. Yet as I look at the thin, smiling woman with bright eyes, I can't bring myself to do it. With a sigh, I shake my head.

"I'm sorry. I can't afford it."

"No?" The lady raises an eyebrow, "Why not?"

"I have no money on me."

"I will hold onto it. When will you get money?" She nods frantically, "It suits your fair skin beautifully. It would be such a shame for you to not have it."

I marvel at the lady's marketing technique. She's good at what she does, I'll give her that. A small smile covers my lips. Perhaps I could accept a little bit of money off of Alessio, just to buy this. But then I will pay him back immediately, so I am not indebted to him. Yes, that's what I'll do.

"I will be back within a week. And I will buy it off you, for the full price." I tell her confidently with a strong smile. The lady nods once, and then twice. I watch as she carefully takes it out of my fingers and slips it into her pocket. She winks at me.

"Of course."

Hope brims in my stomach. I don't know what it is about that bracelet but it's something I itch to have. I've never wanted jewellery before. I of all people know how easy it is to get them stolen. Wearing jewellery is like putting a target on your back. And yet I long for it, like a mother wanting to hold her crying baby.

"Are you ready to go? It's just around the corner from here." Sophia appears out of nowhere. She looks between me and the lady. She offers a small smile to us both before staring down at the bracelets. For a moment, she turns her nose up at them, clearly seeing they are fakes. I smile. All are fake except my bracelet, tucked secretly away in her back pocket.

"Let's go." I give her a quick nod. Her beam multiplies on her face as she takes my hand again. Then, she oddly pulls us down a dark alley way. The buildings either side of us cut out the sun as we walk down the muddy path. My heart longs to return to the bumbling market stools, to the vibrant colours and delicious smells. Why would she bring me down here when there is a city of life out there? She had promised me a surprise, but this feels like a chore.

"Where is it? What is it?" I fumble on my words as I take a large step over what I can only assume to be sick on the floor. The disgust rattles through me and I force bile down.

"Just here." Sophia breathes out with a smile as she quickens her pace. I follow behind her aimlessly like a lost puppy. After what feels like a century, we arrive outside a grey door. It's locked. I strain as I try to spot anything special about this dingy looking door down a dark alleyway. My longing for the market stools intensifies.

"Alexis." She sighs in awe.

"Huh?"

She twists to me and pulls me closer. Then she creates a knocking tune on the door. My eyebrows burrow together, and I frown at her strange activity. What could possibly be behind this door?

Suddenly, a hole in the door appears. A wrinkly face stares back out at us. The sparkling eyes scan Sophia's face before they pull upwards in what I can only assume to be a smile. Shortly afterwards, the door opens. Sophia grins as she pulls me through the threshold.

"Miss Sophia!" He beams. She throws herself into his embrace and they hold onto each other for a long moment. I shuffle awkwardly behind them. Slowly, Sophia pulls away.

"Maya, this is Paul. Paul this is Maya, my Brother's wife."

The man's eyes light up and his lips form an 'O' shape. He stops himself from going in for a hug and instead bows. I can't help the scowl which crosses my face. I am not used to people bowing for me; Hell, I'm not used to people showing me respect.

"Nice to meet you, Miss Maya." He bobs his head. Awkwardly, I peer around at the dark corridor. On the side, there is an old looking lamp shade which softly hums. So far, it's not looking like anything special.

"This way, ladies." Paul says, leading the way down the corridor. Sophia skips ahead and I quickly stumble behind her, careful not to get lost. Slowly, the smell incense wafts up my nose. It's a sweet, enticing smell which makes me want more. A jingle of bells rings around me as we walk through chainmail hanging from the ceiling. And then everything lights up and house music rings around my ears.

A huge room is revealed. My eyes struggle to take it all in; the multicoloured dance floor, the wall-length bar, purple and black booths, a huge stage with a gold rim around it. Despite it only being two o'clock in the afternoon on a Tuesday, the place is buzzing. People from all different types of background either linger by the bar, grind against each other on the dance floor, or sit happily in the booths, lost in their own world of chatter.

Surprisingly, the floor isn't sticky and there isn't that usual tang of alcohol sifting around the room like other clubs. It feels like an incredibly classy club; I've never been to one like it! Where are the asshole men groping unsuspecting women? The barely legal teenagers smuggling in their own alcohol for a cheap night? The thieves?

"Wow." I sigh breathlessly, "I can see why you wanted to bring me here."

"You should see it at night." Sophia grins, "Which is exactly what we are going to do on Friday."

My heart almost skips a beat. Joy fills me. I have always longed for the opportunity to go clubbing like a normal person; just to have fun, let loose and make great memories. But no, my idea of clubbing is a six-hour work shift, stealing off anybody who is too drunk to notice.

"Take a seat, ladies. I'll bring you over two of your usual, Sophia." Paul bobs his head respectfully before disappearing behind the bar. Sophia leads me over to a booth in the corner of the room.

"I used to come here when I was living in Rome." She smiles dreamily, lost in her own world, "My Father never knew, of course. But I'd sneak out and pretend to be a normal, clubbing teenager."

"I understand that feeling."

"Alessio doesn't know about this place, either. Well, at least he doesn't know that I come here regularly whenever I'm in the city. And I'd appreciate it if we keep it that way." She says, before looking at me nervously. Her eyes dance over my face, desperately searching to see if I'll keep her promise.

"Why haven't you told him?"

"Are you kidding me?" She scoffs, "Alessio would flip if he knew we were here unattended. So many things could go wrong."

"But we went to the market unattended? What's different?"

"Did we?" Her lips thin. She casts her gaze around the room and then back to me, "Don't underestimate my Brother. You might not know that you had a follower, but they were there."

"He has someone stalking us?"

"Protecting us." She corrects me stiffly, "And not me. *You.*"

"I don't need protecting." The frown crosses my face. Something in my heart flips. Perhaps it's the shock of the situation, or the lack of privacy which stings my insides. Is there someone I need protecting from that he hasn't told me about? Or does he just not trust my fighting skills? The second option seems to hurt more than the first. I thought I have shown him by now that I am a strong woman, who doesn't need help. I can manage alone.

"Don't worry, we lost them when I took you into the clothes stand. That's why we had to move pretty quickly." She sighs. Paul returns with two large cocktails. They glisten under the large lamp above our heads. I frown at the red liquid with small sprinkles of gold inside it.

"Two strawberry daquiris, made specially for two special women." Paul grins and hands us the drinks. I clutch the cool glass and bring it to my nose. The sweet smell of strawberries makes me groan in approval. It reminds me of when I used to sneak into the corner shop as a child and steal the strawberries. Then, like a squirrel, I'd flee and hide them from everybody, so I didn't have to share. Under a huge oak tree, I'd sit and nibble at the juicy goodness. In those moments, I had been free.

"Enjoy, ladies." He says before returning to the bar.

"Paul is the club owner." Sophia explains, "He knows who we are. Nobody else does. In this club, *Alexis,* we are free to be whoever we want."

I marvel at her. Though she seems strong willed like me, she also has a huge responsibility baring on her shoulders. She is the sister of the mafia boss; does she really have the time to run away clubbing? Does she really have the opportunity to pretend to be somebody else for the night? How does nobody recognise her?

She slurps on her cocktail and excitedly peers around the club. It is none of my business how she does it, as long as she starts including me too.

Chapter Twenty-four

ALESSIO'S POV:

My eyebrows burrow together on my head like two slugs going in for an embrace. I run my fingers through my hair and release a sigh. All morning I've been searching through our finance reports for the month. It isn't looking good. We went well over budget with costs of the Russian prison mission, plus lost too much money from businesses as we had less time to help them. The number of men I had to pull out of jobs to help fight the Russians is looking to be extremely costly.

I drag my mouse to another page. My teeth bare as I look at our costs for this upcoming month. Alongside the usual costs of security, bills and wages, this month has the annual ball.

Each year, there is a charity ball, hosted by the mafia to try and integrate with the community. As far as the community are concerned, if we give back to them, they won't say anything to the police. Not that the police are a problem. It is surprisingly easy to bribe the force; they are human after all. But a more important reason for the ball: if the population remains happy with us in charge, they won't try to overthrow. Contrary to popular opinion, power means nothing if the masses are unhappy with the ruling party. When I took over the mafia from my Father, I upped the costs of giving back to the community. A happy population means they are more likely to give back to us too. The partnership works favourably both ways.

I groan as I look at the overbearing financial figure. It's not like we can just borrow money off people. Loan sharks are constantly swarming mafias, looking for a way in. A way to steal power. My fingers clench into fists. It's not looking good.

"Brother." Mateo smirks as he stumbles in. I take in his dishevelled hair and lazy smile. He staggers towards his usual seat as he buttons up his open shirt. His belt is still undone, and he isn't wearing any shoes. I make a scene of checking the time on my watch.

"I got a little caught up." My Brother sends me a cheeky wink. I groan. I don't want to think about which leggy babe my Brother is leading along this time. They all seem to turn a little psycho after a night with my Brother; one night turns into multiple nights and then begging for dates, texts, updates on his location. This is where he severs the tie. Obviously, it doesn't sit well with the woman who believes she's been used.

"Right." I huff. I push the laptop towards him for him to see himself how much trouble we are in. His eyes widen and he chews on his lower lip nervously. I fall back in my chair and pick up a new folder which has 'urgent' scribbled on it. It's Casper's handwriting, so it will be my weekly update on any information he thinks I should know about. May this be in Italy, or anywhere in the world.

With a sigh, I flip to the first page. It's a boring article on rising stock shares.

"So, what are we going to do about the money problem?" Mateo frowns as he slides my laptop back towards me. I let the folder drop to my lap as I face my Brother.

"I'm going to have to give the business a loan, aren't I?"

"That's risky, Brother." Mateo responds quickly, "I don't like it."

My lips pull downwards. It's true. If I were to offer the mafia some of my own money, it could complicate things. Firstly, I may never get the money back. Secondly, the business should never merge with personal finances, it's complicated on tax reports and legal documents. But most significantly, another mafia may get a whiff of our weak position. If we are deemed to be financially unstable, we are vulnerable to attack.

"Or we could just cut down." I whisper, raising my fingers to my lips, "Reduce security, cut a few people off at the bottom?"

"Seems pretty unethical."

I scoff and peer up at my Brother's smirk. *Ethics.*

Ethics is the term you use to justify your actions or bring down an opponent. Taking food away from a homeless man is unethical. Until you realise that the homeless man is a serial killer and starving him to death is for the greater good. An action can be ethical to me, but not ethical to you. We are an ethical mafia; we provide shelter and food for the homeless, offer jobs and education to the youth, pay off taxes so certain working-class people don't have to. But we also murder, torture and manipulate. Sure, I could start talking about how the people we hurt are bad people, but it isn't always the case. In war, collateral damage is unavoidable. And if I have to hurt an innocent person for another person to spill the information I desperately need, so be it. Ethics is in the eye of the beholder. So, *no.* It isn't unethical to cut a few people out of the business if it means we stay at the top.

"Get to it." I pat my Brother on the back and return to the document in front of me. I flick through it. My eyes jump to page Six's title 'Rising theft rates'. I scan through the paragraphs.

"Wait a second." I tell Mateo who is halfway out of the door. He twists round to face me and raises an eyebrow.

"Have you heard of this new underground stealing ring? It's a global trade." I mumble, stroking my stubbly beard. My eyes jump down to the figure, and I blow out a breath. The illegal activities stole just under two million pounds within a month. That is a serious number; this isn't just a couple petty thefts working for a want-to-be gang boss. This is organised crime.

"Yeah, there have been cases near here. Twenty miles south I believe." My Brother's face contorts in disgust. My fists curl together. If there is one thing I can't stand, it's thieves. Stealing off of other people's hard work is hardly a proud profession. It's cowardly and disgusting. Then my mind drifts to Maya. My beautiful wife. I scowl. I can't imagine her slipping her hands into people's pockets or removing a watch without them knowing. Sure, she is cunning and stubborn and strong. But she isn't deceiving; she speaks her mind too much. speaks her truth *far* too much. Surely that big mouth would reveal her cards before she is ready.

I peer down at the folder again. At the bottom, Casper has highlighted a sentence in red and bold. 'Call Vincent'.

My lips pull into a tight line.

"What are you going to do about it?" My Brother queries. He rests up against the door, propping a foot behind him. He has only just finished re-dressing himself for the day. I hold a finger up to him and call the American mafia boss. He answers on the second ring.

"Alessio?"

"Yes, I'm here, Vincent. Let's talk organised crime." I get straight to the point. In my line of business, you do not waste precious time on useless introductions.

"Perfect." His gruff voice rings through the room. Mateo drops back into the chair and listens intently. This is something he needs to be involved with too.

"So, all I know so far is what I've told Casper. That the gang is profiting well, and the numbers of helpers they have are rising. It's worrying." Vincent says down the phone.

"Where are they targeting?"

"Everywhere. Clubs, pubs, cinemas. You name it." Vincent responds bitterly, "They've been around for a couple weeks now. They're growing stronger and better. What do we do?"

I twiddle with the ring on my finger, it's an anxious tic I have.

Something I've always tried to stop; it's the only thing which reveals my emotions. The tight silver band belonged to my mother; it was her Father's wedding ring. My mother cherished it after his death, and then gave it to me in her will. A piece of my mother is always with me when I wear it. Before Maya, I wore it on my middle finger. Now, it is my wedding ring. If it was good enough for my grandad, it's good enough for me.

"Well, yes, it's organised crime and they seem to be profiting well..." I trail through my thoughts, "But these things always pop up and die within a week or two. They'll steal off the wrong person or land themselves in debt. It will go away on its own."

And, we don't have the fucking money to launch an investigation, I add bitterly in my head. But this isn't something Vincent cannot find out. The fucker is as untrustworthy as they come; we mutually use each other. *And* we mutually distrust each other. My Brother chews on his nails nervously as Vincent falls silent on the other end.

"Give it two weeks." I tell him sternly, "Then, we will act if it's still thriving."

"You're going to let your citizens be stolen from?"

"What would you have us do?" I spit, "Vincent, I've been in the mafia business longer than you. I know exactly how these things work. This gang will not last."

My words are confident and hard, but I silently doubt them. Though my words are true, that most gangs do not last past their third month, this gang seems to be doing very well if they are gaining our attention. I wait for Vincent to speak. Silence is the best tool; there's no use trying to convince him any further, it will look desperate and frantic. The opposite of control, the opposite of confidence. Like a sniffer dog searching for the truth, he will suspect something.

"Fine." He finally relents, "We will give it two weeks, and then make a decision on how we will act."

I release a small sigh. Two weeks gives me enough time to get the charity event over and done with, so I can start pumping extra money into the security sector of my business.

"Perfect." I tell him, "Until then."

Before he has the opportunity to say anything else, I hang up the phone call. Silence drifts around the room. My Brother watches me awkwardly.

"Good save."

"I know." I huff. My eyes scan over the finance numbers again. There is no use in celebrating a small win; there will always be bigger problems which counteract the success. Only on my death bed will I count my victories. Until then, it's back to the drawing board to solve the problems.

"Where is Sophia? If she is staying in Rome for a bit, she can organise the Charity event this year." Mateo offers.

"She's out with Maya. They've gone shopping I think."

"They've gone to town together? Is it safe yet?" Mateo frowns.

"Don't worry, Brother. Angelo and his team have also gone to make sure everything remains under control."

I check my watch and sigh. They've been gone for over four hours now. What could they possibly be shopping for? Something ticks in my gut, like a sense of impending doom. My gut has never been wrong either. I push myself back from my chair. I guess I'll have to go and find out for myself.

"Alessio?" A small voice chirps at the door. Maya sticks her head around the door and smiles at me. I physically jolt with shock.

"You're back!"

"Yes, just got in. Sophia has an entire new wardrobe. I'm sure it will last her for a week." She says with a small smile. Mateo looks between me and my wife. A cocky grin rests on his lips before he raises to his feet.

"I'll leave you to it." He says before exiting the room. Maya gives him an odd look as she slips past him and heads for his vacant seat. I shake my head and pat my lap. She chews her lower lip nervously but doesn't disobey me.

"How has work been?" She whispers as she sits on my legs. I wrap my arms around her and pull her closer. A small sigh slips from her lips and it's as if we both visibly relax now that we are close together.

"Better now that you're here."

She hums in approval. I remove my head from the nape of her neck and scowl.

"What's on your mind Maya? You seem quiet."

"Can't a girl be quiet now and again?" She says anxiously. I bite back a scoff.

"Not when she is my loud wife."

"Okay fine, I'll get to the point." She sighs, "I want a job."

"A job?" I raise an eyebrow suspiciously, "What do you want with a job? If you need money, I have already told you, I will give you my credit cards…"

"No." She interrupts, "I don't want to *take* your money. I want to earn it."

I let the proposition sit in the air for a moment. She continuously turned down my offer of money in the past. And sure, the business is suffering financially but my own bank account is still thriving. My wife shall not go without.

"I won't work for the mafia, though." She adds.

"Then who will you work for?" I frown.

"You."

"Me?"

"Yes, I will be your personal assistant." She says, rising to her feet. She crosses her arms over her chest and feigns confidence.

I dwell on this thought. I can't put her on the mafia business salary due to the financial issues, and I suppose it will be good for her to have something to do during the day. And selfishly, I like the idea of having her near me.

"My personal assistant?" I raise an eyebrow, "And what will this entail?"

This question catches her out. She chews on her lower lip nervously. For the first time, my confident little wife seems anxious in my presence. She doesn't like asking for things, I know that much. My fingers flex and I bare my teeth in a twisted smile; I almost enjoy her squirming under my gaze.

"Filing?" She offers lamely. I can't help but grin like the Cheshire cat. A soft blush coats her cheeks, and she averts her eyes. I pull her closer to me.

"The job will have to entail more than just filing, my dear."

"I can answer the phones too?" She tries again.

"But then you'll be working for the mafia."

"No. I will be working for you. I will be answering your phone and relaying messages. It doesn't matter what the content is. I'm not stupid, Alessio. I've married into the mafia; I can't avoid the subject." She hisses with a little bitterness. My lips pull into a straight line, and I nod my head slowly.

She clearly wants this job. And who am I to say no to such a beauty?

"You're hired."

"I am?" She squeaks, face lighting up. Then, she suddenly plays it cool.

"I mean, yeah, of course I am. I have all the skills necessary."

"And what skills are those?" I groan suggestively, nipping at her ear. My heart pounds louder and louder in my chest. Desire is an understatement for what I feel for her. She shakes the question off and presses her lips to mine.

"When do I start?"

"Now." I growl. She squeals in excitement as I wrap her legs around my waist, the noise of her happiness makes me smile. Then, our lips connect, and it feels perfect. I am drunk on this little siren. Her fingers quickly jump down to my zipper, and she struggles to undo my belt.

Suddenly, the phone rings. I ignore it and encourage her to continue but the rings keep going. Then it stops, only to start again.

"I should get that." She says, biting her lower lip nervously. I rest back in my seat with a smile plastered on my lips. She reaches for the phone and presses it to her ear, all the while still wrapped around my waist.

"Alessio's office, Maya speaking, how can I help?" She says professionally. A throaty chuckle ripples through me as her face scrunches up and relaxes before scrunching up again. Then, she looks at me with a lost look and shrugs. I take the phone from her fingers.

"Alessio speaking." I bark, slightly annoyed my moment with my wife has been interrupted.

"Angelo here, just to let you know there has been another theft close by. Three reported incidents and a couple watches stolen."

I release a long groan and look between the phone and Maya. I want to throw the phone away and continue where we left off but duty calls.

"On my way." I sigh before thrusting the phone back in its holder. Maya doesn't make any effort to move off of me. Instead, she brings her lips to my neck and trails kisses up and down. Her fingers clutch onto my collar. I wrap my arms back around her and hold her in a tight embrace.

"Would you ever go straight?" She whispers so quietly I almost don't hear it.

"What do you mean?" I frown as I trail patterns up and down her back. With a small sigh, she pulls back from me. Her eyes are wide and sad.

"Give this all up? The mafia, the businesses, the illegal activities?"

"No, never." I say within a heartbeat. How could she even suggest such a thing? The mafia is my lifeline, it's everything I've ever wanted and worked towards.

"I'm saying hypothetically, could you give it all up?" She tries again. I watch as her tongue darts out to dampen her lips. A nervousness seeps through her.

I ponder on this thought. Hypothetically speaking, I could pack my bags and leave. But then there is the issue of handing the mafia over to somebody else and who would be a suitable leader? My brother? But even he needs more mentoring before he's ready to stake a claim in the title. Another issue which arises is one of threat. The new mafia leader would have to wipe me out, they couldn't have any chances of me changing my mind and returning to rule again. I grimace and shake my head.

"No, it's not possible."

She visibly deflates. Gently, I take her cheek in the palm of my hand.

"Why are you asking this of me? I know you hate the mafia, Maya, but you know I can't leave. This is my home. *Our* home."

"I know." She whispers in a small voice, "I just wish sometimes we could run away from all of this. I have given up stealing, I want to go clean. I want no more violence, no more illegal activities, Alessio."

I remove the thought before it can fester into something more dangerous. It is not possible. It is not even a matter of not being able to leave the mafia. I do not want to leave. I have everything here, and she must accept this.

Slowly, she climbs off my lap with a sullen expression. I itch to pull her closer and kiss her fears away but the phone rings again.

"I'm coming!" I snap into the receiver before slamming it back down. With one last look at my wife, I disappear to hear an update on the new thefts in the area.

Chapter Twenty-five

MAYA'S POV:

"How was your first week working for my Brother?" Sophia grins as we walk down the alleyway. My cheeks flush red, thinking back to all the devastating things he did with my body each day. The positions, the places he kissed, the ways he touched me. If every week was like this previous one, I'd be the happiest employee ever.

"Good." I squeak, "Just lots of filing and taking notes really."

She casts me a grin and my cheeks flash a deeper red. Most likely everybody in that house heard Alessio and me.

"At least you're getting some." She sighs as we turn left up the alleyway towards the club.

"What happened with Angelo?"

"Well, we went on that date ages ago, but nothing has really come about it since. I thought we had a connection."

"Perhaps he is just shy?" I try to offer some reassurance.

"Or he is intimidated by my Brother." She huffs, taking an extra-large step over a puddle. She makes sure her sparkly heels are not dirtied by the dingy alleyway. I nod in agreement. Alessio has been very stressed this week. He won't tell me why, but I can feel it in the way he touches me. It's as if he needs to be close to relax. Something is eating him up.

"I can talk to him if you'd like?" I raise an eyebrow, "Discreetly, of course. I'll see if Alessio has said anything?"

"No, I don't want to bother you. Besides, if Angelo is that easily persuaded by my Brother, perhaps he didn't like me as much as I thought he did." She sighs dramatically, "I just need to know where I stand with him. He's everything I want, you know? He's funny, loyal and handsome. Plus, he's in the same business as me. What could be better?"

I smile fondly at her but my heart throbs painfully. Of course, them being in the same business would be a huge bonus. They both understand the overpowering responsibilities involved, the sleepless nights and the unethical methods to get what they want. Alessio and I would never be in the same business. He'd never go straight for me. And there is no way I'd join the mafia's activities.

"I think I may be in love with him. Do you think that's possible? We haven't even shared a kiss yet!" Sophia squeals in despair. She halts in her tracks outside the club door and turns to me. Her eyes are frantic.

"Am I crazy?"

I think back to me and Alessio. We told each other we loved each other on that fateful night, when we thought we lost each other. Since then, the four-letter word hadn't been uttered again. There are many reasons why I haven't been able to bring myself to say it. Firstly, I have never been in love before; I wouldn't know what it was if it hit me in the face. Secondly, am I capable of loving someone in his line of business? Someone who mercilessly slaughters, deceives and manipulates others into getting what he wanted. Sure, I stole from people, but I've since stopped. My illegal activities have come to a halt; I am now a new woman. I am no longer a slave to breaking the law. I want to go straight. I want to live a normal, happy life. Settle down in a sweet cottage in the countryside, have a couple children, get a normal job; just live a typical life.

My Alessio can't do that. *Won't* do that. Can you love somebody who goes against every dream you have?

"I don't know." I answer her honestly. Who am I to dictate what is and isn't love? My own feelings are so mixed up. I know that I lust for him. That I long to be around him and to make him happy. But that I *love* him? Love has something beyond its utterance. That feeling is missing.

"Let's just stop thinking about the men tonight." Sophia sighs. She turns to the door and does her signature knock. Like last time, Paul greets us. He swings the door open and quickly ushers us into the club. The pounding music fills my chest, and my bones vibrate in tune to an unfamiliar song.

Chapter Twenty-six

MATEO'S POV:

"That was great." Alice lazily smiles up at me. Her long nails scratch my back in soothing circles. I still fight to regain my breath. I smile into her naked breasts, placing one last kiss to them before pushing myself off the bed. Quickly, I reach for my shirt.

"Want to grab some food?" She says, twisting around to grab her own clothes. I scowl at the wall so she can't see. This arrangement is just sex, and yet after we fuck, she will always ask this question. Well, it changes each time: *Want to grab a drink? Can you drive me home? Shall I call you later?* Nonetheless, she is pressing for a relationship. And it just isn't possible right now.

"Wow. Silent treatment, eh?" She scoffs, "I thought we were above this."

I turn to face her as I button up my shirt. She is stunning with short, dark hair which bobs around her clear complexion, and a thin, athletic body. Alice has the capacity to turn any man into goo with one bat of her eyelids. She had the personality to match too.

It's a shame she is not her sister though.

"You know the rules, Alice." I tell her bitterly before shoving one leg through my trousers.

"I know, it's just sex. But..."

"But what?" I snap.

"Don't use that tone with me, Mateo!" She squeaks, crossing the room. When her small hand touches my arm, I feel like I'm melting into her touch. She takes my cheek with her other hand, and I can't help but nuzzle into it. It feels as though time has slowed down slightly.

"You know what I mean. About the feeling between us."

"We can't, Alice." I whisper, closing my eyes. A lump forms in my throat and I desperately try to push it away. This always happens. It's undeniable that Alice and I have a special connection. I long to be close to her, to hold her up against me, to make her happy. But it just isn't tenable.

"Yes, we can. Alessio will understand eventually." She presses. I clench my eyes together more, forcing the headache away.

"No, Alice. Stop!"

"Fine!" She grows angry, "If you don't want to be with me, cool. But stop fucking calling me every night when you're lonely and missing me! I will not be your secret mistress!"

I grab her by her wrists before she can throw a punch at me. For a second, she looks like her sister, Laura. When Laura was alive that is. Those angry eyes sparkle in the dim lighting of my room and her lips part as she readies herself to spit some insult.

"It's been over a decade, Mateo!"

"Not for Alessio." I bow my head and take another step backwards. I couldn't do that to my Brother. Any reminder of Laura would break him, and we really cannot have him break down now. Especially not with all the financial problems brewing.

"He has a wife now! He has to be over my sister, surely!"

"It's not about that. He doesn't care about your sister." I spit but immediately regret my words as she flinches away from me. The tears burn in her eyes, and it hurts me. I know it's not nice for her. That she has to live in hiding, out of fear. I don't believe my Brother would hurt her, but he would definitely hurt himself if he were reminded of his first love. Alice and Laura look strikingly similar despite the three-year age difference.

"He killed her and yet I'm the one being punished." She says quietly. It breaks my heart.

"Don't say that."

"But it's true!" She yelps. I throw a hand over her mouth, trying to steady her volume. We can't risk waking anybody up.

"Alice, calm down." I tell her warningly, "We are not going to talk about this…"

She opens her mouth to protest but is quickly silenced as a roaring bang echoes around the room. Instinctively, I grab her small body and throw her to the ground. I use my own body as a shield as a couple more bullets rip around outside my window.

"Mateo!" She squeaks in fear. I feel her hands fist my shirt. I lay a hand over her mouth and force her to be quiet. Silence follows the gun shots. For a long moment, I don't move as I try to figure out what's happening.

"Stay there." I hiss to her before crawling off of her. I drag my body closer to the window before peeping my head up. Outside my window, I can see the entrance to the house. Three of the guards are mangled on the floor, blood pouring out of them. My fists clench together in rage as I spot a black SUV speeding out of the driveway.

"Fuck!" I hiss, jumping to my feet, "Stay here and hide!"

Before Alice can say anything more, I sprint out of the room. It's almost two in the morning so everybody should be safely in bed. I bound down into my Brother's room but neither Maya nor Alessio are in bed. A scowl coats my face as I quickly sprint towards his office.

"Brother!" He shrieks as we run into each other. He grabs either arm of mine and he holds me still.

"What happened?"

"We've been shot at!"

"Fuck!" He seethes furiously. Then his rage turns to concern, "Where's Maya?"

Before I can say anything, my Brother charges away. Like a bull in a China shop, he races into every room on this floor, screaming his wife's name. The world around me hums into my heartbeat and the heat washes through me. I quickly search for my sister too. But she's nowhere to find.

The cold air harasses my body as I sprint to the roof top terrace, searching for them. But she isn't here either. My heartbeat quickens and bile rises in my throat. *What if she's been hurt? What if she's been taken?*

I charge back down the stairs, but stumble to a halt as Sophia and Maya stagger out of the cinema room, clutching onto one another. My eyebrows jump together on my forehead and the adrenaline paces through me.

"Where the fuck have you two been?" I hiss, "We've been attacked! You could have been hurt!"

"Relax, Brother, we were watching a film."

I raise an eyebrow at them and shake my head. Even though they are both wearing their pyjamas, their full face of makeup says otherwise. Besides, I had just searched the cinema room and it was empty.

"Tell me the truth." I spit, crossing my arms firmly, "Before I call Alessio up here."

"Mateo, don't! We were just watching a film!" Maya is the one to answer this time. I glare between the two girls menacingly. Neither one backs down under my gaze. My lips pull into a straight line; they must think I'm stupid. Of course, they are up to something. A challenging silence drifts between the three of us as if we are in a Mexican standoff. Finally, I sigh.

"Go and take your makeup off. I'll distract Alessio." I tell them quietly. Relief quickly fills their expressions, and they waste no time storming into the bathroom. My heart races louder and louder as I charge into the office.

I could tell Alessio that I think they've snuck out the house. But what good would that do? My Brother is too firm on both the girls and trapping them in this house will do no good. As long as they are both safe, and learn their lesson from this, it can remain our secret.

"Sophia and Maya were watching a film. They're safe." I tell Alessio as I enter the office. My Brother looks all dishevelled and pale. His eyes light up when he hears my words.

"No, never mind, they're safe. Thank you, Angelo. Call off the search." He says into the phone before throwing it down. He releases a sigh of relief and runs his hands through his hair. My Brother looks like he has aged a decade with his pale, papery skin and sunken eyes.

"I should find Maya, see if she's okay."

"No, wait Brother." I say quickly, "First let's figure out what just happened."

My Brother pauses, silently debating between the two options. I give him stern look, forcing him to take the rational choice.

"Fine." He huffs.

"I heard the gun shots from my room. Four different bullets. Killed three guards." I explain.

"Yes," He nods slowly, "Angelo has informed me. We are searching for the number plate now."

"Who do you think it was?"

My Brother ponders over this thought quietly. He brings his fingers to his lips and taps them anxiously. After a long pause, he shrugs.

"Too many enemies, too little time."

"Do you think they know about our financial situation?" I hear myself ask the dreaded question. My Brother pales again and slumps in his chair.

"I fucking hope not, or something tells me that won't be the last attack on our home."

I gulp. My fingers itch to punch something but I force myself to remain still. Unwillingly, my thoughts drift back to Alice who is probably trembling and afraid in my room. In that moment I had used my own body to shield her. It was a brave move but also incredibly stupid. She will now think more into this; it will be her new ammunition in the war for us to get into a relationship.

Nervously, I peer up at my Brother. Stress has really eaten at him lately; the Russians, Maya's attitude, the financial problems and now being attacked. I pity him, it's not a position I long to be in. A sigh takes a hold of me. I can't add to his worries; at least it answers my next move with Alice- I must get rid of her. It's not safe nor fair to keep her around this place any longer. For her sake, my Brother's and the world's.

Chapter Twenty-seven

ALESSIO'S POV:

My eyes scrunch together as I press a finger against the bridge of my nose. The migraine rocks through me and it feels as though snakes are slithering around my head. They constrict against my temples, inflicting more pain. A guttural groan escapes my lips, but it doesn't sound like me. Well, not the new me anyways.

It reminds me of a beast I've repressed. The hideous monster which howls and snarls when rage bubbles inside of my chest. It beats at my heart, pounding to escape. To wreak havoc on those closest to me.

Trying to distract myself, I tear my eyes around the drawing room. A huge Grandfather clock in the corner of the room mocks me. Its dark wooden structure contrasts the gold trims around the clock face. It ticks. As each second ticks by, my heart rate speeds up. The sound taunts me. Like a marble inside a ball being rattled by some toddler, the sound echoes around my brain, bouncing off my skull. It hurts. My migraine increases.

Time seems to slow down as I rock forward on my armchair. The tumbler with whisky in it explodes against the carpeted floor when I release it from my tight grip. It makes a satisfying thud when it hits the ground. My brain repeats the event over and over again. The way my white knuckles unclench from the glass, how it falls through time like it's tumbling down a rabbit hole, when it kisses the floor in a violent smooch. Then, *bang*. The glass shatters. Like a stone being thrown into water, the glass ripples outwards in a devastating explosion. It stabs into the carpet, and any nearby furniture. Small shards of glass also slice through my suit trousers and dig their teeth into my skin. A slight hiss escapes me, yet I make no effort to remove the invaders. If anything, I welcome their pain. It takes my mind off things. Off the monster.

But it doesn't take my mind off the real reason why I'm hiding away from everybody. Why I'm slouched in this wooden chair, counting my miseries, instead of planning my next business transaction. Or even better, making love to Maya.

Laura haunts my thoughts. Even if I haven't seen her for over a decade, the memory of her squeezes my heart like it's in a vice. I don't even know which emotion hurts most: the loss, or the guilt. The guilt which I can never confess to.

When I searched through the CCTV, trying to find the numberplate for the black SUV, I saw her clear as day, running from my house. She escaped into a taxi and sped away. But it wasn't Laura. It was her sister. *What did she want with my house? Was she behind the attack? Is this Laura's revenge?*

Unwillingly, my brain flashes with images of her mutilated body. Dusty, blonde curls, round, sad eyes and thin, cracked lips, my Laura, bleeding from her pasty skin. Dried blood clinging to her like peeling paint on a wall, bruises scorching her sunken skin. The only colour on her lifeless body was the disgusting clotted blood.

Father called me in to see her corpse. His lips were thin and grim; though I distinctly remember seeing them flick up into a smile when he saw the pain it caused me. He almost sang my name when he summoned me into the bedroom. *Her* bedroom.

"Remember this pain." He had hissed in my ear. His harsh words contrasted the lazy arm which pulled me into a side embrace. Around us, friends and family members of Laura were oblivious to my Father's pep talk. Their mournful sobs drowned out our conversation.

"Remember this pain and never let go of it, son." He growled, "One day, you will be a mafia king. There is no room for love in the mafia. Family is the only thing you'll love."

"What about Mum? Do you not love her?" My voice was clipped with a retort. He snorted and squeezed my arm. The pain burned when his rough nails sliced my skin.

"Of course not. Marriage isn't about love. It's about convenience."

My lips pulled downwards as I glanced again at Laura's dead body. The woman I was learning to love. Her limbs had been snapped backwards and into different directions like branches in a damaged tree. Her cheeks had been sliced up like an onion, and her bruises had bruises. She didn't die painlessly; this would have been an awful death. In front of my Father, I caught a sob in my throat; I couldn't be seen to cry over her. *Mourning*, my Father always said, *is the quickest way into signing your own death contract. It makes you weak. An easy target.*

And yet when I miserably peered down at my beautiful teenage friend, I couldn't help the sinking sensation in my heart. It was as if somebody had stuffed rocks inside of my chest and thrown me into the sea. I was suffocating in misery. The sneaky kisses and awkward teenage glances and fumbling we shared were now nothing but worm food now. My first love was dead. My first, and last love, according to my Father.

Back in the present, I splutter on a cough as I throw myself to my feet. *No.* I can't think about Laura. It has been over a decade since her death. And yet everyday my mind wanders back to her. And how she died. Mysterious circumstances, my Father told me. *Bullshit.* There was nothing mysterious about it. The attraction between her and me was palpable. Dangerous. My Father had to squash the bug before it grew into a bigger virus and infected everybody. The mafia had no room for viruses. It had, and always will, wipe out the weaker ones. And since that day, I had promised myself never to fall in love. Until Maya showed up.

"Brother!" Mateo grunts as he bursts into the room. He bends over, hands on knees, and pants, trying to regain his breath. I raise a curious eyebrow at him.

"What is it?"

"I have bad news and bad bad news." He breathes out in despair, "which would you like first?"

"Don't play with me, Mateo. Spit it out!"

He slowly regains his posture and leans against the door frame. The silence ticks between us and it increases my fury.

"The bad news is that Vincent has pulled out of our trade deals." He eventually answers, "He wants nothing to do with us anymore. He told Aria that he washes his hands of us, that we have dirty business he doesn't want to taint his name with."

"What dirty business?" I snap. My Brother winces at my booming voice but quickly regains his confidence.

"The attack yesterday. He believes it was provoked."

"Provoked? How?"

Mateo shrugs before casting his eyes at the explosion of glass at my feet. He raises an eyebrow but keeps his mouth shut.

"What's the bad bad news, then?" I grunt, running a hand through my hair. It's knotty and resists my fingers but I quickly tear through the inky tendrils. I will deal with Vincent later. I need to know both problems first so I can prioritise.

"Me!" A booming voice calls from behind me. I tear my gaze towards the other door where the intruding noise comes from. My heart drops in my chest like an anchor over a ship.

"Father." I growl menacingly.

With wide arms, my Father enters the room. His tanned, wrinkly skin creates ripples in his papery skin, especially when he gives me a menacing smile. We look alike with raven coloured hair and eyes. But he has put on a lot of weight, evident through his bursting suit where the buttons strain to keep the expensive material together. He also seems shorter than when I last saw him. But then again, I haven't spoken to my Father for half a decade.

"Alessio." He beams, "How are you, Son?"

My lips thin and I give my Brother a wary look. He sends one back. Neither one of us trust him; when he called, he always wanted something. He asked for the world but gave barely a pebble back. My conniving, malicious Father would always take what he wanted, even if that meant murdering his family. Unwillingly, I think back to my Mother. I push her from my mind just as quickly as she appeared.

"What do you want?" I hiss. His wide smile falters and that familiar malicious look returns to his face. Those cold eyes harden as he takes a step forward. As if he owns the place, he points a hand towards the three chairs in my drawing room. I huff and take my usual seat. They both join me, being careful to avoid the smashed glass on the floor. My knuckles turn white as I grip onto the armchair.

"Can a Father not visit his sons?" My Father teases.

"No." I answer quickly, "Spit it out, Father. If you and Sophia are both here, I dread to think which unreliable idiot you've put in charge of *my* southern council."

His eye twitches as my hostility. Desperately, he looks towards Mateo, but he doesn't give my Father any kindness either. With a big huff, my Father falls back in his chair. His entire demeanour changes again; he resorts to the cold, heartless bastard he has always been. Hot and cold. The Morisso family's signature move.

I bounce my knuckles off of the chair, filling the silence.

"Okay, fine." My Father releases a dramatic breath, "I'm here thanks to a tip by a friend."

"A friend?" I raise my eyebrow before reaching for a cigar on the desk. I don't offer my Father one; he would get no hospitality from me in my own home. Mateo leans forward and sticks the lighter in front of my face. Slowly, I hover my cigar over the flame and inhale. The bitterness soothes me instantly. I release a dark smoke cloud and fall back into my seat. Again, my Father winces. He reveals his cards more than he wishes.

"It doesn't matter who, it just matters what they said." He retorts, waving his arms around theatrically, "Rumour has it, you have a wife."

I stiffen in my seat. My beautiful Maya fills my mind; her gorgeous strawberry scent, large doe-like eyes, delicious lips... I frantically push her away. Dread replaces the fond thought.

"And?"

"And rumour has it you started a war with the Russians over her." My Father seethes. Droplets of spit fly from his lips and they miss me narrowly. My head cocks to the side and I dare my Father to continue talking. Pursing his lips, my Father shakes his head slowly. Then a scoff escapes him.

"Something funny, Father?" I hiss, rocking forward. I take another puff of my cigar before balancing my elbows on my knees.

"I thought you learnt your lesson with Laura." My Father leans forward and mocks my posture, "I guess not. How many women will have to die before you learn you cannot love in the Mafia..."

Before he can even finish his sentence, I fly across the room. My fists curl into his suit as I throw him back against the wall. I massively overpower him.

"Fucking talk about my wife like that again." I lower my voice threateningly. Without thinking, I raise a fist to my Father. My entire body trembles with rage and I feel like I'm ready to kill. No, I will not let him near my Maya. He had already ruined Laura for me; he will not hurt her too. Nobody will touch what is mine. *Again.*

"See." My Father hisses, "This is what I'm on about. Your feelings for her has left you vulnerable."

"Last time I checked, you're the one up against the wall." I retort bitterly. My eyes darken and I bare my teeth at him. Like a lion, ready to kill its prey, I ready myself to take the final blow. The world would be better without him in it. My Father tuts and averts his eyes downwards. I frown and look at whatever he is staring at. My stomach twists at the gun pressed firmly into my stomach. In the heat of the moment, the adrenaline hid the weapon's touch.

Fuck.

"See, Son?" My Father tuts. I stumble backwards as he places a hand on my chest. He shakes his head as he pockets the gun.

"Vulnerable." He spits the word. My mind is blank as I stumble over my words. How did I not see that coming? It was such an easy move; wind your opponent up so they make a wrong move. Mentally, I kick myself.

"You're becoming weak." My Father hisses as he circles me. The roles have been reversed. He is the lion, readying himself for the kill.

"You must get rid of her."

"No!" I bark, tearing my gaze towards her. My Father pulls a funny face and looks to my Brother. Mateo remains inscrutable and doesn't back down from my Father's stare.

"Then, you must control her." My Father grunts, "You cannot start wars for women."

"The war is over." Mateo finally pipes up. Another scoff escapes my Father's lips.

"Are you really that naïve? The war will never end. You have slaughtered their leaders, sure. But there is always someone lurking in the shadows ready to take their place." He growls, "You haven't ended the war, you've begun it."

An evil silence drifts around the room. The bile rises in my throat as I realise my Father is right. If both my Father and I were slaughtered, Mateo would rise up. Without him, Sophia. And then it would fall down to my Council ranks. We have contingency plans for our contingency plans. As we speak, the Russians are probably planning their next attack. Perhaps they are responsible for gunning down my security?

A guttural growl leaves my lips. We can't afford to go to war again. We are already in financial ruin.

"What would you have us do?"

"Good." My Father's lips pull into a twisted smirk, "Now you're listening."

"Get to it, Father. My patience is thinning!"

"Reconciliations." He spits quickly, "Apologise to the Russians. It's a cheap and effective option."

"Never! Aren't you the one who taught us to never back down? To never fear anybody else?"

I throw myself backwards and hiss. My migraine feels much worse as more problems beg to be solved. Suddenly, my Father advances towards me. I keep my posture strong and sturdy; he does not scare me. And yet, as those dark eyes twinkle, something squeezes inside of me. I recognise those cold eyes; the exact same ones which ripple through me when I let the monster free.

"I also taught you not to love." He growls, "And look what happened there. You can't pick and choose my advice, Alessio."

"If we apologise, they'll expect a peace offering. They will obviously ask for Maya, to make a point." Mateo frowns. It pulls my Father away from me. I almost long for him to take another step towards me; I'll put the old man in an early grave. Gun or not. May the best predator win.

"No, you're not the ones to apologise to the Russians." My Father snaps. My eyebrows snatch together on my forehead. Mateo's head snaps towards me and we exchange a confused look.

"Maya will not apologise to the Russians." I hiss, "She'd rather die."

"So be it." My Father shrugs, taking a step backwards. He peers around at my gloomy drawing room. Slowly, he scans the dim lights hanging from the walls, the wooden planks decorating the walls, and my expensive dark furniture. This room took the longest to perfect; I wanted a room of mourning. A room to think about the lives taken because of the mafia. And it looks as if this conversation has been a perfect opening gift.

"I like it here." He says but his voice offers no hint of sincerity, "I think I will stay for a bit."

"You're not welcome!" I snap back.

"Oh, but I am. You boys clearly need my advice."

"Leave my house, now!" I bellow in rage, thrusting a threatening finger towards him. Inside, the monster screams to be released. I long to hurt my Father. To hurt everybody who even tries to come near my Maya. My mouth dries and I bare my teeth at my Father. Before I can do anything, My Brother takes a step closer towards me and places a hand on my shoulder. He shakes his head slowly.

"Calm down, Alessio. We are stronger as a unit. Nobody is going to attack us here if the three Morisso's are in one house. They wouldn't dare."

"Exactly." My dad gives him a curt nod before turning to face me, "Get your wife in check. I've heard a lot about her. She needs to learn true Mafia wife etiquette. After all, why would someone go into business with you if you can't even control your own wife?"

I growl at his misogynistic ways. I desire to bring him pain like no other but my hand lowers. My own body betrays my heart. With pursed lips, I think back to my little warrior wife. She won't do as she's told, and she certainly won't apologise to the Russian Mafia even if it got us out of a costly war. My beautiful wife, perfect as she is, is incredibly stubborn.

The beast within me growls at the thought of her saying no to me. With my Father back and Laura's sister creeping around, I feel my rationality slipping. The snarling creature longs to return to a state where blackness reigns and *justice* is just a whispered word to justify murder. My fists curl into fists. My family is right. It's *my* mafia, *my* kingdom, *my* control.

If Maya won't obey my commands out of respect, she'll have to learn in the same way everybody else does. Out of fear. And fuck if the monster longs to rule again.

Chapter Twenty-eight

MAYA'S POV:

I yank the long socks up my thighs, stumbling backwards into the bed as I struggle with them. After what feels like an eternity, the black socks cuddle just above my knee. I run my fingers down the beautiful scarlet skirt with pleats in it and then feel the rich material of my thermal, long-sleeved top. As I put the black boots on, I stagger towards the long mirror. I take a peer in at my outfit, and I can't resist the smile. My long, inky hair curls beautifully and sways by my hips. I have applied a light amount of makeup, just to make me look a little more alive.

My body hums with excitement. Today, Sophia and I were going to return to the beautiful market with the multi-coloured stands. Since vising the other day, that beautiful gold bracelet hasn't let my mind. I long to own it. And now that Alessio has paid me, it's well within sights.

"Where are you off to?" His voice echoes through the room. I peer at him in the gold-rimmed mirror and offer him a smile. *Will he compliment me? Does he think I look good?* I bite my lower lip nervously and take in his reaction. At first, a look of appreciation covers his face. It flickers in his eyes and fills me with hope. However, it is short lived. A sudden cold expression replaces it. He raises a challenging eyebrow. Like somebody has flipped a switch, Alessio changes. He takes a menacing step forward.

"Must I repeat myself?"

I flinch at his hard demeanour and twist to face him properly.

"Sophia and I are off to the market." I say confidently but then the nerves creeps in. His once warm eyes are cold and hard, and his hands are curled into fists. I frown at his strange behaviour.

"No." He spits out the single word. It holds an incredible amount of power.

"No?"

"You heard me." He growls, twisting to exit the room, indicating that he is done with the conversation. Fury floods through me. Who does he think he is talking to me like that? Frantically, I march after him and grab him by the arm to force him to face me again.

"What has crawled up your ass and died?"

"Excuse me?" He glowers. For a moment, it's as if he grows in height and broadness. Like a bear sizing up its prey, Alessio towers over me. As much as I'd hate to admit it, a flicker of fear dances through me as his cheeks flush a crimson colour. It's as if somebody has stepped on my grave. I flinch and shake my head slowly.

"Why are you acting strange? What's going on?"

"You need to respect me more." He says in a low voice. The sound sends shivers through me; It's nothing like my usual Alessio's voice. A dark growl, from a hideous monster. I frown at his cryptic words.

"Respect you more? What do you mean by that?"

"You will not go to the market today. Respect *that* wish, the rest will come eventually." He spits out, taking a step backwards. I retort quickly, not backing down from the fight.

"I don't know what's gotten into you, but I don't like it. You will not speak to me like that! I am your equal!"

He grabs my arm and I yelp in shock. When our gaze meets, I feel nauseous. His eyes are full of hate and despair; I avert my eyes to the strong hand wrapped around my wrist. On his pale cuff, a blood stain sinks into his suit. The words are snatched from my mouth.

"You will not go out; you can't be trusted!"

My heart sinks in my chest. Does he know where we were the other night? Who am I kidding, of course he fucking knows. He's the mafia boss! He knows everything. His eyes are the CCTV cameras. I sink away from him guiltily. He seems to double in size.

"Instead, You will join me and my Father for lunch."

"Your dad is here?" I gawp. He doesn't register my question. Desperately, I try to yank my arm away from his grip but he's much stronger. He doesn't even twitch. Furiously, I throw a finger in his face trying to regain some control over the situation. My body shakes with adrenaline.

"I will not be meeting any mafia men. You know that!"

"And yet you're fucking one." He retorts quickly. Like a bucket of cold water to the face, it takes me by surprise. I frantically scan him, searching for the cause of his hostility. Is he being uptight because his Dad is here? Or is he still miserable about whomever he has just harmed? Whatever the reason, It does not warrant talking to people like their nothing. His wife no less.

"And then, you will apologise to the Russians!"

"What for!" I shriek, trying to throw him off me, "I didn't do anything wrong! They came to hurt me, remember?"

"You will apologise to the next in line and reassure them of peace." He growls. I shake my head frantically.

"I will never apologise to them after what they did to me!" I hiss. His eyes darken and he brings his face closer to mine. I open my mouth to spit an insult, but I'm quickly silenced.

"I suggest you come to dinner with us, *Maya*, we can talk it over then." Another voice ripples around the room. The way my name is said is terrifying. It's like the gruff voice has completely ripped the word from my identity; the name is now his property.

Mortified, I take in an older version of Alessio. He oozes the same amount of power and rage. My gaze snaps back to Alessio. For a moment, he looks miserable, but he quickly fixes a furious scowl on his lips. Alessio's furious behaviour starts to make sense.

"Playing up for daddy, are we?" I spit bitterly in his face. My hair falls into my eyes as I resist against his hold. I shake my body around, like a mouse trying to escape the grip of a constricting snake. Alessio never relents and instead grabs my other arm too, so he has complete control of me. Fear floods through my body; I throw myself around even more frantically and even try to land a couple kicks to his stomach. They're unsuccessful. Alessio's malicious eyes seem to become much worse; like something from my nightmares.

"Let go of me, Alessio!" I whimper, losing my confidence.

"Not until you learn some respect."

His words send me into another furious rage. My fear turns to anger. If he wants to fight, I'll fucking fight. Nobody tells Maya *Carter* what to do, not even her fucking husband! He switches. I switch back.

"Fuck! You!" I say the words slowly so that he gets it in his thick, fucking head. For a moment, he holds my gaze. It's unforgiving. I don't relent and instead challenge the mafia king.

Suddenly, he snaps. His perfectly combed back tendrils of hair jumps free from their position as he lurches forward. I throw myself backwards, stumbling away from him. But I'm locked in his grip. His elbows throw outwards and the buttons on his shirt burst free from the sudden strain. I watch in horror as my husband becomes something beastly. A wild, crazed look burns his face as he pushes me onto the bed. He quickly holds me down with his weight.

"Respect me." He bares his teeth at me. I return the gesture, not backing down. He should know that he cannot scare me more than my Father.

"No!"

Suddenly, he releases my arms and slams the bed either side of my head. The noise is almost deafening. I stop squirming and keep his gaze. If he wants a fight, I'll give him a fucking fight. My head sinks back into the bed before lurching forward. I spit in his face. The saliva smacks him dead on the nose and drips down like foaming water tumbling off a jagged water edge. Any pride bubbling in my stomach quickly evaporates when a low guttural growl escapes his lips.

"I will ruin you, little Maya. It's time you learnt respect." He hisses into my ear. I feel his hot breath on my face, and something twisted inside of me enjoys this moment. The thrill of the fight, of his close, possessive proximity. The way we both fight ruthlessly. Like sparring wolves, we send equal jabs into each other.

"But you won't." I snap, quietly enough so his Father won't hear. Like sand racing through my fingers, I try to grip onto the idea that my fake husband would not actually hurt me. That this is all for show. My safe thought, my safe dream. My Alessio wouldn't do such a thing. *Right?* A scoff leaves his lips.

"Want to make a bet?"

My eyes widen at his devilish question. Our noses almost touch and his scent is intoxicating. I fight the urge to lean up and kiss him, to remove whatever stress is playing on his mind. The other half of me wants to kick him in the balls to teach *him* some respect.

"I do." I say breathlessly. I take a chance on my dream.

Like a wild animal hearing something in the distance, he cocks his head to the side. I can feel the desire seeping from him too. This is a dangerous type of attraction. He is a mafia boss, I will never kid myself, something will always despise him for his occupation. And yet the other part of me longs for him.

"Juliet." He whispers so quietly I almost don't hear it. A strained

expression licks his face. I frown.

"Juliet?"

"Yes. And I'm Romeo." He spits cryptically, "This is a love which will end up with us both dead. And I fucking despise it."

A lump in my throat forms and I try to gulp it down. No matter how much I try to repress the thought, I know deep down that he's right. I choke on a breath. We are incompatible. Star crossed lovers if you will.

"Finally." Alessio's Father sighs in bitter relief, "She's quiet. Good job."

For a long moment, Alessio doesn't move from above me. His body suddenly becomes much heavier on me and I long to squirm away from his gaze. Right now, I can't stand to be near him. I don't have much choice though. He heaves himself up before pulling me to his side. Stunned, I stumble into him. He wraps his arm around me and leads me out of the room.

"Now, let's get some food. I'm starving." His Father says smarmily, leading the way. Alessio's hold around me is possessive but no longer in the desirable way. It's not necessarily a tight grip and yet it burns my skin. I wince as we take a left and then a right, into the dining hall. All the while, I keep my head low. Alessio's words have silenced me. His touch has removed my voice. And his presence has slaughtered my thoughts.

Perhaps he might win that fucking bet after all.

Chapter Twenty-nine

MATEO'S POV:

My head pounds as I make a bee line for my room. Alice's number has been blocked from my phone; I will never allow myself to talk to her again. To let myself be weak for her. Especially after the scene between Alessio and Maya. I must quit whilst I'm ahead.

It doesn't stop the thumping in my brain though.

"Mateo." My Father's voice calls out. I skid to a halt and turn to face him. He holds his large belly, those thick fingers drumming over the swell.

"Father."

"I've just had a lovely lunch with Alessio and Maya."

I hum to show I'm listening but all I want is to disappear to my room. I can't stop replaying the hurt on Alice's face when I told her she had to leave and never come back. I have never seen her cry like that before. And then she fled, like she should have. She fled like her life depended on it. Because it did.

"Well, it was extremely tense. And quiet." My Father corrects himself. He frowns and gets lost in a silent thought. I clear my throat.

"Is there anything I can do for you, Father?"

His beady little eyes light up.

"Yes, actually there is." He points into the drawing room. I gulp and take a seat, my Father close behind me. He loves this room, with all its dark glory. A pregnant pause drifts between us. My Father takes his time getting comfortable in the chair and the shuffling noise gets on my nerves.

"How can I help?" I say, trying to speed this awkward conversation along.

"We need to get rid of Maya." My Father spits bluntly. I jolt in my seat and my jaw hangs low.

"Why?"

"She makes Alessio weak."

I shake my head quickly.

"No, she makes him strong."

"Oh, is that it?" My Father scoffs. The sound sends shivers through me, and it makes me tremble.

"So, the splashing unnecessary cash to save her, consistent fights to get her to do as she's told, and now the attacks, are all signs of strength?"

"I thought you said all she has to do is apologise?" I try to fight for my sister-in-law.

"And do you believe she'll do that?"

I purse my lips and refuse to answer. Of course, Maya will not apologise, it's not in her thieving nature.

"But if she leaves, then what?"

"*When* she leaves." My Father corrects, "You two apologise to the Russians. Offer them a stake in one of the businesses or offer them extra security. I don't know. A bribe. A gift. Whatever you want to call it."

"But why can't we do that with her still here?" I try again. My brain hurts and it all is too much.

"Mateo." My Father releases a sigh of disbelief, "I thought you were much smarter than this."

I don't answer him. Instead, I hang my head and stare at a single shard of glass still embedded in the carpet from my Brother's accident.

"You cannot apologise for her behaviour, for the death of Sasha and his gang, if she is still here. It's patronising. She has to go. Otherwise, you'll be going to war. And we all know you can't afford that. Beside, she will start many more wars with her feisty attitude."

I shoot forward in my chair and scowl at him.

"How do you know about that?"

"Oh, come on, Mateo. You should know by now. I know everything."

"So, you propose we get rid of Maya, push her out of the family and then make reconciliations?" I scowl, ignoring his confession. There is no point in prying the information out of my Father, he'd never reveal his sources. It is simply a waste of effort and breath to try.

"Exactly."

"And how do we get rid of her?"

My Father's lips thin. My jaw drops and I shake my head once, and then more firmly.

"We will not kill her." I hiss, pointing a threatening finger towards my Father. Alessio will not be able to take another lover's death. It would break him. Besides, Maya doesn't deserve death.

"Okay, fine." My Father raises his hands in the air, "We simply have to turn them against each other. He won't let her go on her own accord. I've already done quite a bit already. I just need you to push them too."

"But…"

"She's an expensive liability!" My dad snaps bitterly, "He will understand after that his loss is for the greater good. But for now, they need to hate each other. If she is smart, she'll go running for the hills. That way, Alessio can return to the ruthless killer who doesn't splash unnecessary cash around."

The lump in my throat forms. Just like Alice. Just like what Laura should have done. My fists clench together; *Will Maya become the new Laura? Will the family survive such loss again?*

"You have options, Mateo. Of course, you do." My Father says grimly, "One, she apologises. Two, she leaves the house herself. Three, she dies."

"You won't touch her." I seethe. She shouldn't be slaughtered; it wouldn't be fair. She never wanted to be involved in this life, she had always wanted to leave. Up until Alessio saved her from Sasha, that is.

"Think about it, Alessio is already pushing her too far by forcing her to obey him. He is becoming that monster again. All we need to do is plant more doubts in her head." He presses further.

I gulp. It's true, the cracks are already starting to show. And if it's for the greater good of the mafia, Alessio will understand eventually. With a big sigh, I relent to my Father's plan.

"Making them hate each other, it is."

Chapter Thirty

MAYA'S POV:

Something's different about him. He is no longer the gentleman behind closed doors. The man who'd stroke my back as I fell asleep or would give me a reassuring smile when I felt anxious. I'm not stupid, I know exactly what is happening. The monster is revealing his true colours; and unfortunately, I fell for him. I fell for the lie. A mafia king can never be free. It isn't his occupation, it's his fucking lifestyle. He eats, drinks and breathes for the mafia. He is trying to scare me into obeying him, but it has the opposite effect. I want to run away and escape his toxicity.

Evilness seeps from him now. When I see him walking around the house, I can't help but liken him to a stalking bear. Claws out, teeth bared, and a low, guttural growl leaving him. When his eyes meet mine, I know instantly that I'm prey.

"Maya." Mateo's voice rings through the room. I jolt and try to hide the heels I have in my fingers under the bed covers. He notices my short dress and full face of makeup but doesn't comment. My heart pounds in my chest and I wait for him to summon the beast, to set my husband on me. To scream for the hills that yet again, I am sneaking out of the house.

"Don't worry, I'm not here to get you in trouble. I'm here as your Brother-in-law." He tells me as he crosses the room. He sits on the bed next to me. Despite his comforting words, I can't unfreeze my stiff body.

"I know you and Sophia are sneaking out to Alexis." He sighs, loosening his tie. The breath catches in my throat. I long for the ground to swallow me up to remove me from the conversation.

"I don't blame you." He finally says. My eyes tear towards him in confusion. *Why is he helping us? Why isn't he choosing loyalty to his Brother? His boss?*

"If I were you, I'd go and never come back." He sighs dramatically.

"What?"

He turns to face me and takes my small hand in his. I can feel myself pale under his scrutinising gaze.

"Let's not pretend, Maya. You are not built for this life." He speaks my concerns out loud, "Alessio will never love you the way you long for him. He isn't free to love. He can't love. Do you understand what I'm saying?"

I try to swallow the lump in my throat down, but it doesn't work. The burning tears tease my eyes. I shake my head.

"It doesn't matter." I lie.

"Yes, it does. The way he's treated you recently is unbelievable. Personally, I wouldn't have it. Mother taught us better than to speak to women like that."

I avert my eyes down to the floor. It's true. Alessio has been far from perfect lately. If this were anybody else, I'd leave.

"And it's only going to get worse."

"How do you know?" I squeak, staring up at him in disbelief.

"The monster is finally being awoken from its long slumber."

"What are you on about, Mateo? Why are you telling me all this?"

"Because I care about you." He squeezes my hand reassuringly, "Which is why I need to tell you about Alessio's first love. Laura."

My heart flips in my chest and the breath refuses to sink into my lungs. I slowly shake my head. I want to scream and tell him 'no', that I don't want to hear about my Alessio with any other woman. Ignorance is bliss. But something forces me to stay and listen.

"Alessio and Laura were childhood sweethearts. Their attraction was growing and growing as they grew up. But not long after Alessio's eighteenth birthday, Laura was found dead."

"What happened to her?" My hands jump to my face. I shake my head in disbelief.

Mateo's lips pull together in a grim line. For a moment, pain flickers through his own gaze. He removes his hands from mine as if it hurt him too much to talk about the memory. I shuffle backwards on the bed to get a better look at him.

"What happened, Mateo?"

"It's what's happening to you. At first, Alessio was loving, kind and gentle. Then he became more severe. More violent."

"No!" I shoot to my feet and back away from him when I realise what he is hinting at, "No, Alessio didn't kill her."

"Didn't he?" Mateo joins me and takes my hands in his, "Has he not displayed these traits lately? Alessio is a true killer at heart. How do you think he rose to the top of the mafia so quickly? My Brother is as violent as they get."

My entire body trembles with fear and disbelief. I think back to all the times he held me gently, kissing me lightly and telling me sweet nothings. How he clutched onto me after Sasha tried to kidnap me for the second time. The things he told me then. The agony in his eyes when he thought he lost me.

"It's not true."

"But it is, sweet Maya. I wouldn't be telling you this if it weren't."

Frantically, I spin around to him and point a finger at his chest threateningly.

"Why are you telling me all this, Mateo? What good comes from disloyalty to your Brother!"

For a moment, he looks caught out. A glance of shock covers those rosy cheeks, but they quickly disappear. He takes my hand gently in his and pulls me closer. The smell of his cigar breath curls up my nose.

"Because I care about you in the same way I did for Laura. I can't have it happen again. You can't stick around, Maya."

I'm lost for words. All my thoughts jumble in my brain and inflict too much pain. *Is it true? Is my husband a lover killer? Does he truly want me dead?*

"Okay, let's go." Sophia's voice rings around the room. Blissfully unaware, she stumbles in, fixing her earring in her ear lobe. She looks between me and Mateo and stiffens.

"Mateo, I can explain." She tries to justify our actions for going to the club. He shakes his head and pulls away from me.

"I was just saying to Maya that I don't mind you guys sneaking out as long as you're safe."

"Is that true?" Sophia raises an eyebrow at me. I still feel pale and sick. I can't move nor talk. Mateo nudges me into action.

"Yes, yes it's true." I stumble over my words, a rush hitting me all at once.

"Now, go and have fun, girls." Mateo clasps his hands together, "And remember, don't come back."

A long pause drifts between the room with his cryptic words. His eyes bare into mine and the hairs on the back of my neck stand to attention.

"Until late. You're young. Enjoy it!" He adds merrily before hurrying us out of the room. I stumble as I put my heels on and race to keep up with Sophia. Part of me wants to crawl into bed and cry, or to confront Alessio. But the sensible side of me forces me to escape the mansion for a night.

Who would have thought that a club full of strangers is safer than my own home?

∞∞∞

The music soothes my achy bones and I waste no time pouring alcohol down my throat. Sophia pulls me in all different directions, dancing with anybody who will give us the time of day. Or anyone who will buy us drinks. It's crazy. She has all the money in the world and yet she still searches for more. I think it's a power thing; It's a compliment that they spend their money on her. The minute we step foot in this club, Angelo seems to be a thing of the past for Sophia. Not that I can blame her with how much he has been ignoring her lately.

It's like in the last week, every man in that house has had a sword up their ass.

"Shots?" Sophia raises an eyebrow up at me. I nod eagerly as we head towards the bar. As usual, I quickly push my way to the front. The small bar tender quickly serves us our tequila shots. My heart thumps in my ears. I lick the salt, throw the shot back and then suck on the lime. It burns as it slips down my throat, but I welcome the sting. Anything to get Alessio off my mind. Anything to get my husband out of my head. We have been here almost three hours and still the alcohol is barely affecting me. The adrenaline from Mateo's information pulses through me. I desperately reach for another shot. It burns and I wince. Then, I go for another.

"Woah there." Sophia stops me before I can get my fingers on a stranger's drink, "What's up with you tonight? You seem stressed? If It's about Mateo knowing we sneak out, I wouldn't worry. Mateo is good with secrets…"

"Who is Laura?" I blurt before I can stop myself. Sophia's eyes gloss over and her lip's part. She desperately tears her eyes around, as if to avoid the conversation. I don't know why I ask her; Mateo's voice didn't hint any lies. But something deep in my chest tells me Alessio isn't that same monster. My husband is more than his occupation, more than his past.

"Laura was Alessio's ex-girlfriend." Sophia explains slowly. I nod quickly.

"Yes, and how did she die?"

Sophia winces. She turns her head and order two more drinks for us. All the while, I stare at her paling face. She takes a couple shaky breaths.

"She was murdered."

"By whom?" I press further. Sophia shakes her head quickly and for a moment, I see the fear glisten in her gaze. She stares out into the crowd. I can't help but join her gaze.

"He's here." She squeaks.

In the midst of the crowd, Alessio stands. A furious look rests on his face as he tears his gaze left and then right, searching for us. My heart leap out of my chest like an anchor being tossed into the sea.

"Fuck." Sophia hisses, "We're in so much trouble."

"No, blame this on me, Sophia." I growl as I march towards Alessio. As if he can feel my rage bubbling, he spots me in the crowd. I should be terrified of this beast, of this monster. This murderous, possessive bastard. But I have nothing but fury in my chest. If he did kill Laura, he won't fucking kill me. Not because he loves me, but because I won't let him. I'd kill him first if he laid a finger on me.

Just as I approach him, my attention is snatched by a quick movement behind him.

A familiar face disappears into the crowd. I stumble to a halt and peer around for the man again. Then, I see the mousey locks. My hand slaps to my lips and the tears burn quickly. My Brother, James, weaves in and out of the crowd. He desperately avoids my gaze and storms out the club. He oozes a guilt and fear like never before. I start after him, but Alessio forces me still.

"You're in a lot of trouble, wife." He growls threateningly in my ear. I turn my gaze back to him in confusion. For a long moment, my brain struggles to catch up with what's happening. My mouth opens and closes like a fish out of water.

"What?"

Suddenly, he grabs me by the arm. I resist and throw my body around but he's much stronger.

"Brother!" Sophia squeaks, "Stop it! Stop it! You're drawing attention to us!"

She runs behind us, yanking at her Brother's arm. He barely flinches as we both try to fight back. He kicks the exit door down and the noise sends shivers through me. If I didn't feel sick beforehand, I do now.

"What the fuck are you two playing at?" He seethes, "We are under attack and you're out playing a fucking game!"

"It's my fault!" I hear myself shriek, "I begged to get out of the house. It's lonely trapped in that place, you can't force me to stay!"

"No, Maya!"

"Yes, Sophia, it's true. Don't lie to protect me." I stumble over my words, quickly taking credit. Alessio clearly has an issue with me, not Sophia. I will not let her suffer because of my husband's short fuse.

"Let go of me!" I hiss, digging my feet into the ground. Sophia gives me one last look before she disappears into the night. I watch her in shock as she flees from us. Then, everything gets too much. Mateo's information, my Brother in the crowd, Alessio showing up to our secret hideout. It feels as though the world is against me.

My heart jumps into my mouth.

"I hate you! I hate you! I hate you!" I shriek, earning a throaty laugh from my husband. The sound is sinister.

Perhaps Mateo was right, I should have left and never returned. It would have been safer than being anywhere near this bastard. And now I fear I'm going to learn the hard way.

Chapter Thirty-One

ALESSIO'S POV:

"Has anything been stolen?" Mateo frowns as he charges into the office. I slouch over the desk with my fingers laced in my hair. When we returned from picking the girls up, the house had been broken into. At least four guards had been killed, and many more injured. Frustratingly, there were no witnesses. We had no leads to follow up on.

I peer down at the missing ring on my finger. I had taken it off before the club, as I know how thieves operate. I didn't want to be caught out. But clearly that didn't work. They came into my home to fucking steal it instead. Bitterness swallows me up.

"Mother's ring."

"Why would they take that?"

"It's a threat, isn't it. A reminder that they can break into my home, that they can steal whatever they want." I hiss in despair, "Who the fuck is behind all of this, Brother? The attacks? The theft? We know it's not the Russians, they haven't made a single move yet. Security assures us of this. And there has been no evidence anybody has stepped up in the ranks yet!"

His lips pull into a grim line as he paces back and forth.

"This isn't good."

I don't answer my Brother's stupid comment. Of course, it isn't fucking good. We are in debt, we are in the midst of a war, my Father is breathing down my neck to right the wrongs, and my fucking wife won't obey me. I've tried almost everything in trying to reign her in, to control her a little bit more. My Father will do god knows what if she doesn't just fucking listen.

"How fucking dare she!" I slam my fist into the table. The one thing I ought to be able to control and it seems to be my biggest battle.

"How did they sneak out without knowing?" My Brother scowls, "It just doesn't make sense."

Angrily, I lower my head. My wife will not never this easy for me. It's like she is looking for trouble, desperately searching out any way to ruin me and everything I've worked for.

"How will you punish her?" Mateo raises an eyebrow. I take a long pause to think about it. My fingers itch and then curl into fists. I didn't know how to punish the little devil. Nothing I say nor do will deter this behaviour. I am struggling against an unstoppable force. There is no taming the little creature. Despite the rage I have for her attitude, it excites me at the same time. Did I really want a tameable wife?

Yes. No. *Yes!*

Suddenly, Casper staggers through the door. His eye throbs with a bruise and there are tears streaming down his face. My Father holds him by the scuff of his neck as he leads him in like a lamb to the slaughter.

"What's going on?" Mateo frowns at the two men. I wait silently for an explanation as I drum my fingers against the desk. More bad news, no doubt.

"Go on, tell them what you told me." My Father barks. Casper cowers in fear. Another sob escapes his lips. I sigh impatiently as I look at the trembling wreck of a man in front of me. Casper drops to his knees and clasps his hands together in prayer.

"I let them out." He confesses, "I drove them to the club myself."

Mortified, my Brother's head snaps towards Caper. Then he looks at my Father with an odd look. I ignore it and look at the curly haired mess on the floor. Frustrated, I raise an eyebrow.

"*This* is what you've interrupted me for? A small confession!" I spit in rage, hurling towards my Father. Everybody is shocked by my reaction. I know they expect me to punish Casper, to torture him for allowing my wife and sister out into danger. But truth be told, Maya would have escaped another way. That little devil would have manipulated anyone. Hell, she could even convince my Brother or Father if she tried hard enough. Casper was just in the wrong place at the wrong time clearly. The weak thing didn't stand a chance.

"There's more." My Father growls. I pause and take a couple steps backwards. My eyebrows burrow together, and I stare at Casper expectantly.

"She just came to me for more help." He confesses, "To track someone."

"Who?" I spit, grabbing him by the collar. I heave him to his feet. I resist the urge to spit at him and tell him to have some confidence. I do not hire weak people, but Casper is quickly proving me wrong. And I will not be proved long for much longer.

"Who!" I roar.

"James Carter!" Casper cries out in fear, "Her Brother!"

My fingers release from his clothes, and I let him sink into a puddle on the floor. Confused, I turn to Mateo. He exchanges a similar look. Why would Maya be searching for James? What possible reason could she have? Everything she needs is here in my home.

"I think I might have solved your little theft problem." My Father scowls.

"You think Maya might be behind the break in?"

"Why, of course. Who else knows about the financial difficulties and all the weak spots? It *has* to be her." He presses his knuckle to his lips as he grimaces.

My fingers curl into fists and a red mist settles in front of my eyes. *Fuck!* What if he's right? Maya is uncontrollable and if I've learnt anything in my line of work, it's that you can't untrain a trained dog. Her nature is to steal. Her nature is to deceive. Her nature is to bring pain.

And here I thought she knew better. But two can always play that game. And let's be honest, I'm much fucking better at it.

"Find him!" I seethe angrily, "Find James. I think it's time I met the fucking family properly."

• •

"He's here." Mateo's gruff voice rings through the room. My head snaps upwards towards my malicious looking Brother. A devilish smile licks his lips and a similar one coats mine. The world seems to speed up as the beast crawls free from my chest. Before I know it, I am flying towards the room around the corner from me. Red fills my vision.

"James Carter." I bellow as the door slams behind me. A scruffy looking man, strapped down to a chair in the middle of the room, peers up at me. His eyes almost leap from his head, and he struggles against the restraints. A smile kisses my lips as I pull the gloves up my arms which Mateo hands me.

"How lovely to meet the other Brother." I tease as I slowly drag a chair towards him. It shrieks as it scratches against the floor. My Father hovers behind me on one side, my Brother on the other. They both add to the overpowering sense of danger. Expertly positioned to make James more likely to reveal key information.

He tries to say something, but the duct tape muffles his voice. Having said that, his eyes, full of fear, do all the talking for him. I force the chair downwards and I take a seat. Our knees touch. Like a beast who has heard something in the distance, my head cocks to the side.

"This won't do now. Will it?" I grin evilly as I rip the tape from his mouth. A cry quickly follows from him. Then, his lips purse together. It's as if he regains strength now his mouth is free.

"Tell me, what were you doing in the club tonight?" I bark at him. His lips remain tightly sealed. I give him a moment to decide his next move, but he chooses wrong, he remains silent. With one look towards my Brother, I decide his fate for him.

"Here you go." Mateo says as he hands me the plyers. I fiddle around with the rusty weapon in my fingers.

"Don't make me ask you again."

"You won't hurt me." James says smugly. His Adam's apple bobs in his throat. I open the plyers and press it against it with a wicked smile.

"Oh, yeah? Why's that?"

"Because I'm your wife's Brother. She'll never forgive you if you hurt me." James says smugly. For a moment, I ponder on this thought. Then, I lick my lips and bring my face closer to his ear. He needs to hear every fucking words of this. He needs to get it into his thick skull that nobody tells Alessio Morisso what to do.

"And what makes you think I care about her opinion?"

He gulps. I feel it against my weapon. His strong resolve slowly melts away.

"Tell me, what were you doing at the club tonight?" I hiss. His eyes widen as they tear around the room. Sudden realisation hits him that none of us will relent until we have an answer. Before he can react, I drive a fist into his face. Blood squirts out of his mouth as his head lurches left. A shriek of pain escapes from him but it spurs me on. The monster inside longs to escape for good. It longs for more. Another fist to his face has his entire body rigid in agony.

"Tell me!" I roar, raising another fist. He flinches and tries to move his arms which are firmly secured by his side.

"Okay! Okay!" he relents, "I was looking for my sister!"

"Why?"

His lips purse together. With a snarl, I charge towards the table of weapons on display for me. My fingers trace over the different shapes and sizes of knives and work tools. A cry of despair seeps from James.

"M-my dad, he sent me to talk to her!"

"Why?" I give him another monosyllabic question. I shouldn't have to waste all this breath on him. He should tell me instantly. And yet he doesn't. I settle on a small carving knife before heading back to my chair.

"Tell me, James. This will only get worse for you."

"I can't!"

"No, it is that you won't." I spit bitterly before pressing my knife to his eyelids, "I can go all night long, you know? Soon, you'll be panting from exhaustion and agony. You'll beg for death, beg to go to sleep. But I won't let you."

His chest rises and falls quickly, spurring me on.

"First, I'll cut your eyelids off, so you're forced to watch every second of me mutilating your thieving little body!" I press the knife gently into the thin skin over his eyes as a warning. Then, I drag it down to his lips, "Then I'll take some teeth. Purely for my own enjoyment. After, with each second that ticks by, I'll take a digit. First your fingers then your toes…"

James squirms more and more in his chair.

"Ready to squeal?" I raise an eyebrow up at him. He pales as a singular tear slips down his face. Then, he shakes his head quickly. A sigh escapes my lips.

"Fine, I'll just have to hurt you then."

Just as I go to press my knife into his eyes, a sharp hiss echoes around me.

"Get the fuck away from him!"

Startled, I twist to face my wife. She looks stunning in that black dress, hands curled into fists either side of her body. Her rage excites me. Like Persephone coming to fight Hades.

"You've come to join the party." I beam smugly at her. My little thief glares at me with a hatred like no other.

"I said get away from him!"

"Maya." Mateo steps in front of her to stop her advancing any closer towards me. Fear dances in his own expression. The situation is slowly spiralling out of control. I long for her to come closer, to tempt the beast more. My devious little wife might have staged this entire thing. She could be the reason my business is suffering the way it is. Yet, I couldn't hurt her; I'd never forgive myself if I bruised her perfect skin. Having said that, this doesn't mean I won't torture her Brother, or her entire family if it came to it. What I can't do to her, I can do to them.

"Don't touch me!" She hisses, quickly side stepping him. In defeat, my Brother holds his hands up and takes a step backwards. In the other corner, my Father watches curiously. It's impossible to read his thoughts as he lets the events play out.

"Let him go." Maya says slowly. Fire dances in those dark, menacing eyes. I lick my lips.

"Your Brother was just about to tell me why he's been stalking you. Take a seat, my little Maya and we can find out together."

"You're a monster!" She spits out in disgust. Then, she does something nobody expects. She picks up a weapon from the table. The biggest knife she can find before stalking towards me.

"You're a killer!"

"I am not you enemy, *Juliet*. He is." I say, nodding towards her Brother. Maya shakes her head. Pure rage and pain seeps through her. I silently pray that my words are true. That she isn't my enemy because God knows what I'd have to do if she was. A little piece of me holds onto the idea that she didn't stage the break in, that she has nothing to do with my financial suffering. That she is completely unrelated to all my problems.

"Don't call me that!'" She snaps back, "And you're not particularly my friend either."

"No." I agree, pondering on this for a moment too long. I grab her arm and yank her closer, "I'm your fucking husband."

Her eyes flare with rage. She presses the tip of the knife to my chest. It excites me. I long for her to make another move.

"Maya, what are you doing?" Mateo gawps from the corner, "Don't be stupid! After everything we've do…"

"Silence!" I roar, holding a hand up, "She will do what she wants. Won't you, baby? You've never made a non-selfish move; I don't suppose you'll change now. Go on, save your thieving Brother."

"I hate you, Alessio Morisso." She spits. I give her a devilish smile,

"And I hate you, Maya Morisso."

"Maya, do it!" James cries out, "Just do it!"

Suddenly, her knife points towards her Brother. Like Athena in battle, she holds her weapon bravely as she stalks towards him. The sight of it almost brings me to my knees. For a moment, I honestly thought my Juliet was going to end the family feud. To end our lover's curse with a knife to my chest.

"You." She barks cruelly, "Where have you been?"

It's not hard to hear the pain in her voice. She trembles slightly now, like a leaf in the wind. Her bravery melts as emotion takes over. It's heart breaking. I ache to pull her closer and end her pain and suffering. Perhaps she'll now obey me and respect my commands? Now my Father will see she can stay around?

From the corner of the room, my Brother approaches my Father with a scowl. They whisper something to each other. A nervous look flickers across their face before they quietly exit the room. Ignoring them, I turn my attention back to my wife who holds a knife to her Brother's temple.

"Everywhere, May. You know dad sent me away for a bit, but I was always going to come back. I mean, I'm back now." He waffles a bullshit excuse. I look to Maya, and she clearly picks up on his lies.

"No." Her voice wobbles, "Why were you looking for me?"

"Dad wants you back, May. We all do."

Maya freezes on the spot with her Brother's words. She doesn't even look at me and for a moment I feel weak, helpless even. I can't control the sadness radiating through her. Her lips pop open in disbelief. She considers his answer, scoffs, and she turns back to face me.

"Why is he here, Alessio? What do you want with him?"

I release a sharp breath as her anger turns back onto me.

"We have reasons to believe your family were the ones responsible for the attacks and for the robbery." I tell her slowly. James remains inscrutable as I reveal his crime. Maya's lips pull into a straight line, and I can almost see the cogs in her mind turning as she desperately tries to understand what's happening. Slowly, her gaze flickers between James and me. In this moment, I realise my wife is innocent. She truly has no clue her family was involved. I release a breath of relief.

"Why? What are your reasons." She still stands her ground in fighting for her family. I bite the inside of my cheek.

"Just trust that my reasons are sound, little Maya."

"Let him go!" She says sternly.

"No."

"Yes!" She cries out in desperation. I quickly remove the knife from her fingers before she can harm anyone. Her sanity is slowly slipping, and I can tell it's affecting her more than she cares to admit. Surprisingly enough, she doesn't press further. She lets me take the weapon and then takes a couple steps backwards.

"And you honestly believe my Brother is behind all this?"

"May, stop it! Of course, I'm not." Her Brother tries to protest but I silence him with a single hand.

"Yes." I answer truthfully, "I have many reasons to believe your Father and Brother are trying to overthrow me."

"That's not possible. We hate the mafia. We'd never become part of this shit show."

"We?" I raise an eyebrow, "No, Maya. There is no we in this matter. Your family have abandoned you and now they seek to overthrow us both."

Nervously, she chews on her lower lip. Her eyes dart between us and she scours us for the truth. My body stands rigid and tall as I wait for her to make her decision.

"Think about it, Maya. The attacks on our home are just going to get worse. Who else do you know who'd be up to the challenge of taking my business down? I can't think of any sane, rational person. Can you?" I point my knife towards her Brother, "but crazy people on the other hand? I can see that happening."

"Liar!" James howls. My fist connects with his cheek to silence him. Behind me, Maya startles at the sound. I instantly regret letting my anger get to me. Her entire body starts to shake, and something switches in those dark eyes. Rage turns to fear.

"You really are a murderer, aren't you?"

"Huh?"

She doesn't answer me. Instead, she twists on her heel and charges out of the room.

MAYA'S POV:

I never thought I'd feel guilt like this before. It consumes every inch of my body, pulling me further into a pit of despair. I can't eat, drink or talk. My body sinks into the sofa and I'm frozen. The shrieks and cries of my Brother being tortured rattle around the house. It's been three hours and there has been no sign of the torture stopping. My Brother must be innocent or else he would have confessed by now. *Right?*

I think back to all the times my Father hit us to train us up. To train us to keep our lips quiet. My Brother is simply going through what happened to me in the Russian camp.

Alessio has a right to be mad, he has a right to find out who is threatening him and his mafia. And to an extent, if I cared about something deeply enough like he cares for the mafia, perhaps I'd hurt someone too for the answers. It doesn't make it right though; It doesn't make it fair. Nothing Alessio does is fair.

A particularly long gargle of agony echoes through the walls and the bile rises in my throat. It is a horrifying reminder of what Sophia and Mateo have told me: that my husband is a killer. Worse than that, he is a lover killer. Another cry wracks through my brain and this time I can't take it anymore.

Who have I become? *What* have I become? Not only have I stayed by the side of my potential killer, I am also letting him torture my own Brother. It reveals a frightening truth: I have spent too long around the mafia. It is twisting me into something I'm not.

My Alessio would never go straight for me, he'd never give up the mafia. And I will never be his queen, the woman he desperately needs. We are incompatible. And unfortunately, he is right. This connection we have between us is too dangerous. One of us will end up dead and I can feel it in my bones that it will be me paying the price.

Afraid that I'll change my mind if I hesitate any longer, I charge out of the room and towards the garden door. I skid to a halt in front of it and take a deep breath. It's so warm in here and I can hear the storm sweeping around outside. My heart lurches from my chest as I peer out of the window in the door frame. Rain assaults the world like thick tears from God himself. His children have strayed to the dark side. The Devil has returned in the form of my husband. I gulp and throw the door open.

I send myself sprinting, towards freedom, away from danger. Thick mud and heavy rain makes my body feel that much heavier, but I ignore the pull as I throw myself over the tree. A branch snaps below my feet and I fall. But at least I'm on the right side. Sirens blare. Lights flash. Pain assaults me.

I'm on my feet again, stumbling into the darkness yet I'm frozen still under the awful glare of my husband. A horrified and desperate shriek leaves my lips. He takes a long step towards me, and despite the thundering rain hammering down on us, he seems like he's in total control. My knees threaten to give way; everything hurts and yet I know so much more pain is going to come.

"And where do you think you're going?" He hisses, advancing closer towards me. I stumble backwards, ignoring the puddles splashing up my body.

"I wish I could make you go away!"

"Fucking good luck with that, darling." He growls. Eyes wide, I watch as his fists clench. His eyes are low, and cheeks tainted with an ugly red rash. *Blood*. My Brother's blood. My heart falls in my chest; what if, like Laura, he has killed my Brother?

He silently seethes. Those once calm and collected eyes slowly darken. My Alessio slips away, and he's replaced by the beast. I take a couple steps backwards and hold my arm out at him to keep him at an arms distance. His fist clenches around my wrist. I gasp in horror. He won't let me leave. He can't let me leave.

"Am I suffocating you?" He whispers, yanking me into a frightening embrace. My heart pounds in my chest in fear.

My head lulls to the side as he nudges it to the left.

"Yes." I whimper.

"Am I trampling your dreams?"

"Yes." My voice is small. Desperate. *Terrified.*

"Good." He growls as he nips at my ear. My head shakes in disbelief and another tear slips down my face.

"Let's go home, *wife*." He instructs. The pain in my chest becomes much stronger as he spits the word. It's said with such venom. Such hatred. He owns the word. He owns me. The rain mixes with the tears on my cheeks and the snot dripping down my nose.

My enemy, to lover, is slowly becoming my enemy again. I guess I shouldn't have been so naïve in the beginning. It's true what they say.

Once a prisoner, always a prisoner.

Chapter Thirty-two

MATEO'S POV'S

He's falling apart. Alessio is crumbling like sand. The high and mighty is falling, and his kingdom will quickly follow. My Father's plans have worked a little too well. The background music to the mansion is bickering between Maya and Alessio. It's like two wolves battling for control, battling to be the alpha. Unfortunately, neither of them will back down.

"So, what is the plan for finding my daughter?" My Father's gruff voice brings me back to the present. I peer around the dining room table. Alessio is at the top, silently brooding. His arms are folded defensively across his chest, and he glares daggers into Maya who sits next to him. Her eyes remain fixed on my Father. If looks could kill, she'd be a serial killer right now. Just like her husband, she is in a mood. Her jaw is clenched together, as are her fists. I can almost see her attacking my Father and then Alessio. Perhaps I'd be her third victim.

But I don't blame her; since my dad arrived, her entire relationship and happiness has fallen apart. She is a shell of a person. On her porcelain skin, dark bruises rest. They're joined with scratches and dried blood from her escape last night. I almost longed for her to be successful. To run for the hills, away from this shithole. Unfortunately, for my sister-in-law, and as I quickly learned yesterday, my Brother would never let her leave.

It only left two options: apologise to the Russians. Or death.

Poor girl. The minute she locked eyes with my Brother on the day of her rescue, she was fated to something much worse than death. Her entire marriage would be torture. And in the beginning, I didn't care for her nor her happiness. But as she became integrated into my family, making both my Brother and sister happy, something shifted in my chest. It didn't sit well with me that my Father wanted her gone. She doesn't deserve death. She doesn't deserve exile. She deserves freedom. It is why I left the garden door unlocked for her last night. I never once imagined the fearsome monster my Brother would transform into when he first realised that she had run away.

"Sophia doesn't want to be found. Her phone is off." Alessio grumbles. Beside him, Maya stiffens.

"Or the phone is broken."

"Or stolen." He sends a jab over to her. She keeps his eye contact and challenges him. The air throbs with rage. I roll my eyes and help myself to more of my vodka. To everybody else, it looks as if I'm drinking water from the glass. Little did they know I am drinking the sorrows away. My sister is missing, my sister-in-law won't be around for much longer and the woman I love is banned from coming near me. This is a day of mourning.

"Or taken." Maya responds, referring to her forced marriage. Alessio bares his teeth like a wolf threatening his prey. Opposite them, my Father grins. He enjoys their mutual hatred. He prays Alessio will divorce her and will return to being a monstrous tyrant. I, on the other hand, do not believe Maya will get away so easily.

This isn't what worries me right now. My concerns are for my missing sister. She is probably alone, frightened somewhere, desperate for us to find her. We do not know yet whether she has imposed self-isolation or she has been taken. My rule of thumb is to prepare for the worse and celebrate the better.

"Be quiet, wife." My Brother growls menacingly. It sends me over the edge.

"It doesn't help us find her if you're fucking fighting!" I hear myself shriek and smash a hand into the table. The alcohol offers me more confidence; I rise to my feet and point between the two of them, "Knock it off, the pair of you! For one day, lets act like a happy fucking family and find Sophia!"

Every person at the table gawps. Alessio and Maya look taken aback by my outburst. My Father is shocked that I'm ceasing the fights which could lead to our mutual goal: An undistracted, unstoppable Alessio.

"Have we any news on the last place she went to?" I take control of the situation. Maya looks down guiltily.

"Alexis." She confesses, "She was there with me."

"And did you meet anybody out of the ordinary? Anyone who wants to hurt her? Anyone worth noticing?"

"No." she hangs her head low, "We were having fun."

"Fun!" My Father scoffs. He grips the table menacingly and leans forward. I watch as he shakes in rage.

"Fun has killed my daughter."

"We don't know that yet." Alessio swiftly interrupts the attack. For a moment, that hard exterior softens in pity. However, like Alessio's usual emotions, it doesn't last long. He instantly returns to the moody, brooding leader he is.

"Have you checked CCTV?" Maya raises an eyebrow. Yet again, my Father scoffs.

"Yes, *child*. Of course, we have." He tears his gaze around to Alessio and me, "Can I ask why she has to join? She's hardly any help. If anything, she is the problem here. She has caused all these issues."

"What issues?" She shoots back quickly. I don't know whether she's stupid for picking a fight with my Father, or brave. Either way, it brings a small smile to my lips. As much as I hate to admit it, she really is perfect for my Brother. A mix of fiery and loyal. And though she'd hate to see it, she has perfect traits for being a mafia queen. If only she could put her differences to the side and step up, perhaps then we wouldn't be in this awkward situation of having to dispose of the weak.

"Don't play coy with me now, girl. You think I don't know your game." My Father slowly loses his cool. I glare at him and silently pray for him to stop talking. He's revealing too many things and I fear that famous Morisso temper will ruin this entire plan.

"Don't patronise me, fucker." She hisses. I visibly flinch in my chair. I think I have my answer; she's stupid. Does she really think she can insult my Father like that and walk out of here alive? He will eat her alive for dinner.

"What did you call me?" He seethes. She raises to her feet and doesn't back down.

"Tell me." She snarls, "What is my game? Why do you hate me so much? Am I not good enough for your little Alessio, is that it?"

"Maya." My Brother growls. The word sends visible shivers through her, but she bats it off. She's too far gone now to listen to reason.

"You come into his house, feigning to be some poor little victim, to seduce him. Then your family start shooting the place up in all the secret weak spots. Places only people inside the house know about. And now Sophia is missing. Riddle me that." My Father stupidly rants all his thoughts. My heart runs cold as he bares his teeth.

"No." Maya laughs in disbelief. Only she would laugh in the face of three Morisso members, all armed and ready to kill.

"That's not true at all. I was rescued from the Russian prison, sure. Then I was forced into a marriage I really didn't want to be in. They can tell you that." She points at me and Alessio bitterly, "Then I thought I fell in love with Alessio. But turns out he's a cold, blooded killer just like the rest of you. I thought he was different, and I was wrong. Why would I want to stick around for that? When I try to leave, I'm caught and dragged back down into Hell!"

"You tried to leave?" My Father look stunned as he turns to me. He was the only person not around for the drama last night. I didn't bother to ask what he was doing; he wouldn't disclose his activities anyways. I give him a small nod and then avert my eyes. He will most likely tear my ear off later for not helping her leave more effectively. We had been so close to getting rid of her.

"Whatever. Despite that, you have motive. You hate him and want him dead. You want your family in, instead. Is that it?" My Father provokes her. Meanwhile, Alessio is frozen. He hasn't even blinked as he listens intently to the argument. Despite his physical body being glued to the chair, the rage seeping out of his body is palpable. Everybody can see it drifting through the room like a red mist. Though I'm not sure which direction the rage is pointed at.

"I hate the mafia." Maya seethes, leaning over the table menacingly, "And I hate my family. I don't want to be with either of you."

"Then leave. *Again*." My Father spits his final proposition.

"When Sophia is returned safe, I will leave."

My Father smirks. The corners of his lips pull upwards in some sort of twisted, satisfied smile. I can't bring myself to enjoy his happiness. We got what we wanted. She will finally leave and let Alessio return to being a cold-hearted ruler. And yet there is a hole in my heart at this prospect.

"Did you get any information out of James?" She turns her attention to me. She oozes control and power in this moment.

"No. Either he actually had nothing to do with the attacks, or he is good at hiding it. We let him go. He's no doubt running back and telling your family everything." I tell her nervously. My Father's head almost explodes with rage. His plan is slowly falling apart as the truth seeps in. Maya's family might not have anything to do with it after all.

"Hang on, what about the gang of thieves? Your family were involved in that!" My Father points out. Maya nods her head slowly.

"Thieves work together. That proves nothing about the attacks or who has Sophia."

"It proves they have connections to the people who are against us." Alessio raises a stern point. Maya's lips pull together in a straight line. Any hope dissipates from her. A pregnant pause sifts between each of us.

"Fine, I have a plan then."

"You're not going home. It's too dangerous." My Brother snaps before she can speak. The two of them are unbelievably connected, it's like words do not be spoken to get a point across. They reach each other's minds. And hearts.

He grabs her hand and forces her to sit down. Despite his harsh words, it's clear he still cares.

"Says who?" She retorts. His eyes darken.

"Your husband."

"Not for long."

The tension in the air slices through everybody. Alessio leaps to his feet. For a second, I think he might flip the table in rage. That famous temper of his has always destroyed things when he is mad. And yet, he has met his match with Maya. She thrusts a menacing finger towards him.

"I was a thief; I know all their tricks and trades. Plus, it's my fucking family operating there. I can find out more!" Maya rises to her feet quickly. Their bodies almost touch as they glare at each other. It takes my breath away.

"You won't leave this house."

"I say we let her." My Father calls out. I scowl at him in disgust. He is so transparent; he wants her gone. Whether that's alive or dead. Then I hear myself speak.

"I agree."

My Father's head snaps at me, and he gives me a satisfied nod.

"With Alessio." I add, "Maya you cannot go back to your family. You'll be killed for betraying them."

Her fists curl when she turns to me.

"So, you all want me gone but you also want me to stay? Make it make sense."

"There are better ways to go about this situation." Alessio's low voice rings around the room. Maya throws her hands to her hips.

"Like what?"

Silence follows. I scratch the back of my head awkwardly. We have already tried tracing her phone, searching through CCTV, contacting anybody in the area who might have seen something. We are desperately running out of options. An inside person would help.

"I thought as much." She sighs, "So, I will return home tomorrow and talk to my Dad. I will see what he wants. And we can go from there…"

"Can't you just call him?" Alessio's desperate voice interrupts her. I flinch at how weak he sounds. My Father grunts as he also picks up on it. I silently pray for my Brother to stop talking.

"No. It needs to be in person. He needs to think I trust him again." Maya shakes her head, "I will see if he knows anything about Sophia. I will be back in the evening for a debrief. Alessio, I need you to keep monitoring CCTV."

"Who is to say this isn't a ploy to feedback information to your Father?" My Father spits at her. She raises a suggestive eyebrow up at him.

"Well, you're going to have to use that little thing called trust."

I can't help the smile which teases my lips. He looks mortified at her sarcastic remark and wants to answer back but she starts talking again,

"And I need a list of all the thieves operating in the area plus what they've stolen. Oh, and if there has been any suspicious activity of human trafficking again. Perhaps reviewing the Russian's tactics will be a good start?"

I blow out a breath of surprise at how well she can delegate and think of solutions.

"You got it." I nod at her. We don't have any other choice; this may be our best and final option at getting my sister back. Beside me, my Father scoffs.

"I don't take orders from a woman."

"In the past." Maya quickly retorts. My Father's eyebrows burrow together.

"What?"

"I said, you didn't take orders from a woman in the past. You do now."

My heart skips a beat as she talks to my Father like he's a mere slave. My lips pop as I go to say something, to protect my Father's ego, to avoid a fight. However, Alessio rests a hand against the small of her back. His lips are pursed together, but he doesn't need to say anything. He has visibly shown whose side he is on.

"I don't think you heard me right." My Father growls as he walks around the table towards her. I clench my jaw together and wait for the impending fight.

"I don't take orders from a woman." He says slowly, as if to spell it out for her. My own fists clench together in rage. Maya doesn't deserve this type of treatment. She has proved herself worthy with this sacrifice, with her confidence and decision-making skills. Alessio physically shakes with rage now. Like a beast inside a cage, he is desperate to escape and go hunting. I rise to my feet and hold my hands in the air.

"Let us not fight. We have a solid plan."

"She is not in charge." My Father spits, "Maybe she needs to be taught who *is* in charge."

The anger bubbles inside of me at the thought of anybody physically hurting Maya. She is a best friend to Sophia. She is like a sister to me too. I take another step towards my Father, readying myself for the fight. But Maya and Alessio are there first. Simultaneously, she pulls her gun out of her waist band and he grabs my Father.

"You fucking will if it's my wife." Alessio growls as he forces my Father to his knees. I gasp in horror as Maya presses the barrel of the gun to his forehead. Shocked, my Father casts his gaze to me, waiting for me to get involved. But I can't. I'm glued to the floor. On the one hand, he is the solution to our financial and security problems. On the other hand, the world will be better off without him.

"Say it." Maya spits, "Say you'll obey me."

He pauses for a second, deciding whether he'll choose life or his ego. Maya's finger jumps to the safety button, and she clicks it off. It makes a startling noise. Alessio forces our Father's head upwards to look at his wife. Father makes no effort to fight back; he isn't strong enough to take them both on. Plus, he's not stupid enough to continue a fight when there is a gun to his head.

For a moment, Maya and Alessio fall into each other's gaze. A small, trusting smile rests on each of their lips. I don't miss the exchanged look. My heart sinks in my chest and the guilt claws at me for trying to break them up. The reality is that this is an equal marriage. It's a no brainier. She holds the gun; he holds the victim. They are stronger together.

"I..." My dad stutters. Maya's finger jumps to the trigger.

"Three." She says impatiently. My dad's eyes grow in shock, and he surveys the room once more as if to check that this is actually happening. Maya doesn't relent.

"Two."

"Okay! Fine!" He shrieks, "I'll take orders from you."

"Good." She smiles proudly, removing the gun from his forehead. She slots it back into her waistband. Then, she turns to the room and demands our attention.

"Just a heads up. To all of you." She barks, "I will only respect you if you respect me."

And with that, she marches out the room. My heart pounds in my chest and I hear the blood rush through me. She has silenced the room. Nervously, I look at my Brother. He stares after her, a look of longing and despair in those dark eyes. It's as if he has just learnt that Maya is perfect for him. And I couldn't agree more.

As much as they will both hate to admit it, a mafia king requires a mafia queen, regardless of the consequences.

Chapter Thirty-three

MAYA'S POV

He loves me. That much I know. But he loves me too much. And everybody knows you shouldn't smother someone with love. That's not love. That's an obsession. An *addiction*.

And Alessio is addicted to me. Not in the healthy way, no. This love is toxic, disgusting. It's a feeling which wraps its dark tendrils around our necks and then squeezes. Tighter. Tighter. Until we are both gasping and begging for mercy. Then it tightens more.

He might be pretending to avoid me in the house. If I walk into a room, he will walk out. If I join a conversation, he leaves it. But I see his lingering gaze. That broken look. Those soft lip's part to say something but then he'll notice me staring. Just as quickly as he looks at me, he'll look away. It's impossible to know what he's thinking. Why is he pushing me away? What have I done to him?

From across the library, I can feel his presence. He doesn't know that I know he's there, lingering behind the bookshelf. I cross my legs and get comfortable on the sofa. A new book is in my fingers, and I pretend to read it. He'll have to come out at some point to go to work. He will have to face me before I go and see my Father. I want at least one conversation with my husband before I risk my life to save his sister. I shuffle further into the sofa to let him know I'm not going anywhere.

After a long pause, I hear him huff. The sound is followed by the shuffling of feet. Before he can escape the room, I shoot upwards towards him.

"You're avoiding me!" I snap.

His wide eyes enlarge as he takes me in. Then they flutter left, then right, as if he's searching for a getaway. Since last night, he has been distant with me. Before the argument with his Father, Alessio was mad at me. Furious. Raging. And now he seems broken, timid, shy. As if the gun was pointed at him.

"Why?" I press a finger into his chest, "Why are you avoiding me?"

He chews on his lower lip. It's as if he looks through me.

"I'm not."

"Yes, you are. Why are you lying?"

"Get out. I was here first." He snaps.

"It's my home, I can go where I want." I retort but my efforts are quickly closed off when he takes a step closer. His jaw hardens and it makes me skip a breath. How is he so beautiful?

"It's *my* home." He corrects me.

"It was your house until I said *I do*. Now we share it."

His eyes twinkle with something magnetic. Then they quickly harden. My mouth dries as I lift my hand to cup his cheek.

"Maya." His voice cracks. I frown as I try to read his face. He seems so lost, so heart broken.

"I..." He trails off, "I can't do this."

"Can't do what?"

"This." He points between us. My heart flips in my stomach. *Is he breaking up with me? Does he want me gone? Was Mateo right, will he toss me to the side now that he's gotten what he wants?*

Suddenly, the timid stranger in front of me changes. Alessio presses me up against the bookshelf. What was a heart wrenching moment suddenly transforms into something more passionate, desperate. Dark eyes stare into my soul.

"I fear for your safety in this house." He whispers harshly, "You're not safe."

"I am not safe anywhere it seems."

"I thought I could protect you, Maya." He seethes, "I thought I could keep you hidden from my Father, but it seems he is in control. He has everybody on his side. I trusted Sophia would keep you safe too, and now she's gone. And I fear my Brother has betrayed us too."

"We will get her back, Alessio! Don't say those things." I tell him confidently. My hand jumps to his arm and I can't help but squeeze to reassure him. A low groan escapes his lips before he leans his forehead against mine.

"I showed him yesterday. *We* showed him." I try again, "You don't have to worry about me with your Father."

He shakes his head. Then, I hear him choke on a sob. It wracks his whole body like a tide frantically smashing into a cliff. Over and over, his shoulders bob up and down.

"I tried to hate you. I wanted you to hate me. You needed to escape, for many reasons. But I couldn't let you go."

"I did hate you." I tell him firmly, "You treated me like shit, Alessio."

His big, red eyes jump up into my gaze. It takes me by surprise. My husband has never shown this type of emotion before. He is broken, ruined.

"Do you still hate me?"

I ponder on his question. My entire body screams to tell him *no*; that how can I hate somebody who tried so hard to love me in the beginning? Who makes me feel things that nobody else has made me feel. But it would be a lie. He is also the man who imprisoned me into marriage, forced me into a mafia role, tortured my family. The same man who hurt me over and over again until I couldn't see what was love and what was an addiction.

"Yes." I spit firmly. The word is like a bullet to the chest, though

I'm not sure which of us is firing the gun. He jolts forward. I take his chin in my fingers and force him to keep eye contact with me.

"I don't think I've hated someone as much as you. I trusted you and you betrayed me."

"N-no."

"Yes, Alessio. You let the monster escape. You let the monster hurt your wife. I will never forgive you for that."

His bottom lip wobbles as his eyes desperately search my own. He is looking for an answer. Am I leaving him? I should be. I have every right to. He has been my tormentor, my capturer, my nightmare. And yet something within me is anchored to him. Like our souls have been stitched together in fire and blood.

Without warning, he presses his lips to mine. The kiss reminds me of everything good. The desire and care we have for one another. The supressed feelings we are not allowed to express.

My fingers jump to his shirt, and I desperately tug it off of him. He groans into the kiss. One of his large arms wrap around my naked torso, pulling me closer if it is possible.

"This doesn't change anything." I tell him sternly, pulling back for a second's breath. It doesn't last long; he presses those sinful lips back to mine.

"Good. I want you to hate me, Maya. Know that I am incapable of true love."

Those words should break my heart. They should have me falling to my knees, clutching my chest in agony. Or I should be fleeing from the room. So why have I removed my trousers?

This is what I mean by toxic love. There is an emotion drifting between us, an unbreakable connection. There is also a mutual hatred. A love so full of rage. And if I'm being honest with myself, I wouldn't have it any other way. I *can't* have it any other way. We have both been trained to hate everything and everyone.

And yet I choose him over oxygen. I'll always choose him. He parts my lips with his tongue, and I moan in approval. I've missed his taste so much. Too much. It's been too long since he touched me, and now those rough fingers curl into my hips. The sensation is too much I could combust on the spot. Then my senses return to me. I press my palms into his chest to try and pry him off. It's all too much; my emotions explode.

"Maya." He growls into the kiss. Whatever resolve I had before my name was said, it now gone. I throw myself into it. I have missed him, there is no denying that.

His rough fingers yank at my blouse and the buttons go soaring through the air. It takes me by surprise, and I gasp into the kiss; he uses the opportunity to slip his tongue into the kiss. I am drunk on his taste. Frantically, I strip him of his clothes too.

Then, those sinful fingers grasp at my breasts. They squeeze and play before twiddling the nipple. My body jolts forward at the intimate touch.

"Alessio." I moan. A guttural groan escapes from him and it just makes my body react even more to him. His other hand jumps down between my legs. Usually, he'd tease me, make me shiver and beg for more. Not this time. This is a hate fuck.

Before I can say anything, he lifts me in the air and thrusts his huge cock inside of me. I scream in pleasure and grip onto his shoulders violently. My nails create beautiful patterns down his arms and back. The pain seems to spur him on.

"That's it." He nips my ear as he slowly thrusts in and out, "Good girl. Take it all."

His slow thrusts become faster and harder. I feel my body repeatedly slam against the bookshelf as he enters and pulls out. One of his arms wraps around my body to keep me in the air, and the other uses it's devilish fingers to play with my clit. The pleasure is just too much.

"Alessio, I'm close!"

"Already?" He grins as he trails kisses all down my face and neck. My eyes squeeze shut, and I try to hold off the impending orgasm. I want to last longer; I want him to stay inside of me forever if possible.

But with a change in pace, I quickly fall over the edge. His lips attack mine and he devours me as I ride the high. It's the most violent and pleasurable orgasm I've ever had, and it just keeps going.

"Cum again for me." He growls into my ear. I shake my head as I feel all lightheaded. It's not possible, surely not. Then, he slams into me. Instantly, my body shakes and a scream leaves my lips as he sends me back over the edge. This time, he joins me in riding the high.

Both our heads lull back as we cling onto each other tightly. My traitorous body groans for more but my head pulls back from him. I quickly pick up my broken clothes and exit the room without so much as a look back at him. That moment would be nothing more than a memory in my heart; it will never happen again.

Chapter thirty-four

MAYA'S POV:

My entire body shakes like a leaf in the wind. I never thought for a moment that I'd be returning to face my Father after everything that I've been through. But for Sophia's sake, I have to. What if they are right? What if my family are actually behind all the attacks?

My fingers curl into a fist as I ready myself to knock on the door. Just as I move my hand, the door flies open. Cole stands there, wide eyed.

"Maya!" He snaps, pushing me out of the doorway. I get a quick glimpse at the awful, damp apartment they've been staying in. It stinks of rot and wastage. I turn my nose up at the conditions and return my attention to my Brother.

"Where is dad?"

"No, Maya. Leave!" My Brother snaps, "You have to go!"

"No, Cole, it's fine now. The Russians are gone, I can return home. I just need to ask Dad a few questions, to clear his name."

"Maya, you're not welcome in this house!" My Brother roars, pushing me at an arm's distance. I stumble backwards as his fist connects with my shoulder. The pain pulses through me but the adrenaline drowns it out.

"What are you on about Cole?"

"You let your husband torture James? What are you thinking? What happened to loyalty!" His eyebrows burrow together as he rambles on. I do not back down from his outburst.

"Loyalty!" I scoff bitterly, "Where the fuck was loyalty when I was being passed from prison to prison!"

My Brother's lips slam shut. He doesn't dare to argue back with that sound logic. My fingers remain tightly fisted at my side.

"Tell me, tell me now! Do you have anything to do with the theft ring running around?"

"No." Cole says firmly.

"Are you sure?"

"Positive." He breathes out with frustration. I feel as though my heart has exploded a couple times as I stagger backwards. Cole doesn't have a reason to lie to me- *right?* We have always been unconditionally close. He is like a true Father to me.

But then that leaves a worse option: that Alessio was lying to me. It's as if somebody has kicked me in the stomach.

"Do you know where Sophia is?" I try a new question. My Brother shakes his head once and then twice more firmly. This time, I release a squeal of frustration. *Then what am I doing here? Accusing my own family of kidnapping?*

"Did you guys break into Alessio's home?"

"Maya!" My Brother finally snaps, "No, no and no! Of course, I didn't."

My ears prick. His face falls as he realises what he's said.

"So, *you* didn't." I point out slowly, "But the family might have."

Cole has never been a good liar. He has always been excellent at bending the truth or diverting the interrogation, but he has never been able to lie to me.

"I don't know!" He panics.

"Yes, you do. Cole don't do this right now! This is a matter of life and death. Answer me clearly and honestly!"

"I shouldn't be talking to you." He spits bitterly before attempting to slam the door in my face. I thrust my foot in and let it slam on my ankle. A spark of pain floods through me but I quickly push it away.

"Let me in, Cole."

"Leave, Maya!" He shrieks. Then his eyes cast left before back to me.

"We don't want you here!"

"Y-yes I know that." I stumble over my words.

"Go back to your precious life with your rich husband and leave us be. *Traitor*." He spits with such venom. I am shocked by the way he talks to me. My head shakes slowly.

"You don't mean that. Who is home? Let me speak to James, I'll apologise. Let me speak to Dad!"

"No, they are out walking Chip. But I don't want you here." My Brother spits. This is like a boulder dropped on my chest. My Brother is in danger. My dog, Chip, died seven years ago. When I was younger, my Brother said that if I ever ran into any danger, in a situation where I couldn't make it obvious that I was in trouble, I could call him and ask how my dog is. That way he would know if I needed help.

And he used it. He used the code word! For a moment, his eyes flicker with despair when I take a step forward.

"Leave, Maya!" He booms. This time, I do as I'm told. Slowly, I back away.

"Fine."

The words are like mud in my teeth. Gritty and awful to keep in but worse to spit out or else they will cling to my gums and lips. My Brother sends me one last look before he slams the door in my face. Everything aches as I sprint back to the car.

"Alessio, you have to help him!" I pant, "He's in danger."

Alessio scowls at me but quickly exits the car.

"He used a code word for when he's in trouble." I ramble, "You need to..."

"Get in the car and keep your head low. I'll go and see what's happening."

Something tells me I'll only slow him down if I go with him so instead I do as I'm told. I jump into the black car and slide down in the seat. My head pops up through the window only slightly so I can see him approach the door. Alessio whips out his gun before kicking the door down. He wastes no time invading.

For a moment, my breath is snatched. He fought for me and my family without a wasted second. He still believes that they are responsible for all the awful things happening to him, and yet, as I tell him they need help, he is on it. Does this mean he trusts me?

He disappears for a moment, and it is silent. After ten minutes of me holding my breath and praying, Alessio stumbles out of the house looking confused.

"What happened? Is there someone there with him?" I panic as he slides into the car. He taps the driver on the shoulder to signal him to pull away.

"What? Where are we going? My Brother is in trouble!" I try again desperately. I can feel it deep in my bones that my Brother needs us.

"Maya, he's on the sofa watching telly. I searched everywhere in the house. Nobody else is there."

"What? Why would he use the code word if he is in trouble?"

"I don't know." He frowns, "I will get someone stationed around the house to keep an eye on him to make sure he's safe. But did you get any information out of him?"

"He said it wasn't him. But then wouldn't clarify if my family were involved or not."

"Fuck." He hisses, "We need to find who is sending the attacks, Maya."

I nod slowly and fall into his open arms. He pulls me close, and the smell of his musky aftershave fills my nose. For the first time in a while, his intoxicating smell doesn't relax me. I'm too worked up on adrenaline and fear.

Chapter thirty-five

MAYA'S POV:

"I don't know why we are still running this fucking thing." I hear Mateo snap. He can't see me yet, he's in the other room with his Brother. I didn't mean to eavesdrop, it just happened. My feet are glued to the floor and my hand is locked in a fist which was just about to knock on the door. The other hand grips onto the beautiful silk dress which I found resting on the bed earlier. A beautiful emerald colour licks the long, trailing dress and small, silver patterns snake up the sides, creating beautiful flowery decorations. When I first put it on, I instantly saw the connection between the dress and a leaf out of the garden of Eden. My dark hair sashays by my sides, and I wear a light coating of makeup on my pale face. The more I stared at myself in the mirror, the more I realised I wasn't a leaf out of the garden of Eden. I was Eve.

"Because we can't let the community down." Alessio answers his Brother coldly. Between the gap in the door, I can see him buttoning up his crisp, white shirt. My breath is taken away when his tan chest flashes in view. He truly is a handsome man. My Adam. Or is he the snake which leads Eve into temptation? To danger?

"Come in, wife. It's rude to eavesdrop." His voice rings through the corridor. I startle and ready myself to run away. How did he know I was here?

"Must I repeat myself?"

Before he can say anything else, I scurry into the room. When his eyes land on me, they sparkle mischievously. He busies himself by putting on his suit jacket and then correcting his tie. All the while, his gaze never leaves me, a longing look pulsing through him. I struggle to regulate my breathing as I look at sin incarnate in front of me. It should be illegal to look that good.

"I'll meet you down there." Mateo nods at both of us. A cheeky smile teases his lips as he exits the room. I watch him leave, not for any reason other than to distract myself from Alessio's burning gaze.

"I have something for you." He tells me before heading towards the bedside counter. I nervously shuffle towards the bed and take a seat. He takes his time digging down the draw before removing a gorgeous sparkling box. It's the size of a fist and surprisingly light when he hands it to me.

"What is it?"

"Open it and find out." He smirks at me. Then, he takes a seat next to me. The bed dips under his weight and makes me slide into him. Anxiously, I bite my lower lip and look between him and the gift. I didn't like accepting gifts from people; it usually meant I had to return something. But as I peer back at Alessio's soft gaze, I can tell this isn't one of those moments.

"Go on. It doesn't bite." He gently urges me on. I can't take the tension any longer. Quickly, I pop the lid open on the box and a velvety black bag is revealed. My eyebrows knit together as I pull the bag out. Then I open the draw string. When the present is revealed, my heart skips a couple beats.

"H-How did you know?" I gasp, tearing my gaze towards him. He smirks and those gorgeous dimples shoot out of his cheeks. Shocked, I look down at the beautiful emerald bracelet that I fell in love with at the market.

"Here." He offers, taking the bracelet from me. Without hesitation, I thrust my wrist out to him to let him put it on me. When his skin touches mine, it's like electricity has exploded between us. My eyes are glued to the beautiful gift.

"Oh, Alessio!" I say in disbelief. Before he can react, I throw myself into his arms. It's the best present anybody could ever give me.

"Anything for you, my dear." He whispers into the embrace. Slowly, I pull back and play with it.

"But how?"

"CCTV reveals many things. And when I saw you lingering around the stand, and how your face lit up when you touched it, I knew I had to get it for you." He tells me almost dreamily. I push back the threatening tears. As my shock slowly subsides, my rationality seeps back in. I will have to pay him back for this. I can't be indebted to him.

"And before you say it, no, you will not be paying me back." He reads my mind. My mouth rounds into an 'O'.

"It's a gift. And I know it doesn't make up for how I treated you, in my poor attempt of trying to get my Father off your back, but I hope it's a start. It shows my determination in trying to win you back." He looks at me in despair. Before he can say anything more, I press my lips to his. It's a passionate kiss, my way of thanking him silently. He groans into the kiss and for a second, I feel us both slip into a kiss more desperate.

"No." He whispers, "Not yet. Later, I promise."

Panting, I pull back slowly. I long for more, for more of him. I no longer have to fear him, to pretend that I hate him completely. The truth is, there are some redeeming features in this mafia boss.

"Let's go, darling." He says in a hoarse voice. He leads the way, gently holding my hand to guide me down to the ballroom. I stumble after him, intoxicated by his sweet nickname.

The ballroom has transformed into something other worldly. I can't describe how beautiful it looks with draping golden ribbon, weaving in and out of the fairy lights on one side of the room. Heavenly beings have been painted onto the walls and the celestial beings watch over everybody with a kind look. On the other, dark, sparkly lights glisten. Dark shadows have been painted these walls, intermingled with red ribbon. It's hard to make out what creates there are, but deep down I know it's something devilish.

Round tables have been dotted around the room, decorated divinely by the richest red robes. White, leather chairs accompany the tables, and names have been written on each chair, letting us know where our place is. Stunningly dressed people linger around the room, deeply engrossed in their conversations. I grip Alessio's hand tighter. For some reason, I feel nervous. I know it's for a good cause the charity event, but it still feels like I'm mingling with the mafia tribe.

"This way." Alessio tells me in his low voice as he guides me towards the far table. Before I can reach for my own seat, he extends his hand out to pull the chair back for me. I give him a small look before taking the seat. He slides me into the table before joining me at my side.

"What is the theme?" I whisper.

"Heaven and Hell."

"That doesn't seem very charitable." I scowl at him.

"I didn't do it for them."

He doesn't need to spell the words out anymore. It is clear that he's designed this room for me. The contrast between the happiness and misery. It's a metaphor for our love.

"Brother." Mateo says, nodding as advances towards us. Alessio scowls and looks past him.

"Where is Father?"

"Searching for Sophia."

He tenses up beside me and lowers his gaze. A guilty look

washes through him. We are here celebrating and having fun, and Sophia might be in trouble. No matter how many times Alessio told us he believes Sophia has run away and just needs time to cool down, nobody believed him. There was a sense of something more sinister drifting around.

"Right." He sighs, "Well, collect as many donations as you can. We can use all the help."

"You're stealing charity money?" I gawp at my husband. My gaze flicks towards the sign on the wall which says this fundraiser is for Children in need. Would he really take money away from them?

"Not quite."

"Huh?"

"It's business, Maya. The money earnt tonight goes back into the mafia, so we have some money in the business. And then I will pay the charity out of my own pocket. I'll even double the costs." He keeps his voice low as he watches my expression. I don't fully understand the justifications, but Alessio seems to know what he is on about. And who am I to protest the way he runs his business?

The night slowly passes, and everybody becomes drunker and drunker. The sound of laughter and poorly cracked jokes seems to grow louder until I desire to throw my hands over my ears. I haven't left the seat; I haven't wanted to. The more I watch the guests mingle, the more I realise this isn't a charity event per se. It's a networking opportunity. Nobody is here to donate money to a good cause; they are here for an open bar and a good time. It makes me feel sick. The community is just as fucked up as the mafia itself; no wonder my Father never let us mingle with people outside the family.

"Having fun, my dear?" Alessio's voice hums in my ear. I feel my heart miss a beat in shock but I quickly right myself.

"Always." I respond somewhat bitterly. He quickly takes a seat by my side and pulls my hand in his, "Smile, it looks good on you."

I give him the fakest smile I can possibly muster which earns me a chuckle. The sound is like music to my ears. I long for another one.

"Why don't I introduce you to some of the guests, then you can see they're not all bad." He offers with a small smile. I shake my head quickly.

"I'm good here, thank you. Go and enjoy the party. I'm just waiting for the minutes to tick by until it's socially acceptable to leave."

"Life of the party." He teases me and sends a small nudge into my side. For a moment, as we gaze into each other's eyes, I feel all the tension slip. As if we haven't been dragged through hell these last couple weeks. He rests a gentle hand on my shoulder. I nuzzle my cheek into it.

"Well, let me walk you up to your room then." He offers. I nod my head, suddenly feeling much more fatigued than before. Stifling a yawn, I rise to my feet, but I quickly freeze as the ballroom doors fly open.

Cole stumbles in, panic crossing his face. Frightened, I throw myself towards him.

"Cole?" I try but he doesn't respond. He is oddly pale, and lips are blue. Suddenly, he drops to his knees with a huge thud. I'm racing towards him within the next moment. Before he can fall on his face, I grab him and pull him onto my lap. My mind races one hundred miles an hour and the breath in my lung's stings.

"Cole? Cole?" I slap his blueing face frantically, "Help!"

My eyes glare up at my husband who stands there stiffly. He doesn't even blink as he watches my Brother die in my arms.

"M-Maya." Cole finally splutters, blood pouring out of his lips.

"Oh my God, no!" I panic and quickly wipe it away. The rage fills me as the room goes quiet. Everybody stands and watches the scene. *Why aren't they getting help? Why aren't they trying to save my Brother?*

"It's Sophia." He wheezes, "O-our family aren't i-involved after all."

His eyes flick downwards but I don't understand what he's talking about. I shake my head. This doesn't stop his gaze jumping up and down. Then, out of nowhere, he starts shaking. Like someone has put him on vibrate mode, my Brother trembles faster and faster. Froth spills from his mouth just as quickly and his eye's role back in his head.

"No!" I shriek as the tears pool down my face, "No! No! Don't do this, Cole. Don't leave me!"

Alessio tries to pull me away from my Brother, but I won't release him. This is all my fault. I visited my family and now my Brother is dying! After what feels like a century, Cole stops trembling. He stops frothing. It's replaced with blood. Soon after, my Brother takes his last breath.

I'm not even given a second to mourn as Mateo comes over and dives down his pockets.

"What are you doing!" My voice cracks in despair as I watch him, "Leave him alone!"

My anger towards Mateo only increases. What did he think he was doing? Desperately, I try to pull my Brother's corpse away from him, but Cole is too heavy to budge. Finally, Mateo pulls something out of Cole's pocket. A scrunched-up piece of paper. Quickly, he unravels it and holds it to the light. Instantly, his lips pull into a grim line.

"Looks like Sophia has reached out to us." He says before handing the note to Alessio. I try to grab it out of his hands, but I fail.

"What does it say?"

"Fuck." Alessio hisses as he peers down at the note, "It says: *stop looking for me.*"

"I fear our sister might be more caught up in trouble than we first thought." Mateo seethes as he peers down at Cole. I long to throw myself on my Brother's body to stop the morbid glances towards him but I'm frozen to the ground. A sob gets caught in my throat.

"S-she killed my Brother?"

It's all too much, I can't understand it. Sophia was my best friend. She was the only one there for me when Alessio turned into a beast. And now she is slaughtering my family. She was my last hope for trusting the mafia.

Alessio flips the note around and frowns as he finds another clue.

"It seems Sophia isn't *just* killing people now." He grumbles, "It seems our sister is plotting against us."

Mateo's eyebrows burrow together on his forehead as he takes the note. Yet again, the boys leave me out of the picture.

"Well, at least we know who is behind the attacks then." He grumbles before dropping the note down to me. Frantically, I scramble to pick it up and read the message. On the back, scribbled in Sophia's handwriting the words *'I'm coming for you'*.

Thirty-Six

ALESSIO'S POV:

"It just doesn't make sense!" Mateo hisses as he rocks back and forth on the chair. Since learning the truth about our sister's betrayal, he hasn't returned to his usual rosy cheeks. He looks physically sick. And as he should be. Sophia has broken rule one of being in the mafia: loyalty to family.

"B-but perhaps she isn't?" Maya shakes her head, "It might be a misunderstanding."

Nobody answers her. Personally, I need to keep my lips shut or else I might make her cry with the truth. Sophia has always been a runaway child, and she, like Mateo and me, longs for power. It's in our blood, our DNA. I don't blame her for this hunger. But I shall hold her accountable for the deaths in the wake of our war.

"No, you have too many enemies for it to be Sophia." She squeaks, "My family, the Russians…"

"Who's to say they're not all working together?" Mateo interrupts. This thought makes me feel sick; three against one financially insecure business is not good news. Then, I shake my head.

"No, Cole said it isn't your family. And I believe him. James only told us about small scale theft. And CCTV proves they haven't come near our house."

Maya stiffens as she realises her family had been innocent. All this time, we were pointing an accusing family at her own Father and Brother. When we should have been targeting our own family.

"I've pinged her location." Aria declares as she storms into the room. Silently, she sets up her laptop and connects it to the board so we can all see. My eyes widen when the little blue dot appears.

"She's in Russia."

"She's not the only one." Aria says bitterly before frantically typing away at something. A new screen pulls up.

"Angelo and your Father are there too."

Rage consumes me. I can't resist, my fists flies into the table and a booming noise echoes around the room. So, the Russians have made a deal with my own family.

"Anybody else wants to betray me?" I roar, throwing myself to my feet, "Now is a great time!"

"Alessio!" Maya hisses. She shoots up from her chair and advances towards me. I hold my breath as she snakes her arms around my neck.

"Be rational. They want you to lose your head and make a mistake."

Deep down, I know she's right. Of course, she is right. But rage has no reason. I itch to cause more destruction. Has my Father played me all along? Did he return to whisper awful things into our ears to destroy this mafia, just so he can rule his own? And I let him convince me!

"Fuck! It's all so clear now!" I hiss, "They were trying to break us up. Sophia got you in trouble through sneaking out. They used Laura's name too. And then my Father convinced me the Russians and your family were out to get us. All this time, it was him and my sister!"

Opposite me, my Brother stiffens. A guilty look washes across his face. My heart drops in my chest and despair fills me. He doesn't need to tell me what he's done, the truth oozes from him.

My eye twitches as I watch him. He lowers his head guilty.

"He promised he'd fix the financial is…" My Brother begins but I quickly cut him off.

"No use in apologising now Brother."

"Alessio!" Maya snaps as I tower over him. She grabs me by the shoulder and pulls me away from him.

"Sit down, now!"

For the first time in my life, I do as I'm told. Like a scolded schoolboy, I return to my seat, though I do not stop the daggers which I send my Brother.

"Mateo was just doing what was best for the mafia. There shouldn't be any hard feelings." She barks, "Your Father has manipulated everybody. He's good at what he does."

Everybody in the room is shocked by her calmness. I raise an eyebrow at her. Surely, she should feel the rage I do. I almost lost her due to the own villainous acts of my family. The same awful acts which ended up in her Brother being murdered.

"Don't you worry." She hisses, eyes suddenly full of flames, "I'll get my revenge. Trust me I will. But now is not the time for finger pointing. It's for planning."

My breath is snatched as my beautiful wife takes control. It is such a shame she doesn't want any part in the mafia; she'd be the most ruthless queen. Something in my stomach flips at the idea of her standing beside me, both of us towering over our people. I cross my legs and repress the urges.

"Does anyone have any ideas?" She starts as she paces back and forth, "So we know that we have been turned against one another. It's easier to conquer a mafia one by one than as a unit. To what end though?"

"Power." I explain with a hoarse voice, "Your Brother's death was their declaration of war. I have no doubt they'll be coming after us soon enough. The Russian mafia isn't enough for them.

They'll want both."

"And do you really think Sophia wants to do all this?" Mateo runs his fingers through his growing beard. I ponder on this thought. Though everybody in this family longs for power, my sister had always been different. She loved living in Southern Italy, she adored the lifestyle and the daily activities. Why would she give up this freedom for a job with more restrictions and responsibilities?

"Father is using her like he used us." Mateo declares, "But why? What does he have over her?"

"We have to save her." I hiss, slamming my fist into the table. My Father had no loyalties to any of his children. Sure, he lived close to Sophia in the South, and they occasionally bumped into each other during work, but my Father was still a misogynist and power hungry. If he had a favourite, it would either be me, the mafia boss, or my Brother, the second in charge. But the way he has played us against each other lately is too perfect. It shows favourites are really a thing of the past. The only person he favours is himself.

This means Sophia is not safe. Whatever my Father has over her could be deadly.

"But she sent the note. My Brother." Maya squeaks in disbelief. I shake my head once and then twice,

"Sophia doesn't kill people. Sure, it was her handwriting, but for all we know there was a gun to her head as she wrote it. She is in trouble."

"What do you propose we do?"

"We have to go after her. We have her location; we need to break her free." I bark. Maya lurches forward and holds my hand.

"No, what about your Father? Who is to say this isn't another trap?"

Her eyes bear into mine and for a second, I see the fear. My fingers curl around her hand and I give her a reassuring squeeze.

"I'll be fine. Mateo and you will stay here. I will go with the rest of the council."

"I want to go." Mateo barks but I quickly silence him with a hand.

"No, not after what happened with the Russians. Maya will not be left alone."

"Then let me come too." She tries desperately. My heart aches as I ponder on this question. What if everything goes wrong out there? What if she ends up getting hurt? I'd never forgive myself.

"Please, Alessio. I can help." She begs with large, pleading eyes. My resolve slowly slips. With a half nod, I let her join us. Slowly, I rise to my feet.

"We leave in five minutes for Russia. Gather your armies." I begin to give out the instructions but the doors to the office suddenly slam open. Alice stumbles in, clutching a tape in her fingers. This time, I can't resist the rage that flies through me.

"Get out!" I boom. The short-haired woman trembles and skids to a halt. Her uncanniness to Laura sends agony through me. I can't even look at her without feeling weak in the knees. The guilt, the pain- it's all too much. I do not need her causing any weakness before we go.

Her nervous eyes flicker between Mateo and me.

"Alessio!" She cries out warily, "Just listen to me!"

"I said get out!"

Maya slowly backs away from me in shock. I can see the cogs turning in her head as she pieces everything together.

"I have valuable information!" She tries again but I'm not having it. Laura's face flashes into mind over and over again. The image speeds up and intensifies like a fire burning through a dry forest. My lips feel chapped and my head heavy. No. I can't have Alice near me. She is too much of a reminder of what I've lost. What I could lose again. Menacingly, I take another step closer, but I'm quickly stopped.

"You won't touch her, Brother." Mateo growls. His voice is low and stern. My eyebrows burrow together as the questions flood through me. Then, it clicks. *That's* why Alice was here the other night. She's the new thing my Brother is fucking.

"Great." I scoff, "Just fucking great."

"I know you didn't kill my sister."

"Oh yeah?" I grunt, "How do you know that?"

Even now as I peer down at my hands, I can see flashbacks of blood staining my skin. Sure, I know I didn't pull the trigger or snap her bones back. I wasn't the person who killed her. But I sure was the fucking catalyst. The reason she died. And that is why the blood is on my hands.

"Because of this." She spits, charging towards us. Aria stumbles backwards as Alice opens the tape and plugs it into the computer. For a moment, I'm too stunned to say anything. Laura's face appears on screen. It's like a knife to the heart.

"No." I hear my voice squeak. My legs give way and I fist my fingers through my hair. This can't be happening. I don't want to see her again. I never want to see her again, the woman I loved. The one I hurt.

"Hello, Alice." Laura's soft voice rings through the room, "I don't have much time to talk, but I need to get something off my chest. And if you're seeing this, well, it means something bad has happened to me. The truth is, I'm frightened, sis. I'm terrified. He is out to get me; I can feel it in my bones."

"No!" I cry out, throwing my hands over my ears. It doesn't work, Laura's voice still bounces around the room.

"He lingers around my food, my drink. He watches me too intently when I'm putting on lotion or when I'm spraying deodorant. There is just that feeling that he's waiting for me to notice something is different. That something is wrong."

Laura scowls as she works through her thoughts. My eyes catch Maya's shocked expression. She looks as if she's seen a ghost with her pale cheeks. A frightened gaze tears between my dead ex-girlfriend and me. A lump forms in my throat. Is this how she discovers the truth? That I really am a cold-blooded killer, incapable of love? Incapable of being trusted due to my mafia nature? Everything I love turns to dust. What if she is next?

"I can't do it anymore, Alice. I fear that he is going to kill me." Laura chokes on a sob, "Alessio's Father is really going to kill me."

My head shoots upwards. The shock ripples through everybody's expressions. It was totally the wrong answer. And yet deep down it was clearly the right answer! I knew he did it! My fingers curl into fists.

"He hates me. Fine, he hasn't told me he hates me in those words, but I can feel it. I know I'm not good enough for his son, I know I'm not wanted in the family, and I know I will not be around much longer. He offered me money to leave, you know?" Her eyes widen and she bobs her head quickly as she speaks, "It's true, Alice. I honestly think he's going to hurt me. Sophia too."

The lump in my throat worsens at the mention of my little sister's name. She would have only been sixteen at the time; what does she have to do with Laura's death?

"A couple days ago I saw her pour powder into my tea. She said it was sugar. Sugar!" Laura squeaks in disbelief, "Of course, I pretended to drink it. But for the rest of the day, they both stalked me around the house, waiting for me to drop dead. But what do I do? I can't leave, it's not safe. I fear they will always be out to get me."

"Laura!" I hear my own voice call out in the video, searching for her, but I do not come into view.

A tear slips down my cheek as Laura panics with the camera in her fingers.

"I've got to go. But you just need to know, that I love you. And whatever you do, run. Never trust a Morisso man."

Then, the film ends with static music. Silence pierces through the room; how can you respond to perhaps my ex-girlfriend's last moments?

"I only just found this." Alice whispers before wiping her snotty nose on the back of her jumper, "I am so sorry, Alessio, that we never believed you."

I can't answer her. The world around me spins and an awful heat floods through me. I was right, all that time, I was right! I am not a lover killer, I am not cold blooded, I am not the predator. Nobody what rumours sifted around this house; I didn't do it. And now everybody knows the truth!

"What do we do with this?" Mateo frowns, asking the rational question. Alice's mouth open and shuts like a fish out of water. Then, she casts her gaze away from my Brother; I don't miss how hurt he looks.

"This, this is what your Father has on Sophia."

My face pales as I realise the truth behind her words. Blackmail! My Father is threatening Sophia with the truth of Laura's death. She is wise to be afraid, to run away from the truth. If I ever found out she was the one behind my first love's death...

Red fills my vision. Laura died for nothing. She died because of my vicious family!

"Brother." Mateo steps in front of me, "Deep breaths."

"Fuck, deep breaths!"

I punch a hole in the table in front of me, letting all my rage out. How could she do this to me? I expected it from my Father, but from my little sister too? And is that why she was growing close to Maya? Was she planning on doing the same thing?

From across the room, I make eye contact with my beautiful wife. A horrified look spreads through her as she realises the truth.

"Alessio!" Carlos cries out as he storms into the room. Panic seeps into his face as he skids to a halt.

"They're here!"

My heart drops in my chest at the realisation the war has started much quicker than first planned. I don't have much choice in including my wife now.

"Fuck." Mateo hisses, pulling his gun out of his back pocket. Everybody copies him, clutching onto their weapons. I pace back and forth.

"How many are there of them?"

"At least one hundred."

Like an anchor being thrown off a boat into the ocean, my heart drops in my chest with a thud. Nervously, I peer around at the room. Maya, Alice, Carlos, Mateo, and Aria. That makes six of us against one hundred of them.

"How long have we got?" I bark, checking my watch.

"Five!" A booming voice calls from the other door, "Four."

Frantically, I twist to face my Father but my heart leaps out of my chest. One of his arms are wrapped around Maya's neck and the other holds a gun to her head. At first, she squirms and bucks against him, but the flick of a safety switch has her freezing on the spot.

"Three." My Father cackles.

"Stop!" I bark at him. Rage floods through me as I watch the vulnerable position the woman, I love is in. "What do you want Father? Let her go. I'll give you anything."

Behind him, Sophia stalks into the room. With a slight tremble, she holds her gun firmly pointed at everyone.

"Put the guns down." My Father barks at us, "Or I'll pull the trigger."

Without hesitation, I place my gun on the floor before turning to face my team. Mateo holds my gaze for a second too long. He silently tells me he doesn't trust giving up the weapon. I bare my teeth at him and give him a stern look. My Father has a gun pressed against Maya's head. He is in control here. And unfortunately, this means we must obey his demands. Finally, Mateo lays his weapon down on the table and takes a step away from it.

Suddenly, a bang echoes through the room. My head snaps back towards Maya as a cry of fear leaves my lips. But it's not her who is bleeding. Opposite, Carlos falls to his knees and clutches the hole in his heart. A string of painful moans leaves his lips, but he dies quickly.

"Fuck!" Aria cries out as she looks at her co-worker's dead body. I turn to face my Father and his smoking gun which has been returned to Maya's head. The reality of the situation increases.

"What do you want?" I boom to my Father and sister. They will not hear me be weak, they will not win this war. If they harm a hair on Maya's head, I'll wreak havoc on earth. They think they've seen the full monster. Not at all.

"We want the mafia. We want control." My sister replies with just as much strength. I turn my gaze to her and resist the urge to attack. The monster within me pants and claws to get out. I'd torture my sister into the next life for what she's done to us.

"Have it." I declare nonchalantly.

"Alessio!" Mateo spits behind me. I raise a hand to him to silence him. Slowly, I advance towards my family. My entire body shakes in fear of losing Maya. I have put her in too many situations like this. If I had just gone straight, like she asked, we wouldn't be in this situation. I wouldn't be risking her life.

"Have the mafia. Have the control. Just let her go."

"Ah, the problem is." My Father snarls, pressing his arm tighter into Maya's neck. She gasps for air and claws at him with both hands. Her gun is on the floor in front of her from where he caught her by surprise.

"We can't let any of you live, now, can we?" He continues, "You'll always be a threat. A virus. And we need to wipe you out."

"What happened to family loyalty in the mafia?" Mateo spits venom. Sophia raises her weapon at him, a cold, blank look in her eyes. She is inscrutable.

"No!" Alice gasps. I internally flinch as my Father's awful gaze turns to Alice. For a moment, his face lights up in shock, and then delight.

"Oh, this has just become interesting!"

"Leave her alone!" Mateo barks, taking a step closer towards Alice. Sophia flicks the safety switch off and silently orders him to remain still. With a grim line on his face, Mateo stills.

My eyes are firmly fixed on Maya who watches me back. We exchange a longing, desperate look. It feels as though there is a boulder resting on my chest at her vulnerability. And yet she doesn't shed a single tear or appears in despair. Far from it, my wife oozes rage and power.

"Or what?" My Father spits at Mateo. Then, he turns to face Sophia and gives her a half nod. For a moment, Sophia stiffens but then quickly does as she's told. She marches over to Alice and kicks her to the floor. With a thud, Alice lands on her knees. Her head remains low and her entire body shakes as she sobs. Sophia presses the gun to the back of her head.

"No!" Mateo blurts out before his hands jump to his mouth, "Sophia, don't! This isn't you! Don't fucking pull that trigger!"

"Do it." My Father spits from the other corner. My heart drops in my chest for my Brother; he is about to witness the pain which love brings. Sophia gulps and peers back around at everybody, then she gathers her wits and takes a deep breath. Just as her finger jumps to the trigger, chaos explodes.

Mateo charges towards her and tackles her to the ground.

Everybody leaps towards their guns and gun shots ring around the room. Glass shatters, bullets tear through flesh and furniture and the screams of agony pounds through the air.

It's as if time slows down as I leap towards Maya. She throws her head back and smashes my Father in the nose before she leaps towards the gun on the floor. Every sound around me dulls into a throbbing of my heart as I fire two shots. It doesn't matter. My Father is quicker. He fires more rounds. My body smashes against the ground and as does Maya's.

Behind us, my Father drops to the floor, clutching his chest. I can't focus on him right now; the pain is awful as it tears through my flesh.

My body skids towards her and comes to a stop as our faces are opposite one another. Her lips slowly open and close in disbelief and a cloudy look stains her expression. Red stains my vision, but it's not rage. It's blood. She is covered in the awful sticky stuff. As am I. Pain is an understatement, but it's not from the bullet holes in my body. It's the fact she has bullets in hers.

"A-Alessio." She gawps, taking shaky, sharp breaths. Her face is pale, and lips are slowing draining of their rosy colour.

"Maya." I whimper, reaching for her face. I have no energy to do anything other than stare at my beautiful dying wife as she watches me back.

"I d-don't hate y-you." She stutters. Her eyes flutter close and open and a shiver takes hold of her body. In my mind, I pull her close to me and cuddle her.

"Don't." I gasp before choking. My whole-body wracks as blood squirts from my lips in a cough. She shuffles closer and places a kiss to my lips, not caring about the fluids.

"I love you. More than anything." She whispers. With all my energy, I return her kiss.

"I love you too."

It's not a surprise that our story ends this way. We were always fated to die. Romeo and Juliet never killed each other; it was their families which pulled the metaphorical trigger. It just so happens that my family had access literal weapons.

Perhaps in another life, I'd be free from the mafia. It would release its awful tendrils from around my neck. And maybe in another life, Maya wouldn't have had to come into contact with me. That way, Romeo and Juliet may have lived.

Books By This Author

Death's New Pet

A revenge-driven woman. A bitter Death-incarnate. And the Death Trials.

The Devil decides Death needs a new pet to keep him company in Hell. The way to find the perfect candidate: through a series of deadly trials to whittle ten mortals down to one. The winning human will be able to make a deal with the Devil.

Scarlet Larson enters the trials with the intent to make her abuser suffer. She desperately craves revenge against the man who held her hostage for eight years. However, as each trial passes, she begins to lose focus as she engages in a steamy love affair with Death.
She knows she should stop. She knows she should concentrate on the trials. But how can you say no to Death when he tempts you?
However, as the mortal begins to develop immortal powers, Death, alongside his Hellish family, begin to wonder who, or what, is Scarlet Larson?

Five Red Flags

She is a hard-working Bubble member. He is a blasphemous Freedom Fighter. Yet they both end up in the Red Flag Trials, fighting for their lives against the impossible odds.

Set in the year 2202, cancel culture is potent. The ruling elite had to prevent the misery and despair which wrecked their cities. Offence had to go. Change needed to happen. Happiness must be restored.

Once a diligent young worker, Arabella's perfect life crashes and burns when she first meets the new and intimidating arrival to her bubble- Isaac. His scandalous words and promises eventually land them into trouble with the ruling elite's new rules.

Forced to compete in a series of death trials with five other disgraced bubble members, Arabella can't help but question why she strayed from her perfect life beforehand. As each trial passes, the people around her that she grew to trust, wither away. Fear and friendship are indistinguishable in the Red Flag Trials, and hope is nothing but a four-letter word whispered in the dark.

Despite all this, Arabella can't help wondering what the bigger threat is... The trials themselves, or her mysterious lover who seems a little too knowledgeable about them.

The Hit

Isla Morris, alongside her brother and father, are contracted killers. Their job includes infiltrating their target's lives to gain more information and then make a clean kill, all in the name of money. However, when Isla falls in love with the man she is supposed to murder, trouble stirs.
Will she choose to stick to the mission, or will she betray her family in the name of love?

In the future, her decision haunts her in a new mission. And when a handsome, mystery man called Toby shows up and threatens to reveal all her secrets, she must make more fateful choices.

With a blooming love triangle and everyone around her turning out to not be who she expected, Isla finds herself lost and in despair. She was supposed to play them, but now all the men in her life are playing her...

Time's Up

An innocent girl has died in the hands of many.

It seems she was just a small pawn in a much larger game of wealth and greed. Now it's up to Isla, Tyler, and Toby to avenge her tragic story. They've already killed off the majority of people who wronged the girl, but with one man left and a new rule in play, the stakes grow higher.

No more killing. To right the wrongs of the past, Isla, Toby and Tyler agree that there will be no more deaths involved in their final case together. Too much irreversible damage has been done. Instead, their final target shall suffer greatly as his whole life falls apart.

But when a hit is placed on Isla's head, the case becomes much more complicated. Without her father's protection, she creeps closer to death every day.

One question remains: How can you complete your final job when you might not be alive at the end of it?

Printed in Great Britain
by Amazon